PERILOUS RELATIONS

Also by Carole Epstein

Perilous Friends

PERILOUS RELATIONS

A Barbara Simons Mystery

CAROLE EPSTEIN

WALKER AND COMPANY

NEW YORK

First published in the United States of America in 1997 by Walker Publishing Company, Inc.

Published simultaneously in Canada by Thomas Allen & Son Canada, Limited, Markham, Ontario

Library of Congress Cataloging-in-Publication Data
Epstein, Carole.
Perilous relations : a Barbara Simons mystery / Carole Epstein.
p.   cm.
ISBN 0-8027-3309-3
I. Title.
PR9199.3.E65P47   1997
813'.54—dc21   97-30885
CIP

Printed in the United States of America
2 4 6 8 10 9 7 5 3 1

For my sister, Wendy Katz

BARBARA FREIHEIT READ and criticized. Martha Oppenheim did, too, engaging me in a battle about commas. Many thanks to Michael O'Connell, who supplied airline information, and Lois Hutchison, who told me how to bury an Anglican, in detail.

PERILOUS RELATIONS

1

"COME FOR DINNER tomorrow night," Susan said, plowing right in. Never the "Hello, how are you?" that generally begins polite phone conversations. "Robert has something very important to discuss with you."

"Is he standing right beside you?"

"Of course, and he would like an immediate answer. The only reason I'm the one calling is he's afraid he'll give it away on the phone."

"Sure I'll come. But I want pizza." Robert loves pizza as much as he loves me. He's eight years old and my godson and we are passionate about each other. We have our own little secrets that I sometimes choose not to share with his mother, but this didn't seem to be one of them. Since the death of his father we'd grown even closer, which satisfied me to my core. He's a wonderful little boy, the image of his mother, right down to the streaked blond hair that Susan emulates at great expense.

After being instructed to arrive promptly at seven I said my good-byes since I'm obviously more polite than she, and went back to preparing dinner. I found some frozen chili in the freezer and nuked it until it was bubbly and aromatic. Settled at the kitchen table, I clicked on the television to see if my friend Joanne Cowan had a segment on the news. I hadn't spoken to her today, so there was probably something that had kept her too busy to call. We usually connect on a daily basis, but there's no point in my calling her, since she's rarely behind her desk and if she's out on assignment she'll phone me when she has the time. That's after her piece has aired so I can critique it. On slow days she'll call five times or so to pretend to look busy. I know this since at any point she'll break into what I consider gibberish about something political or equally uninteresting to impress the person who has walked into her office. I'm sure nobody is fooled, but Joanne has a lot of clout at the station, so no one ever calls her on it.

It hadn't always been this way. Now that I am theoretically unemployed I have more time to pay attention to my friends and enjoy the benefits of liberty. Somebody, and sometimes even I, always has an amusing tidbit to relate. And I guess I'm only technically unemployed, as I have two years' severance pay socked away, earning nice interest and dividends. Life is also cheaper now that I'm not toiling away in industry; no need for the expensive clothes that I love. And I even found that I don't miss them, a fact that a few months ago I would have considered inconceivable. Also, I'd recently had two short-term freelance jobs that paid well, so I was ahead of the game and more secure about my fiscal viability. All in all, life was pretty good.

After dinner, visually accompanied by Joanne telling me that someone had just been busted for embezzling a couple of million dollars on a pyramid scam, which I thought pretty clever and that he had to have been very greedy to get caught, I took a nap so I would be prepared for my next adventure.

When I was still vice president in charge of Corporate and Public Relations at PanCanada Airlines, one of my duties had been to be very visible and represent the company at all sorts of functions. I liked this aspect, because I was usually so busy at my job that I didn't have much free time and it gave me the opportunity to socialize and catch up with people. On one occasion—a charity auction where everything fetched double its value in the name of ovarian cancer—I had placed the winning bid for a Ride-Along with the police department, and tonight was my night. It had sounded like a lot of fun then but had preceded my recent encounters with the police, and now it didn't seem quite the lark I had first envisaged. I had at the time selected the overnight shift, eagerly figuring there would be more activity in my quest for action and excitement. Now, in my new laid-back, somewhat lethargic mode, the idea of being awake the whole night didn't seem as appealing. I can remember how easy it used to be to spend the night out carousing, dancing, and talking a blue streak. But that was my twenties and now was my forties—if just barely—and it didn't seem as much fun. Oh well, tomorrow I would be the one to relate the stories.

I lay down and was asleep within seconds. I've always been blessed with the ability to fall asleep anywhere, anytime, and it's served me well on long flights across the Atlantic and Pacific and crisscrossing the nation. Working for an airline implies lots of travel, both business and personal, and being a vice president rates you first class, which generally means no screaming babies. I had set the alarm clock for eleven, which should give me a good three and a half hours of sleep.

I awoke to someone on AM radio discussing the political situation in a less than calm voice. His agitation brought me back to reality in a second, and I snapped the radio off. These days someone is *always* complaining about the powers that be on the talk shows, and I could pick up the thread anytime I chose to tune in. Now was not that time. Tonight there was no need to get upset to start the adrenaline pumping. I had an adventure to look forward to and was wide awake and only slightly nervous.

First thing to do was select the proper attire. There were a lot of things to consider; the weather could be iffy in early May. Although we could hope for warm days, there was still the danger of night frost. Or it could be boiling. The smart thing would be to go back to bed and give in to the sleep that my body demanded. It had been tricked into thinking it could lie there like a lump all night, and the sudden arousal confused it. I was getting no cooperation at all from my brain.

I finally decided on true Montreal style. Black pants, black turtleneck, black boots. Perfect gear for a trendy St. Lawrence Street restaurant but equally acceptable to my destination. I looked too wan and couldn't stand it, so I added a bright red belt and grabbed my red leather jacket in case I froze. Black leather gloves got jammed into the pockets. I tied my hair back in an effort to look tough but auburn just isn't a mean enough color, so the look wasn't as effective as I'd hoped. Mascara, a soupçon of eyeliner, and pale lipstick completed the ensemble.

Dress-up has always been fun for me. I love to disguise myself into the person I choose to be. Tonight was streetwise, sassy broad. A last glance in the mirror showed close but no cigar. With the costumes come the clichés.

I DROVE WEST through the dark streets, surprised at the number of people out strolling even though it was almost midnight. We'd shed our winter skin and were out celebrating spring.

A few blocks away I crossed the invisible border into the municipality of Westmount. It's an upscale community that originated miles away from the pollution of Montreal but was surrounded as the city expanded westward. There are quite a few of these independent townships in what is known as Greater Montreal, and they cling fiercely to their independence, electing vocal mayors who do battle with the big city that threatens to swallow them. Since the early seventies, police services are under the auspices of their larger neighbor, but the municipalities each have independent fire departments that they pool in case of emergencies, often rushing miles away to offer assistance, while a well-equipped Montreal fire station lies only blocks away from the scene of imminent destruction. The residents seem to have no problem with this and cling to their village ways.

There are lots of fabulous homes in Westmount, but I didn't pass any on my short drive west on Sherbrooke Street, only solid apartment buildings of gray or brown stone and a lovely lawn bowling green, still yellow after the long winter. At the imposing stone castlelike Westmount City Hall I turned right, heading to Stanton Street and the hodgepodge of connected buildings that housed the police department, municipal courts, and the fire department.

I parked around the back in a spot reserved for a judge, figuring he wouldn't be using it. There is no night court in Westmount. The traffic violations, neighbor disputes mainly about obstructed sight lines, and assorted other minor infractions are dealt with during the day, at a civilized hour. A sense of calm pervades the city. There is a lack of urgency, explained by the knowledge that reason will take care of everything in an orderly fashion. It's a nice illusion and a nice place to live if you have the big bucks necessary.

I had been to Police Station 23 before but had paid little attention to my surroundings. When I got inside I realized why: There was nothing much to pay attention to. I found myself in a large lobbylike area with tons of doors leading somewhere and a counter on the right-hand side behind which were three desks, twelve tiny darkened surveillance monitors, and one person. I assumed that during the day the desks would all be manned and there would be some sense of business being conducted, but for now all was quiet and the officer behind the only inhabited desk was engrossed in a manual, which he held upright. I suspected it housed a paperback book.

"Hello. I'm Barbara Simons and I'm scheduled for a Ride-Along."

"Yeah, the auction winner. Please sign these papers," he said in a not too friendly manner. He didn't sneer, but it was close.

I had been surprised when I had only had to pay fifty dollars for this privilege, and this officer seemed to be well aware of the bargain price fetched; hence the attitude. He obviously felt that the station's largesse should have raised more money, but it's not my fault no one else present had a sense of adventure. To that particular middle-aged, stuffy crowd, adventure was golfing in Arizona or skiing in the Alps.

I took the papers from him, then fished through my cavernous purse for a pen since none was proffered. I came up with a neat one that said "Reed a Book Today." I love the fact that it had been a promotional piece for the library and carry it with me everywhere; I will be sorry when the ink runs out.

I signed the copies quickly, having given up reading the French-only text a quarter of the way through. In essence, I absolved the police department of everything up to, and including, loss of life. Should the inevitable occur, it would be up to my heirs to challenge this flimsy document of absolution. Still, it was a little scary.

Unsure as to whether I had been too hasty in not reading

all the fine print, I nevertheless returned the papers to the officer, who, still engrossed in his fake manual, looked annoyed when I cleared my throat to get his attention. I was too timid to be vocal, which should have told me I had no business doing this in the first place. He then went to a phone on one of the desks, punched in three numbers, and announced my presence to someone. Kind of like a doorman in an expensive apartment building. He added something else that I didn't catch since he turned his back to me and lowered his voice. I could tell it was about me and it wasn't nice. They sure were doing a good job of making me feel unwelcome. Perhaps I should offer some additional money, but I was too intimidated to chance committing some other faux pas.

And it didn't get any better. From one of the myriad doors came two officers, all spit and polish and sharply creased pants. A man of about thirty and a woman who looked like a man of about twenty-five.

In an effort to get off to a good start I plastered a huge grin on my face and said, "Hi. I'm Barbara Simons." I stuck my hand out, but after waiting expectantly for a few beats, shoved it back into my pocket when no one showed any sign of shaking it.

"Constable La Pierre."

"Constable Beaubien."

They said that at the same time, so I had difficulty catching the names. They looked at each other and smiled, acknowledging a coup over the civilian.

So that was how it was going to be. Not easy.

I was eventually led to the garage and bundled into the back of a spotless blue-and-white police car. Whoever had their car wash contract must be eating very well. The interior was equally spotless, contrary to my expectations, which had been honed by years of cop shows on television. Although I appreciated the lack of expected stench I was disappointed; the tidiness and order might be the harbinger of a dull night.

La Pierre drove while his partner fiddled with the rearview mirror so as to apply some lipstick. I thought of telling her it wouldn't help, but I didn't. She had a gun.

They ignored me, and at this point I couldn't have cared less. All I wanted to do was either get this over with as painlessly as possible or see some action, or better yet, get some food. Not accustomed to beginning an eight-hour shift at midnight, I was unprepared for how hungry I found myself. I rummaged through my bag but could come up with nothing edible, although there were lots of interesting, weird things in there that I promised myself I would throw away tomorrow. Having come from a white-collar world populated with efficient secretaries, I wasn't as yet attuned to the practicalities of life. I should have taken my cue from Joanne; her purse is always loaded with goodies.

Maybe if I asked very nicely they could be coaxed into stopping for pizza or a hamburger. I wouldn't have dared suggest a doughnut shop, as I am sensitive to implied insults and stereotypes. Also, they could get mad at me, so I kept my mouth shut and listened to my stomach gurgle for want of conversation.

We drove through the now empty streets in silence, the police band radio crackling unintelligible sounds every now and then, which they ignored. When we passed some illegally parked cars they looked at each other and reached a silent decision; they shrugged simultaneously and drove on. There were some lucky people sleeping blissfully away, totally unaware of their good fortune and thirty bucks richer. I thought this was a good example of community cooperation to set for the passenger in the backseat, but I kept quiet. After all, my precious 560 SL Mercedes is not exactly unobtrusive and it was parked in a judge's spot behind their station, so I had no intention of attracting any tickets of my own. When there is the danger of parting me from my money for no reward I can be quite circumspect.

After about an hour of this seemingly interminable boredom a word was spoken. " 'Ungry?"

I didn't respond, since he couldn't possibly be speaking to me. They had probably forgotten I existed. At first, while still at the station, I'd tried to make conversation by asking pertinent, interested questions. After all, I was going to spend a long time with these two, and anyway, I'd always thought it would be intriguing to be a cop. But fifty bucks hadn't earned me the right to conversation, so I'd been silent and obedient since and was about to pop. This was, however, an interesting development. I eyed them both, eagerly awaiting a positive response since I was close to starving to death. Hyperbole comes to me naturally but is accentuated by being bored to tears.

Nothing. Maybe she was as bored as I and had disappeared in her head to another place with lots of excitement. I wished she'd tell me where it was, since I could use some entertainment. Also, if she didn't acquiesce soon I'd get out at the next light.

"Madame, I ask you if you are 'ungry?"

He was talking to *me*. I felt on the verge of a major breakthrough here, but I had to tread carefully, not seem too overexcited or he would shut down again. If I had to endure seven more hours of silence I'd go mad.

"Sure. Whatever you guys say." Five words and all of them wrong. It wasn't the nature of the response, it was the delivery. They had been politely speaking to me in English and I had answered in French, which could lead them to believe that I was mocking their English. Language is a delicate and convoluted issue in this province, a minefield fraught with implications of insult. The occasional blunder is to be expected, but this was not the optimum occasion. I hastily repeated myself in English and they let it pass. At least he did. She snorted. He patted her hand, which was good since I now had fodder for the next seven hours. I could speculate about the sexual permutations and combinations of these two, an idea that hadn't crossed my mind, since she seemed so asexual.

"Hokay," he said, and smiled for the first time. This was obviously the favorite part of the tour.

As we pulled into the parking lot of a Dunkin' Donuts—I guess some things really are true—the radio crackled again.

"Merde," he said, as we took off with a lurch and sped out of the lot. I hadn't been able to decipher a word, but it was obviously meant for us, and we were gone. I wasn't sure if I was happy with this turn of events. On the one hand, I was starving and those doughnuts sure did look good to me, since I know calories consumed in the middle of the night don't count, as don't calories consumed on airplanes or those eaten standing up. On the other hand, I was going to see Montreal's finest at work and there might be blood and adventure. Hunger was getting to me.

He turned on the flashing lights but, to my disappointment, not the siren. There was no traffic, and without the siren there was no sense of urgency, so I dismissed the idea of blood, which was really better since it could ruin my appetite. Basically, this tour thing wasn't anywhere near as exciting as I had envisioned when I plunked down my fifty dollars. At least it went to charity and was tax deductible.

We sped back along Sherbrooke Street, the road that takes you east to west across the island, and stopped in front of a convenience store at the very western edge of Westmount. They got out with no great exigency and drew their guns, strolling into the deserted-looking store. Totally forgotten, I sprang off after them; no way was I going to miss this.

A small, timid man with tiny black scared eyes stood behind the counter, the empty cash register open in front of him. He was dressed in a cheap gray suit with a pressed white shirt and dark green tie and looked totally incongruous with his surroundings. He was really short and really frightened. No genius needed here to figure out what had happened.

"What happened?" asked Beaubien.

The response came in a torrent, accompanied by much gesticulating. Agitated words ran together in interminable sentences, all of them incomprehensible to the cops.

"*En français, s'il vous plait,*" she said. I guess they're taught to be polite to victims.

The shopkeeper prattled on, oblivious to her request. The hand gestures were getting wider and wilder, and she stepped back to avoid being inadvertently bopped. The cops exchanged looks of long suffering.

"Excuse me," I interrupted in a quiet voice. "I think he's speaking Italian."

"Yeah? So what 'e say?" she asked, none too pleased with my interjection and willing to show me up as an idiot.

"Let me ask him." Which I did in passable form for the middle of the night and rusty skills.

"*Erano due. Uno gigante e uno pigmeo.*"

Anyone of just normal height would be a giant to this vertically challenged man, so that was no help. The pygmy had been shorter than he, which meant he might really have been one. They were white, spoke French, got sixty-three dollars from the till, and had a huge gun. I couldn't get him to describe exactly how huge since as soon as it was pointed at him, it kept growing. Having been in a similar situation, I could empathize.

I translated all this for the cops, who were staring at me. What did they think? The fact that they were so astonished that I showed any usable talent pissed me off. This whole

Ride-Along had been organized to improve the relationship between the police and the population. It sure wasn't working. "Ask him where the regular clerk is." Use me—yes; respect me—no. But I obeyed. "It's his son, and he's home studying for exams." At that moment, the door flew open and the son exploded into the store. It had to be him; he looked exactly like his father, with an extra six inches that made him on the average-short side. His eyes were just as black but not at all scared. The anger was apparent as he spoke to his father in rapid dialect that I had trouble following, although I tried my damnedest as the cops watched me listen. Basically, Poppa was fine, just shaken up, and he was sorry to have troubled his son.

Much calmer but just as angry, the son turned to the police. "Same ones. It's the second time this month. I shouldn'ta left him alone here, but I have a philosophy exam in the morning, and he insisted. I got hit last week, so I didn't think they'd come back so soon. Last time they waited a month. My boss is gonna blame me, like it woulda made a difference who was working, me or my father. A gun is a gun. Soon as this term is over I'm gonna quit. It's not worth it."

The cops were pragmatic. They told him to lock up, take his shaken father home, and come down to the station the next day to fill out the necessary reports. It was my suspicious little mind that led me to the understanding that they had fobbed off all the tedious paperwork onto someone on the day shift. Very clever.

On the way out I snagged a Diet Coke for which the father insisted I not be allowed to pay. If I had been a little younger he would have forced his son to marry me, so grateful was he that I had understood and sympathized with him.

We said polite good-byes as though we were leaving a tea party. This was not the blood-and-guts, "knock a few heads in" tour I had anticipated. We headed back to the car, with me sucking down great gulps of Diet Coke. If I couldn't get any food I'd try to trick my stomach into thinking it was getting sustenance. Any second now the cops in the front seat would be treated to a loud belch, and I truly didn't care. When I went to put the empty can into my bag I found another full one there. Silently toasting the gnome-sized gentleman, I downed that one equally fast, then burped a good one, which the guys up front ignored but I enjoyed immensely.

I thought they would now talk to me since I had been of such great assistance, but no such luck. I sat sullenly back in the seat and burped again to punctuate my annoyance. I was on the verge of giving up and asking them to drop me off at the station, when I heard them mention food again. My fit of pique could wait. Also, I would soon be in dire need of a bathroom.

Just as we were pulling back into the same parking lot we had a déjà vu experience. Only, it was real. The radio crackled and I recognized the car number but couldn't discern the coded message. I could see the doughnuts through the window, all in a row, iced in decorative colors, all calling to me. The washroom pictograph beckoned me, and it was with great longing that I averted my eyes as we headed out. We drove back east along Sherbrooke Street to Belmont Avenue, a pretty street in the middle level. Westmount is nestled into one of the twin humps of Mount Royal, a really, really ancient extinct volcano. It was once a great mountain a million-billion years ago, but now Westmount is just a vertical residential area with the house prices climbing as the hill rises. And it *is* only a hill.

We pulled up in front of a beautiful gray flagstone house. It was gracefully designed and meant to sit on a much larger plot of land. The house was on the east side of the street, which meant it backed onto Murray Hill Park and was thus prime real estate. The entrance was to the right, with three steps leading up to a large indented porch boasting a bright blue door. It was the only sign of color; even the grass was still yellow after the cold winter freeze. Standing on the walk, midway down, I saw a gray-haired woman beckoning us. Aside from her there was no sign of any movement. "Stay 'ere," ordered Constable Beaubien. In her dreams. After the nonexcitement of our last call I had deduced that the most dangerous thing that could happen to me tonight was that I would either perish from hunger or have to pee in some bushes, the latter being more imminent and more terrifying.

I sprinted out after them, keeping my distance as I watched them approach the woman, who now began gesturing toward the house. She handed something over, which I presumed to be the key, since I saw them unlock the door with said object. She remained fixed, and as soon as the cops were out of the way I proceeded slowly toward her, exchanging my sprint for a slow walk. I didn't want Beaubien or La Pierre to see me speaking to her and order me back to the car. I'd been good with the old man, so maybe I could be of some use here or I could find out something interesting. It was clear and cold outside, and she looked so pathetic standing there, shivering visibly. As I neared I saw that she wasn't really gray, she had sandy blond hair shot with white, the kind that is called dishwater in books. I recognized it as upper-middle-class-de-rigueur WASP. Like "I'm too busy walking my dogs and doing Martha Stewart–type things to be bothered with superficial things like dyeing my hair." I hope that never happens to me. I've warned my friends to be on the lookout and the minute I do something "craftsy" they are ordered to shake me violently and begin deprogramming.

Just as I reached her, she spoke.

"Barbara?"

"Beth?"

"Barbara?"

Not scintillating, yet shocking.

BETH WHITESTONE, STILL trembling, wrapped her arms around me and clung. This was an altogether strange turn of events. I had worked on various committees with Beth and she had always struck me as the strong, no-nonsense type of woman who could handle anything. I had never seen her display any type of emotion; she handled everything with the kind of aplomb I can never seem to muster. In truth, I was a little scared of her; she is always so self-assured and well poised. She's a great organizer and I had liked volunteering under her, since I knew the work would get done efficiently and we wouldn't fritter away my then precious time on social chitchat.

I had been to this house before, I now realized. Once a year for the past five years for the ritual Vice Presidents' Dinner. Walter Whitestone, Beth's husband, had been my boss. My ex-boss, to be exact. Walter Whitestone was the president of PanCanada Airlines. Not the horrible man who had terminated me but a man I liked and respected, a man I had come to consider an ally and almost a friend. Subsequent to my dismissal I went into a massive funk and locked myself in my house to wallow. When he'd realized I wasn't responding to the messages on my answering machine he'd sent me a letter explaining how sorry he was at the turn of affairs, and that although he'd tried to protect me, it was all part of the takeover deal. I believed him. I'd believed him but hadn't responded, afraid I would burst into tears if I spoke to him. I'd been planning to write him a note now that I was over it but hadn't gotten around to it yet since I still hated to think about the whole thing. It was over. Part of my past.

"Beth, what happened?"

"We've been burglarized." Not robbed as most people would say, but burglarized, the correct form for the occurrence. "It's a mess in there. I don't know . . . It's shaken me so. I feel violated, defenseless. . . ." She shrugged away the thoughts and continued, calmer. "As soon as I went inside I saw the living room was topsy-turvy. Then I ran out and called nine-one-one on my cell phone. I couldn't go back in. I waited out here for the police to arrive. They were quite prompt."

I had a thought. "Where's Walter?" I hoped the answer would be "out of town" so I would have time to formulate an apology or explanation for my breach of etiquette in nomenclature. I'd always called him Walter in private but was careful to say Mr. Whitestone elsewhere. The Whitestones have impeccable manners.

"Walter! I forgot about him. He should be at home!"

"Wait here," I ordered, and damned if she didn't obey. Nice reversal of roles, but I didn't have time to savor it as I rushed inside to alert the police to the fact that Walter might possibly be found in the basement or somewhere, bound and gagged.

There was no sound from the ground floor, but I could hear people walking around upstairs. A cursory glance into the living room confirmed that the place was indeed a mess.

I remembered a powder room near the front door and availed myself of the facilities as quickly as possible. There might have been a brigade of robbers in the house, but the police were somewhere in there too and I seriously had to go. Diet Coke on an empty stomach sure can go through you fast.

Rather than search the basement alone I headed for the sound of voices and safety. I'd never been upstairs before. As I climbed I noticed the carpets were worn thin, something I hadn't seen since the poorer days of my youth. The sculpted cabbage rose pattern was visible only at the edges, having eroded to a smooth path in the center. It was almost two-tone, original mushroom color on the sides and dingy gray in the middle. I recognized it to be a fifties-style sculpted broadloom and marveled at how someone could live with the same carpeting for over forty years. And someone who supposedly had a lot of money.

The two police officers were in the master bedroom, where I assumed they'd found Walter. I was right. As I reached the doorway, prepared to make my no longer important announcement, I came to an abrupt halt, dumbfounded. There was Walter, crumpled onto the floor, a large, black knife handle protruding from his back. He was folded over in a kneeling position, head touching the floor as though in prayer to Allah.

"Don't touch nutting and get hout," shouted Constable Beaubien, who noticed I was there only after my voluble gasp. She looked as alarmed as I, and slightly green to boot. It was a good thing we hadn't had time to stop for doughnuts.

I didn't move. My eyes were riveted to Walter's back and the red stain. He was wearing a dressing gown, a beautiful emerald-green silk with black satin collar and a black satin sash. The cuffs were probably also black, but I couldn't see them, as his hands were clutched to his stomach area and not visible. La Pierre was on the phone with someone describing the scene, a handkerchief protecting the handset so as not to ruin any fingerprints.

I broke Walter's hold on me and looked around the room. It was a testament to wanton devastation or great rage. Everything had been swept off the dressers, some of the drawers had been overturned, and one chair was upended. But it looked strange. I have seen what a room looks like after it has been systematically searched, and this bore no resemblance. It seemed more a haphazard afterthought or real anger. A picture of Beth and Walter in all their wedding finery lay at my feet, the glass smashed into thousands of tiny slivers, some of them mashed into the photograph.

I remembered shaken Beth alone outside and went racing back downstairs. It was good to get out of the bedroom, since it reeked of Walter's insides and warm blood. He couldn't have been dead long.

"Beth, Beth," I cried, as I erupted out the door, much too loud for the still night.

She stopped trembling. The alarm in my voice seemed to calm her; I was about to relay some tangible information that she could process and would then behave accordingly. She's always been so controlled. I was still so shocked that I hadn't taken the time to reflect on the possible consequences of my statement, and I blurted it out with no consideration for her feelings.

"It's Walter. Beth, he's dead!"

"Walter?"

"Yeah, Walter. He's been stabbed to death."

"Good heavens, how horrible."

I had to wonder at Beth, who seemed virtually unaffected by the news. And this was not my first corpse. Yet she was taking it better than I. Well, she hadn't seen him.

"Who would do this?" Not a particularly bright question, but it was the middle of the night and I meant it sincerely.

I'd always liked Walter; he'd been a good president and a nice man, always making himself available to discuss problems and very devoted to the airline.

"How would I know, Barbara? I wasn't there. The burglars, I assume."

It was a totally inappropriate answer, and I stared at her, nonplussed. No emotion whatsoever crossed her bland face. She just stood there, looking me right in the eye as though waiting for me to say or do something.

Before I had the chance to say something else inappropriate and possibly unkind, a patrol car pulled up and two more cops got out. One came up to us and hesitated only long enough to order us to stay there as the other rushed by. About three seconds after they entered, Constable Beaubien came reeling out, getting greener by the minute. She came to stand with us, ostensibly to prevent us from leaving, but I think more in need of live human companionship. I was sure this was her first body, and she wasn't taking it well. A major blow to her macho image.

We ignored her, and Beth proceeded to inspect the paving stones as I proceeded to inspect Beth. She sure was calm.

After about five minutes, during which time Beaubien composed herself, she spoke. She asked Beth where she'd been all evening. I should have thought of that. Usually I'm so curious about everything, and the fact that I hadn't been bombarding Beth with questions was testament to how shook up I was.

"I went to a film. Then I drove around for a while. It's such a beautiful night, spring at last, that I didn't feel like coming straight home. Walter was expecting someone from the office, so I wanted to wait until I was certain he'd be gone. I wasn't in the mood for socializing. I just drove around and looked at people's plantings. You know, what they're doing in their front gardens this year. Everything is just starting to come up, and soon it will all be so pretty."

Even the latest movies let out at about eleven-thirty on weekdays, and she hadn't shown up until nearly two. That's a lot of driving around and a lot of unawakened spring gardens to visit in the dark.

Constable Beaubien seemed to be of the same mind, as evidenced by the downturn of her mouth, and she started to say something when another car pulled up, this one unmarked and regulation boxy shape. The men, obviously plainclothes detectives even to the eye not as attuned as mine, approached us. My heart thumped wildly and I tried to keep a poker face, which is not one of my long suits.

"Barbara?"

"Greg?"

"Her!"

There was a lot of naming going on tonight.

Before me stood a surprised Detective-Sergeant Gregory Allard and a none too pleased and very suspicious Detective-Sergeant Fernand Boucherville, both of the homicide squad and with whom I'd had some dealings. I hadn't heard from either of them in the intervening three months (it was two months and and twenty-one days, to be precise, but I wasn't going to admit to even myself that I was counting). I'd been disappointed and confused at the silence. About Greg, not Boucherville, whom I disliked almost as much as he disliked me.

"What are you doing here?" Greg asked, his wonderful blue eyes looking directly into mine. I wondered where he had been when he got this call, since he was dressed in what, to my practiced eye, was a bespoke charcoal gray suit, white shirt, and colorful silk tie. No overcoat, but he didn't look cold. I sneaked a peek downward and there they were: his ubiquitous, incongruous, dirty Reeboks, in total contrast with the rest of his impeccable attire. They might rightly have belonged to his partner, whose battered trench coat sported numerous stains, some suspiciously resembling dried blood, or maybe ketchup. Either way, they were an unlikely duo. Greg looked happy to see me, but it was dark in the middle of the walk and I could have been projecting. Even under such dreadful circumstances I was glad to see him. Walter Whitestone had always been kind and generous to me, and now, in death, he'd brought me Greg. He's really majorly attractive.

Before I could even consider batting my eyelashes, Constable Beaubien answered. "She wit' us."

Greg looked surprised but said nothing. Boucherville snorted, glad that I'd at last been arrested for something, and tugged Allard away toward the house. They had a job to do, and that broad (meaning me) was not going to interfere if he could help it. Near the door, Boucherville turned around and called out, "Wait 'ere." That phrase was wearing a bit thin and beginning to annoy me, but I obeyed, as there was an armed woman present to ensure that I did.

No sooner had they gone inside than a station wagon arrived, the revolving light on the roof flashing. It pulled up and double-parked beside the police cruisers. Three people jumped out and slammed the doors loudly, in testament to their importance and the urgency of their mission. As the neighbors were being awakened by the repeated car doors slamming, lights were popping on in the surrounding houses on both sides of the street. They were quickly doused when the spectators realized there was good stuff going on out there and they should watch. Human silhouettes could be seen lurking behind half-drawn drapes, illuminated by the bright streetlights. The enterprising couple directly across the way had armed themselves with binoculars.

Three men and one woman headed our way.

At least she didn't say "Barbara?" That one was also getting old fast. What Joanne Cowan, ace reporter, said was,

"What the hell are you doing here, and put on some lipstick so you'll look presentable on camera."

Constable Beaubien looked stunned or maybe suspicious; I seemed to know everyone. Beth looked at her budding tulips, and I cracked up.

"How did you get here so fast? But more important, do you have anything to eat?"

Joanne always has some food secreted about her person somewhere.

"Sure," she said, dipping into her briefcase. "Hmm, what do we have here? Chips, a chocolate bar, some brownies. Sorry, that's all. I left on short notice."

"Beth?" I asked in offering.

"Nothing, thank you. I ate earlier."

"Officer?"

I had her. Constable Beaubien was now well and truly my new best friend. She smiled for the first time that night, a not unpleasant sight, and said tentatively, "Brownies, please."

Joanne handed one over. If she hadn't known that the policewoman could be a good source for her story, it is possible that Joanne would have denied possession of any comestibles. She had once told me that she always carries around a stash of goodies to feed the cops she encounters because they're always hungry. None of them has as yet twigged to the fact that it's just another form of bribery. Nor did Beaubien, who now loved Joanne and liked me for knowing her. Beth remained stoic. Maybe she was in an advanced state of shock.

"Here," Joanne said as she tossed me the chips, knowing my preferences. We'd been friends since kindergarten and knew way too much about each other.

"Okay, so what happened?" Joanne asked. The question was directed at Beaubien, but I knew more and felt the need to show off in front of my friend Joanne and her crew, who were now busily setting up their equipment. They had made no move to enter the house, well aware that they'd be summarily ejected if they did.

"It's Walter Whitestone," I gushed. "He's dead."

"Barbara, I asked you what happened. Tell me something I don't know."

"Well, how did you know?" I pouted. I was hurt. My great news was old news.

"Police band radios? Heard of 'em? The address and the code for homicide were a dead giveaway, if you'll pardon the pun."

Her crew obviously found her hilarious, as they fell about laughing. I didn't.

"It could have been Beth," I countered, which was stupid and cruel since Beth was standing there beside us. For a second Beth looked alarmed at the possibility, but her face quickly reverted to its implacable stare.

"What do you do? Sleep with your ear glued to the radio? Headphones? Your husband must really love that."

"No, silly," she said, laughing. She seemed to find me very amusing. "The station called. It's too big an event to let some second stringer handle, so I hustled the guys and we made it over here fast. The other stations and papers will arrive any second, so what can you tell me quickly?"

Constable Beaubien had apparently lost interest in us and was munching away on her brownie. Joanne gave her another one to keep her docile. Beth continued with her mental weeding.

"I went inside. The house has been ransacked, but it doesn't look like a robbery. I mean everything's a mess, but it looks random, like it may have been done afterward. Walter, Mr. Whitestone I mean, was killed in the master bedroom. He was run through with a knife. And not long ago."

I sounded like a game of Clue.

I'd used Walter's surname since I didn't want Beth to

think that we were that cozy. I didn't want her to envisage any hanky-panky. Walter had a tight yet laid-back style of management, and was on a first-name basis with all his vice presidents. It made for a friendly work environment.

I shouldn't have been concerned about Beth's feelings; I don't think she even heard me. I was beginning to get worried. Her apathy was alarming, and I feared she had disappeared into another space.

Joanne ordered me to "wait here" as she went back to her crew, who were just finishing their setup. She took the mike, faced the camera, and ran through her opening remarks. I was curious to hear what she was going to say, but I was distracted by the sound of yet another car door.

An elderly woman got out, this time not slamming the door but closing it quietly and locking it. She was dressed in a cream-colored blouse under a brown tailored suit with the requisite pearls adorning her neck. Fashionable but sensible brown-and-white oxfords with a matching handbag. Quite the matronly fashion plate for the middle of the night. Her short white hair was still damp about the edges, indicating she'd taken the time to shower before she came. At two o'clock in the morning. "Beth, dear, I came as soon as I got your message. What is going on here? Who are all these people?"

"Let me introduce you. This is Officer—? Sorry, I didn't quite catch your name."

"Constable Beaubien." She was the one who now looked in shock.

"And this is Barbara Simons. You might remember her from the Yellow Ribbon campaign. Also, she works for Walter."

"Worked," I muttered, although no one paid attention except Beaubien, who now stared at *me*. Outside was sure better than all that messy stuff inside. She'd have a lot to write in her report.

"Barbara, you remember Beverly Warfield. She chaired the committee. She's also Walter's sister." Also? This woman was definitely over the edge.

"Beverly," she continued calmly, "Walter's been killed. I know it's tragic, but we have to be strong."

What kind of line was that from a woman whose husband has just been murdered? If she did do it, it was a hell of a way to allay suspicion. Beaubien was staring at her with narrowed eyes, watching. Beverly, on the other hand, looked suitably astonished. Her hand flew to her mouth and she gasped loudly. Beaubien moved in behind her in case she fainted.

"How? What happened? When? Why?"

"Dear, calm down. The police are still inside. When they come out I'm sure they'll tell us all. Meanwhile, in the morning I'd like you to alert the children, as I'll be occupied with the funeral arrangements." In the first show of any emotion since my arrival, Beth went to Beverly and wrapped her arms around her. She patted her soothingly on the back and said quietly, "Bevy, I'm really sorry for you. I know how close the two of you were. We'll all miss him."

She sounded like a matron in the receiving line of a funeral service for a distant cousin. Beaubien's eyes got narrower.

Joanne, never one to miss a trick, had been eavesdropping while she was rehearsing. She approached Beth and asked her to do a brief camera appearance. Beth was appalled. "It would not be dignified!" Now, that was the Beth I knew.

Joanne shrugged her shoulders and grabbed me by the arm, dragging me to her preferred location. By now, more news media had shown up and lots of people were milling around outside. A French network had sent a very pretty boy to do their segment, and he and Joanne eyed each other. I'd have to remember to ask about that later. I couldn't see Joanne consorting with the competition, but I could well see her leading him on. Everyone hushed up when the morgue van arrived. They'd all probably seen it many times, but in the dead of night it was still a chilling sight, a reminder of how elusive and fragile life can be. As soon as the two men had gone into the house and closed the door, it was back to business as usual.

The camera whirred and Joanne asked me how I'd come to be there. It was likely just a warm-up question to put me at ease, since it was irrelevant, but it worked. I was on a roll. To hear me tell it I'd single-handedly led the cops through the dangerous streets of Westmount to this very location. And not a mention of Dunkin' Donuts. She asked me to describe the murder scene, and I was about to sail into a gory description when a hand grabbed the mike away from Joanne. We both wheeled around to see who had committed this heinous crime. I knew I wouldn't be getting my allotted fifteen minutes of fame, but I had been counting on fifteen seconds.

"Sorry, Ms. Cowan. Not until we've spoken to Ms. Simons first." Greg the Stuffy Snot had reverted to formal usage of last names. And he didn't seem quite so happy to see me now.

"Ms. Simons, Mrs. Whitestone, please come with me."

"Where?" I wasn't going to be acquiescent to his bossing me around. Joanne was one thing—there was history there—but he was something else. If he was going to pretend that he hardly knew me, I wasn't going to obey meekly. I knew he had a gun, but I doubted he'd use it on me. Especially with so many witnesses.

"There are too many people around, and I'd like to speak to each of you privately. If you would accompany me to the station I would be very thankful."

Mr. Formality. He and Beth were going to get along great. Beth had a few words with Beverly and proceeded to follow him. After a quick assessment I figured I'd better tag along. I'd really like to know what Beth had to say about the situation and I wanted the opportunity to talk to Greg one-on-one. See what the picture was, since he was still gorgeous to me. In the time I hadn't spoken to him I'd nearly, but not quite, forgotten about him or at least tried to, and I wondered how he felt about me. His body language when we were alone would tell all.

Joanne came rushing up as I got into the car. Detective-Sergeant Boucherville was tapping impatiently on the horn, but the car was not started, so no sound came out. The message was clear though. The good-looking French reporter was trying to engage him in conversation, peppering Boucherville with questions to which the only response was a shrug of the shoulders.

"Call me as soon as you wake up tomorrow," Joanne said, one eye on her confrere.

I ignored her. She wouldn't wait for my call anyway. She'd decide when I had slept enough and then call me. I'd do the same, since I wanted to know more about that French guy. Joanne had been faithful to her husband Jacques for an inordinately long time, it seemed to me. Perhaps my vicarious life was beginning anew; it was something to look forward to.

Beth sat in the backseat with me, impassive as ever.

3

WE ARRIVED AT the station, where there was now an abundance of people milling about the lobby, mostly media, in contrast to the lone officer of my earlier visit. Walter Whitestone was big news in this city, and everyone had sent someone. Since they couldn't get information at the scene of the crime they had descended on the precinct house. I noticed Joanne wasn't there. There were two or three people from my public relations days, but thankfully they either didn't recognize me or were distracted by Beth's arrival. Microphones were shoved into her face, and she looked as if she was going to faint. She still said nothing.

We were separated. Beth got Greg and I got Detective-Sergeant Fernand Boucherville, a man not high on my list of favorite people. He flushes red and gets irritated with great frequency and for no particular reason that I can ever discern. One has to tread very carefully with him; he's a political policeman, but not in the usual sense of department politics. He personally carries the flag for the separatists of the province and is quick to take offense at any insult, real or imagined, to his precious flag or language. Westmount, having a large Anglophone population, would not be his favorite location for an investigation. I'm not even sure if he can speak English, since I never heard him do so. Often, this is too tempting for me to ignore. I take the position that this is my country too, and I'm still legally entitled to speak the official language of my choice. We Anglophones have begun to dig in our heels, and we're not at all the nice docile population that we once were. It's a pretty mean-spirited attitude and we're not proud of it, but somehow the government has created us by their restrictive legislation. We're a minority in a province that is a minority in the country. Circles within circles.

However, I was tired and he's just too easy to bait. I generally like to see him redden to the point of imminent cardiac arrest, but it takes so little effort he makes no sport of it. Virtually every word I say has that effect on him. And he's only about my height, five feet eight, which must further enrage him. So I spoke in French and told him exactly what I saw. Right down to the emerald-green bathrobe and broken eyeglasses on the floor. Walter wore reading glasses, and usually had them perched on his forehead, making him look singularly silly. He'd worked out some sort of code with his secretary, which I never figured out. All I know is that he would look over at her and the offending lenses would suddenly reappear either on his eyes or on the desk in front of him. Boucherville, true to his nature, was suspicious of my tale. What was I doing there in the first place? I repeated the auction story, and he wanted to know when and where it had occurred. I could remember where but not when, and he looked as if he'd caught me and cracked the case. It was very tedious.

I was furious that Greg had foisted him on me. But it was probably a lot better for Beth, who was from Alberta originally and could barely speak French. I know. I'd heard her try it out on delivery and service people in a true effort to be gracious and fit in. Didn't work. They looked at her as if she was speaking Greek and either switched to English if they could, or ignored her. She was very frustrated about this and tried harder and harder, with funnier and funnier results. Her vocabulary improved in direct inversion to her accent. I don't know who was coaching her, but I suspect it was someone from the large Haitian population in the city, whose Creole-French is indecipherable to the rest of the world at large. The sight of superwhite Beth spouting black Creole brought many snickers, but to my knowledge, no one, including me, ever told her.

Boucherville asked me a few more stupid questions and then told me I could go. Which I did, but the wrong way. He didn't have the courtesy to see me back to the front desk, and so I wandered on my own. I hadn't paid enough attention to where I was going on the way in. Somehow I'd forgotten that I'd come up a flight of stairs, so I found myself in a large room full of desks, all of them empty and some of them quite messy. On further inspection I divined that I was in the detectives' room, the nameplates displayed on the desks being helpful. This was interesting. I snooped around someone's papers but found nothing entertaining. A couple of reports on some break-ins and some stolen-bicycle queries. These guys sure had dull jobs.

Just as I was about to open drawers to look for something more fascinating, I heard someone come up the stairs. It's not that I was really prying, it's just that the temptation was overwhelming. I like to know things, and this seemed like a great place to find them out. It's this insatiable thirst for knowledge that has led others to accuse me of being nosy. But I am only in semipublic places, like offices. I wouldn't dream of going through anyone's drawers at home. Anyone I liked, that is.

However, as for most people, the medicine cabinet is always fair game.

I quickly went into the hall to greet my visitor and did an excellent impersonation of a very dumb broad who couldn't find her way out of anywhere. He directed me condescendingly and I didn't even say anything snarky as I followed his directions, with him suspiciously accompanying me. I don't think he quite bought it.

Beth was already there, Greg at her side. He was fiddling with some papers, and she still looked catatonic. Boucherville had kept me longer than Greg had kept Beth, and I hadn't had anything to offer. The man really didn't like me, and I never could figure out why. On the other hand, I had a hundred reasons for not liking him.

"I'll drive you ladies back," Greg said.

"Don't bother," I answered. It came out colder than I meant. "My car is here in the back. I'll take Beth. Thanks anyway." I tried to sound nicer. It was okay for me to be pissed off at him, but I didn't want the reverse.

He flashed a big grin, causing the corners of his eyes to crinkle attractively. How old was he, anyway? I'd always assumed around forty-two, but then I like them to be just a little older than I am, unlike Joanne, who likes them a lot younger, except for her husbands.

"I'll see you out." This was good.

We said nothing as we walked around the building to the back. Greg held the car door for Beth and then came around to my side. I was already seated, but the door was still open.

"I'll call you."

He probably just wanted to know about Walter. He knew I'd worked at PanCanada, a detail I'd deliberately omitted to mention to Detective-Sergeant Boucherville for fear he'd never let me go. I had answered every question, only telling him what I saw and offering no speculation. It had been dif-

ficult since I had tons of theories to test, but I knew
Boucherville would be infuriated by what he'd consider my
interference; and it was late, and I had to go to the bathroom
again and just wanted to go home. He was going to be angry
when he found out.

Nevertheless, I was elated. It was very late, I was very
tired, and Greg was going to call me. The exhaustion had
caused a reversion to teenage emotions. If he'd been any more
flirtatious I might have sprouted a pimple on the spot.

"I can't go back there tonight," Beth said. "Beverly suggested I stay with her."

"Sure. I understand. Where does she live?" I hoped it
was close. I was not in any condition to start driving to the
outer edges of the island, much less over some bridge.

"Not far. The Glen Eagles."

No address needed. The Glen Eagles is an early-twenti-
eth-century apartment building on Cote-des-Neiges Road,
originally built for wealthy people who wanted the convenience of services without too many servants. The apartments
were of course equipped with enough servants' quarters for
a small nursing home by today's standards, because it would
have been unheard of to have none. Most of these huge lodg-
ings had been broken up into smaller billets over the years,
yet it was still a desirable rental address in a city where most
high-caliber buildings had long since gone condo. It was a
perfectly appropriate building for the sister of Walter
Whitestone, although I was surprised she rented.

"What does Beverly's husband do?" I asked, trying to
make the drive bearable. Her stony countenance was implacable, and I had the strong urge to slap her out of it.

"Winston is an insurance broker. With Levesque
Johnson."

"Beth, what did Detective-Sergeant Allard ask you?" I
said, abruptly changing the subject. Who cared what Bev-

erly's husband did for a living? I'd only asked the innocuous question to measure how Beth was responding. There were more important things to explore, and it was a short drive.

"He asked where I was. I told him the same story I told you."

"And he believed you?"

"Why shouldn't he? It's the truth." She looked steadfastly out the front window.

"Beth, it's not a great story. It doesn't make much sense. Think about it." I let it go at that. For tonight. The poor woman's husband had just been murdered. I'd have another go tomorrow.

Beth had more to say. For someone who had spent the greater part of our time together staring off into space, she was suddenly loquacious.

"Beverly will have to tell Mother Whitestone about this. Not that she'll understand, of course."

Lots of information in that sentence. Mother Whitestone? People actually called their in-laws that in real life? These WASPs sure were living up to all the stereotypes. And Mother Whitestone wasn't all there.

"Alzheimer's?"

"Yes. She's quite near the end. Beverly visits her every day at the hospital, and the doctors say she hasn't much time left. Walter wasn't the son he should have been." She sighed deeply. It was the first sign of caring for anyone that she had so far exhibited. "He said it upset him too much to visit her, since she rarely recognized him and consequently only went once a week, early Monday evening, and only for a short time. We'd dine late that day if he didn't have a business appointment following, which he frequently did. He had probably just got home when this dreadful thing happened."

It didn't track. Earlier she'd said that Walter had been expecting someone, which had been the excuse for her solitary meandering. Now she speculated that he'd likely just arrived home. She could have thought that he'd been killed earlier in the evening, before his appointment, but that didn't seem logical either. I also thought he'd been murdered later rather than earlier, as I'd seen the body and it had looked fresh and recent to me. I'd have to ask Greg about the time of death and try to find out who had been expected, if he ever called me and if I could finagle him into disclosing the details. I cheered up a little when I realized this could give me the excuse to call him.

Beth was already talking about Walter in the past tense. I had serious reservations about the relationship between Walter and his wife. I've never been married, but I would like to think that if my husband, current or ex, were suddenly murdered I'd be visibly upset. Even if I hated him I'd show some kind of emotion. Beth was the coldest woman I had ever met or a genius at hiding her feelings.

I sighed, too, at I don't know what. The atmosphere in the car was heavy and portentous and too much to think about. I was happy to pull up in front of the Glen Eagles and dump Beth into the care of a doorman. Let her be someone else's problem for a while.

By the time I got home I was drained and exhausted. The message button on my answering machine was flashing, but I wisely ignored it, which is very difficult for me. I always think it could be the call of my life, Ed McMahon calling to tell me I'd won a trillion dollars even though I'd never sent the wretched envelope back, since I could never find all the parts you had to affix to various locations on the form. Or some gorgeous rich man calling to tell me he'd fallen in love with me from a distance and wanted to sweep me off my feet and whisk me away to Florence for the weekend to shower me with gifts and diamonds. Since it wasn't likely that either of those two people would have called between eleven P.M. and four A.M., I resisted the temptation to listen.

WHEN I AWOKE at eleven-fifteen the next morning I was refreshed and ready for another day until the memory of the previous evening washed over me. There was information I needed and one sure way to get it. Why I needed to know anything about an affair that was none of my business is one of the defects of my otherwise sensible personality. I have to know everything about everything, especially if there is some glamour or mystery attached to the situation. I feel it helps me be a more well-rounded, empathic person.

After gathering my breakfast essentials, Diet Coke and a cigarette recently supplemented with a multivitamin, calcium, and vitamin E in deference to my advancing years, I settled in to begin the day. My instincts told me to call Joanne at home since she'd had a later night than I, but then, my instincts don't know her as well as I. Joanne is a true professional, more devoted to her job than any of the three husbands she's had or all her hard-bodied dalliances. So I called her at work and was lucky enough to find her at her desk.

"I was hoping you'd call soon. I was going to give you another half hour and then run the risk of waking you up. You'd have had enough sleep by then."

Joanne was obviously seeking information from me, since she would have otherwise called anytime she felt like it with nary a concern about my interrupted sleep. Which meant I had the upper hand in this lifelong jousting match, which pleased me enormously.

I seized the opportunity to get the first question in.

"Okay, so what did you learn?"

"About what?" Coy but useless.

"I didn't see you at the police station. And that means you stayed back to talk to either Beverly or a servant."

"They don't have any servants. Not even a live-out or a weekly. Beverly says Walter didn't like strangers touching his things and insisted it was Beth's job to keep everything in order. She went on about this at length. It was weird. She spoke in such a flat, clipped tone that I couldn't tell if she approved of this enslavement or not."

Joanne feels that money entitles her to a lackey to clean up. What with her busy schedule and Jacques being on call or at the hospital operating much of the time, I can see where it would be a necessity. I sort of have the same attitude, but I don't consider my twice-a-week cleaning lady an indentured servant; to me she's more like a savior.

"How'd you get Beverly to talk? She seems almost as buttoned up as Beth."

"You mean Lady Macbeth. With her catatonic staring I thought at any moment she'd start wringing her hands and spout a Shakespearean monologue. It looked like a set theater piece to me. What do you know about her?"

"Not much, really. But you know me, I'll find out. What about Beverly?" I was not going to be deflected into revealing anything about Beth until I got the scoop on Beverly. Joanne was magnanimous in her defeat.

"After you all wandered off, the good-looking Gregory Allard in the lead, I followed her back to her car. By the way, he looks at you a lot. I think he's interested."

"Really?" She nearly got me. I was about to ask her why she said that and what it could mean, but stopped myself. One of the few secrets I had managed to keep from her was the circumstances of Greg and my last meeting. It was truly none of her business and could damage us both.

"Not now. On with your story."

"It's a good one. I'll want something in return. Just as she was about to get into her car I accosted her. Nicely. She sort of recognized me, but not from television. She thought she knew me because I was your friend."

"How would she know we're friends?"

"Well, I sort of implied it. I said I saw her talking to you and wondered if I could be of any assistance since you had left."

"And she fell for it?"

"I'm very convincing. You know that. She looked pleased and thanked me but said there was nothing. I suggested she use my phone to contact the cleaning lady to roust her out of bed and coerce her to come over immediately so Beth wouldn't have to face the mess when she returned. That's when I learned there wasn't one. Then, if you can believe it, I offered to go in there and help tidy up."

"*You* offered to clean up someone else's mess?" She was right; I didn't believe it.

"I figured if I got inside I could snoop around, or at the very least, I could build on the budding camaraderie and pry some information out of her."

"Obviously she turned you down."

"Yep. She said Beth could deal with it in the morning. It wasn't her responsibility. Not very sisterly, in my opinion."

"Sister-in-lawly," I corrected.

"Right." Joanne stopped there, waiting for a prompt. Her turn for control.

"And?"

"And then I asked her how this terrible thing could happen, all the solicitous sycophant. And she blurted out, 'She did it.' "

"She who?"

"My question exactly. 'She' turns out to be his mistress."

"What?" Old habits die hard. I thought I'd cured myself of that particular phrase, but evidently not.

"Your old boss, the perfect Walter Whitestone, had a mistress. And his sister, Beverly, knew about it, so you can be damned sure his wife did, too. Unfortunately, Beverly clammed up. It dawned on her who I really was and to whom she was blurting, so she brought herself up short. Her eyes were furious little slits. Your mission, and you *will* choose to accept it, is to find out everything about said mistress."

"Me? How?"

"You. By reconnecting with your old network at the airline. Look, I know you're pissed because you didn't know about it before and you pride yourself on knowing everything, but now's your chance to vindicate your breach of knowledge and get all the dirt. Unless, of course, you're holding out on me."

"No. I'm not. You're right, though. How could I not have known? He's obviously a master of discretion, since I never heard a whisper about it. Someone there has to have some information. Time to explore the old secretary network. I'll give them some time to digest the fact that Mr. Whitestone has passed on and then make a few not-so-discreet calls. Let me think about this. I'll get back to you. You know, it's strange, I was really upset about Walter, but what you just told me makes me angry. I'd always thought he was such a straight-arrow kind of guy, and I'm disappointed in his behavior. It doesn't seem right."

"It isn't. Mistress implies a long-standing commitment and not a one-night stand or short fling. It's disloyal."

Joanne of the boy-toys has a code of morality that is convoluted but does exist. And it was true. No one could ever denigrate or dismiss her husband, and she adores him. She just has a very short attention span and a low resistance factor. I'd lately suspected that Jacques was aware of her escapades but never broached the subject to either of them. I like them both too much to endanger the friendship by such a breach of trust, as they seem to have worked it out between themselves and it was none of my business.

"Okay. Gotta go anyway," she said. "There's the editing of last night's tape to do. Speak to you later. By the way, nice duds last night. You always manage to wear the appropriate thing. Black with red, perfect for a murder. Bye." She rang off in her breezy way, her mind already on the next topic. One of Joanne's attributes is that she says what she needs to and then moves on. You're never bored.

As I hung up I noticed the red light blinking on my answering machine. Now was the time to find out who had called me in the middle of the night expecting me to be intelligible. The horrible, high-pitched fax tone was amplified by the recorder and screeched through the apartment, nearly causing me to spill my Diet Coke. I won't even begin to describe my reaction to that sound; suffice it to say that whoever had caused that was really lucky I didn't have caller ID. Whoever it was would have joined Walter Whitestone, and no jury would have convicted me.

4

EVEN THOUGH I had to circle the underground parking lot a few times, I found a space near the door and made it to the gym with exactly enough time. The disruption of my regular routine had almost made me forget my obligations. While I was working I seemed to be able to do a thousand different things in a day, all efficiently and effectively. Now all my planning and executing skills had eluded me. Or else my mind was turning to mush. There was never that much to do in a day, yet I still found I barely had time for it all. I guess the biggest change was that I now actually enjoyed the things I chose to do. *Chose* being the operative word. I was learning that the world was a pretty nice place to be when you could do what you wanted to, pretty much when you wanted to. I was also turning into a nicer person. I no longer heard the phrase "bitch on wheels" muttered as I left a room. I wasn't sure if this was a good thing but thought I'd go with it for a while.

I still had responsibilities. I had to manage my investments with great care and attention, and I had to watch out for my parents, who were now back from their winter sojourn in Florida because my sister lives in Philadelphia and my brother is a boy. I have never understood that last one, but it seems perfectly clear to my mother, who repeats it to me often. I was about to do the thing I hate most yet still do religiously. I really like food (not quite as much as Joanne, but that's a whole other story), and in order to consume enough of it to satisfy myself, I must pay penance, which means going to the gym and working out strenuously at least three times a week. I don't take classes but try to make it interesting by calling my competitive side to the fore. It's me against the machines, and once the battle is engaged it's a toss-up as to who will win.

I try to go at off-hours, not wanting to encounter anyone I know, but since everyone I know seems to belong there, it's often difficult. It's a fancy, yuppie, every-service-and-activity-you-could-ask-for type of place that caters to the serious bodybuilder, the housewife who takes classes during the day, and the dilettante who sits around the juice bar, which has suspiciously begun to serve alcohol of late. The bar is often full of guys on the lookout but pretending not to be, and women with hair too perfect and nails too long to have put in any serious gym time. The whole scene intimidates me, and I stay out of there after five P.M.

My preferred locker is a hidden and relatively inaccessible one that no one else wants since it's out of the line of vision of the routine security patrols and therefore vulnerable to break-ins, but I never have anything of much value with me, so I'm willing to run the risk. Lately, though, I'd noticed other people were getting the same idea and I was irked to find that today someone had already usurped my personal public space. I fanned the flames of the snit I was working on by imagining horrible things I was going to do to the inadvertent thief. This was all very therapeutic and effective as

I attacked the machines with a vengeance and completed the requisite workout, sweating and beaming. Not one machine had gotten the best of me, and I hadn't even had a good night's sleep.

I was appropriately energized for my next session. A few weeks prior, after a series of frightening newspaper headlines, I had realized that even though I was in good shape, I was still a prime target for an attacker (a nearly middle-aged woman who drove an expensive car and liked jewelry although she didn't have any that qualified as "important" pieces in her humble opinion, but the attacker's concept of "important" might differ significantly). I fought like a girl, with much arm waving and fear of doing any bodily harm, and decided it was time to learn to protect my investments and myself.

For a while I had scoped out the weight room and finally settled on the biggest, baddest guy I could find. He had shoulders as wide as a doorway and thighs larger than mine, although his were all muscle. I couldn't find a neck, which I took to be a good sign. When I approached him I discovered that his ego was in direct inverse ratio to his intelligence. Full of bravado, he scoffed at me, told me girls didn't have to know how to fight since there were guys out there to protect them. All said with very bad grammar. It wasn't my position to correct him, what with all those muscles; nevertheless, I pleaded my case, playing up to him in a totally disgusting fashion. He decided to be magnanimous and said, "I'll test you. Come at me and I'll give you a few pointers. But, lady, an old broad like you don't have to worry. It's the pretty young chicks what got something to be scared of."

Which was the perfect thing to say to me, since it made me furious. I may have been sweaty from working out, and I admit my hair wasn't so great either, but old? I took great exception. He must have been expecting me to take a swing at him, but I didn't. I lowered my head and barreled into him at top speed, knocking him over. He collapsed in a pile onto the floor, stunned. I had counted on physics, and I'd counted right. He was so top-heavy that once he was knocked off balance he went down easily.

But it didn't help my situation. He gave me a malevolent glare and slunk off to the locker room, hopping on one foot while adjusting his shoelace. He was obviously trying to convince anyone who had witnessed his embarrassment that his downfall was due to a technical difficulty. I stood there watching his retreating back, trying to figure out what to do next.

"Effective," a voice from behind me said.

I turned around to face a skinny guy I had seen before when I'd been checking out the possibilities. I had dismissed him because he was so thin. I'd watched him work out a few times, thinking that he might be all sinew and strength and speed. But he used low-level weights and demonstrated no special ability. He stood about six feet, had streaked blond hair tied back into a ponytail with a multicolored striped ribbon, and had the sweetest little face. All rosy and soft. He looked about fourteen years old, although I knew he couldn't be since he was always there during school hours and the exorbitant membership dues excluded most students. If he'd been there by the grace of his rich parents I'm sure they would have insisted on school attendance. Actually, I'd pretty much assumed that he was gay, since he was so angelic looking and I'm sometimes victim to stereotyping.

"Thanks. I think it surprised me as much as it did him."

"Well, it surprised him, all right."

"Is he going to be mad?" I had visions of him waiting for me by my car. Exactly the reason I wanted these damned lessons in the first place. This wasn't going well.

"I don't think he'll come after you. You're a girl. And it was a fluke shot. And his shoelaces were almost untied."

I burst out laughing. "It's going to take his little brain a long time to gather the necessary defense argument. Any of his friends around to witness the debacle?"

"Nah. He's a bodybuilder. Pretty much a loner."

"Oh, good."

"I can probably help you, but why do you want to learn to fight?"

"Fight dirty," I said in clarification.

"Smart. The martial arts are excellent for balanced opponents, and there aren't that many attackers who have the discipline."

"My problem exactly. Little discipline and a short attention span. And virtually no patience."

It was his turn to laugh. He looked so sweet, I wanted to hug him.

"Hi, I'm Barbara Simons."

"Rick Fogarty."

"Rick, can you really teach me? And fast?"

I must have sounded more dubious than I felt. A slow, lazy smile spread across his face. He now looked like the winner of the Angel Beautiful Babies pageant, if they had them up there.

"When you look like me you learn to take care of yourself at a young age. Pretty faces on guys who live in the St. Henri district make it tough in school. My credentials are that I've reached the age of thirty-six and am still pretty. I'm straight, but a lot of gay bashers out there don't take the time to ask. Yeah, I can fight. And yeah, I can win. It's not hard. Come, I'll show you a few tricks."

And so began my lessons. This was the fourth and last one, and Rick had proclaimed me a natural. At first I beamed at the compliment, but when the implications set in I wasn't so sure.

The bonus was Rick himself. He was a gentle, bright guy

with a great sense of humor. The reason I'd seen him there in the daytime was that he worked mostly at night and in the mornings doing strange things on overseas and Asian commodities markets. He obviously made a lot of money at it, since he wore expensive clothes and drove a Lexus and the ribbon that tied his hair back was always fresh and eclectic. I've tried to train myself not to notice these superficial things, but it seems impossible, although I have learned not to share these musings with others.

He liked me and I liked him, and it looked to be the beginning of a nice friendship. It took a few tries, but I successfully executed my final maneuver, which was pretty disgusting, calling for the use of digits in orifices I don't like to think about. He'd advised me to keep my nails medium length and take glycerine tablets to keep them hard. If I didn't want to wear colored polish (he'd seen me stare in disdain at the acrylic wonders of the perfect bodies in skimpy leotards), I should coat my nails with several layers of clear, hardening varnish. Nails were great legal weapons.

By the time I hit the showers I was hot, sweaty, dirty, and happy. There was something very appealing about knowing how to fight like a guy. A mean, dirty, low-down kinda guy. It was a primal kind of high, a back-to-nature, he-man macho kind of thing. And here I was, sharing the experience. It was fabulous.

I washed off the grit and grime (the floor mats weren't as clean as my hefty dues should have entitled me to), noticed the latest batch of bruises Rick had inflicted on me, and stayed under the hot stream for a long time, loosening my muscles. My body was a delightful blend of blacks, blues, yellows, and greens. I could have had Rick arrested.

When we met in the bar to celebrate my graduation we both looked completely different. He was in his louche mode, a beige silk shirt, beige linen pants, a tooled black leather belt, and beige silk socks with black Italian loafers. His hair was tied with a multicolored silk ribbon for that little flash of color. I was wearing my regulation daytime going-nowhere uniform: jeans, white T-shirt, and blazer, which today was red instead of the usual navy. My little bit of color in honor of my elevation to the rank of professional sneaky person.

"You look better. Your hair's great." A feminine comment, but it came from him. I realized he'd always seen me in my gym attire, which consisted of knee-length leotards and a very used T-shirt. Our sessions took place after a workout, so my face would have been flushed and my tied-back hair frizzing out and sans ribbon. Now it was loose and clean, the auburn accentuated by the pinpoint lighting. Lipstick and mascara helped.

"You look fabulous. Why are you all dressed up?" I asked. It was obvious he'd made a big effort.

He blushed. Fourteen became twelve. "I have a date later and some things to do first, so I won't have time to go home and change."

A date. I'd never considered that side of him.

"First date?"

"How'd you know?"

"Aside from the ribbons you don't seem the vain type to me, but a lot of thought went into that casual-yet-elegant outfit. Who's the woman and where did you meet her? You don't have to answer. I always ask questions like that and never get insulted when rebuffed. It's amazing how much people will tell you if you ask a direct question."

"You should know how to fight if you're that blunt."

"Yep," I said with a disarming grin. "So who's the girl?" He looked so young to me that I couldn't possibly imagine a woman. More a counterculture Gen-Xer who dressed all in black but had no tattoos or nose rings. She likely wrote dark poetry.

The waitress chose that moment to come take our order,

and Rick looked relieved. I had the regulation Diet Coke and he had a juice concoction loaded with calories.

"I have trouble keeping weight on," he said, as though he needed an excuse. While I can't eat all the good stuff in the world, I don't mind watching others indulge. It's interesting that people often feel guilty ordering something fattening and feel the obligation to explain. In Rick's case he may have simply been trying to divert my attention. If he fought sneaky, he'd likely think sneaky.

Didn't work. "So who's the girl?"

"I've been politely trying to tell you it's none of your business, but I see you can't take a hint."

"Nope."

"Well," he began. I thought I had him. "I will not tell you, since I can't see what possible good it would do. Maybe if something develops."

"Okay, then. Where do you live?"

He started to laugh. "If you can't get some information you'll go for any. Let me first tell you that I am a very private person. I have few friends and fewer acquaintances. I manage to keep myself busy and entertained without littering the field with companions."

"So why'd you start talking to me and volunteer to teach me?" This time the deflection worked. I really wanted to know, and could always get back to the other.

"I've seen you here often. You attack the machines with diligence and concentration and rarely talk to anyone. I thought it was interesting that you would want to learn. Most people would never even think of it. It takes a warped kind of mendacity, which I appreciate. Also, you took down that huge hulk one-two-three, operating only on instinct, and I liked that you showed no fear. You sized your opponent up in a flash and knew he'd never hurt a *girl*, and so you had the advantage."

I noted that he had a large vocabulary and good sentence

structure. Must have gone to a private school, which premise belied his St. Henri roots. A great many of the local denizens could hardly afford food, much less private school. He'd probably been beaten up a lot as a kid.

"I didn't know I thought all that."

"You did, and it intrigued me. I'm glad I approached you. I like you, and you may yet become one of my few friends."

I beamed. "So where do you live?"

He nearly sprayed juice on his shirt. "Okay, okay. I shouldn't have complimented you. It made you cocky."

I didn't say anything, simply nodded. If I'd answered I'd have had to repeat the question, and this time it would have been annoying. Years of labor negotiations have taught me when not to press my advantage. Most of the time.

"The Chateau." Another building that needs no street address. I'd have to consider moving to one of those. You never have to explain to anyone how to get there.

"Hey, that's near me. I'm at the top of the hill."

"I know."

"What do you mean, you know?"

"I followed you home one time."

"What?" That pesky word again. "You followed me? That's disgraceful. But good. Why?"

"I wanted to know more about the person who's going to be my friend."

"I think I'm supposed to be flattered and thus not annoyed."

"Yeah." He blushed at the confession. It had obviously taken a lot out of him, as he looked like a ten-year-old who'd been caught peeking into the girls' bathroom.

"And just when did this stalking occur?"

"The day I first met you. After I offered to help you."

"And you, very private person who doesn't let anyone get close, decided on the spot that I was going to be your friend?"

"Yeah."

I let him off the hook. Actually I was pleased. I liked him and was glad to add him to my odd assortment of friends.

"Let's celebrate this grand concession. Would you like to have dinner one night?" I hadn't asked a man out in years. Actually, ever. In high school I was too terrified of the probable rejection to even consider the possibility. In college I was too much the intellectual to reduce myself to such mundane, childish things. Even later, I could never bring myself to do it. Maybe I was born in the wrong decade; I would have made a perfect fifties teenager.

"Sure. That'd be fun. Sometime soon," he said, as he gathered his things. "I have to leave now. Things to do."

As I watched his receding back I wondered why I didn't find some easier people. This was going to be a lot like my relationship with Joanne. Or even my friend Susan. I never seem to have the upper hand in these associations, but on the whole, they're stimulating, entertaining, and long lasting. I'd been friends with Joanne since kindergarten, and Susan dated from the high school years. On reflection, I hadn't made any new friends in a long time, so this was definitely going to be a bonus.

I went to pay the bill and discovered Rick had taken care of it. I thought it was my turn to be sneaky and asked the bartender what she knew about Rick.

"Nothing much. He comes in here almost every day, drinks the same thing, is very polite, and never talks to anyone. If someone tries to talk to him he's pleasant enough, but cuts it short. You're the first person I've seen him socialize with. Lots of women try to talk to him—he is a hunk—but it never goes anywhere."

No help there. I'd have followed him just to pay him back if I'd thought of it in time, but he was long gone by the time I reached my car and I didn't think a Mercedes was a good tailing car. I'd have to get ahold of one.

5

B Y T H E T I M E I got home it was a little after four and I was exhausted. The annoying light on my answering machine flashed, and try as I might, as usual it was too much for me to resist.

First up was Joanne. "Watch the six o'clock news. You made the final cut. Find out anything?"

Next was equally interesting. "Hello, Barbara. This is Beverly Warfield. I'm calling on behalf of Beth Whitestone. There will be some friends over at her house this evening, and she wondered if you could make it. No need to RSVP. Just show up anytime after seven if you can. Look forward to seeing you."

Very bizarre. A formal invitation to what I presumed to be some sort of wakelike affair. All full names, as though I wouldn't recognize the people involved. And why did Beverly call me? Why not Beth? Why me? I had nothing to do with this, so why did she want me there? It's not like we were close or anything; she'd barely said six words to me last night.

I was too tired to puzzle it out. I'd find out later, because no way was I going to miss this conclave. There were things to find out, and I suspected a lot of alcohol would be consumed. If I played my cards right I could finagle a lot of information out of some drunk uncle or something.

The choice was an extra hour of sleep or some food. I debated the question for a while, then figured Beth would have some platters set out to feed the folks, and I could probably manage to eat more than my fair share without being obvious. A student of sneaky Rick on all occasions.

I knew I had made the right decision when I woke up almost an hour and a half later, craving even more sleep. In the nick of time I remembered to switch on the news. The screen filled with Joanne, looking better than she had in the flesh, her serious tortoiseshell glasses perched on her nose. This was her television eyewear, fitted with special nonreflective lenses so as not to distort the image. She owns tons and tons of pairs of glasses and always has one for every outfit or mood. But on TV she always wears these. When I asked her about it she said she didn't want to appear frivolous and always carried them to be prepared for any camera eventuality. A pro all the way through.

Joanne reported the demise of Walter Whitestone. Behind her, the body was being carried out on a stretcher and placed into the coroner's van. This stand-up must have been taped after I was gone, because the body was still upstairs when Beth and I left for the police station. Joanne said that Walter had been stabbed and there were as yet no suspects. The camera then switched to a doubles shot of us, with me looking into the camera, gushing, "He had this huge knife sticking out of his back." Oh, shit. This was not good. Joanne was dead meat—although I will admit it made for good television and I didn't look half bad. There was no more of me, as that was the only good sentence I'd managed before Detective-Sergeant Allard grabbed the microphone from me.

Whereas I'd cursed him the night before for doing it, now I was furious he hadn't gotten there sooner. Me, Barbara Simons, in charge of public relations for a huge airline, shooting off her mouth like the village idiot. This was not good. I'd become much too laid-back.

I switched it off and went on to a more pleasant task: wardrobe choice. What did one wear to one's very first wake? All black, while chic, was too funereal. Save that for the actual service. Too short was in bad taste. Pants were not appropriate. A big problem to consider as I wandered through my closet, the best feature of my apartment. It had been the clincher when I was considering whether to buy. It was enormous—bigger than those of my friends who had huge houses. The architect had wisely decided that the large bedroom could be slightly smaller and the closet enormous. Consequently, my model of apartment had been the fastest seller in the whole building, and everyone I knew was jealous. If ever I had people over, it became a focal point for the women: prime stop on the not so grand tour.

Since I had so much space I rarely threw anything out, and it was full and an embarrassment. I'd promised myself that now that I had the time I would weed through it and there would be a lot of poor, battered Montreal women soon wearing very expensive clothes. Well, it would be good for their morale and court appearances.

I chose an ankle-length navy-and-cream flowered skirt that was not my usual style but had somehow found its way into my closet following a trip to New York and Barney's. It had never been worn, so it took some time to figure out what went with it. I finally decided on a cream silk knit T-shirt and a navy crepe jacket. Very springy. Looking in the mirror, I decided there was some merit to these long lean skirts; I looked positively thin, which was a good thing.

It took a few moments to get the hang of walking, what

with the skirt flapping around my ankles, but I got used to it once I changed into more comfortable shoes. Wedge heels may look good, but they are a difficult balancing act, and combined with the material at my ankles, boded an undignified sprawl across Beth's living room. And I'd already made a public spectacle of myself once today.

I matched my navy blue car perfectly. As I drove down Beth's quiet street I couldn't help but notice all the cars parked around her house. Quite the crowd to console the bereaved widow. The front door was ajar, so I let myself in without ringing the doorbell, thinking I'd reconnoiter before I made my presence known. I didn't know if anyone present had seen my televised blunder and needed the moment to compose myself before I faced Beth again.

Everyone was in the living room, and it was a large number of everyone. About thirty people were congregated in the ample space. The house had been designed with entertaining in mind, a generous cross-floor, dining-living room plan. I wondered how long they'd owned it: at least for the past twelve years, to my knowledge. Had the scruffy, faded stair carpeting been there when they bought it, or had it been a family home forever? I knew the mother was in a nursing home, so maybe it had been hers.

The downstairs was no match for the up-. Last night's upheaval had been righted, by the nonweeping widow herself, according to Joanne's information. Everything here was beautiful. Crystal vases full of fresh-cut flowers were scattered about, warming the large space. The furniture was sparse yet sumptuously upholstered, with a burgundy and navy Regency striped fabric covering the larger pieces. This was a room clearly designed for large cocktail parties, with lots of space and small mahogany tables strategically placed for empty glasses.

"Barbara!" came a loud roar behind me. I didn't have to

turn around to recognize that voice. One of my favorite people in the whole wide world, Pietr Korlinski. Of course, I should have expected to see him here; he was head of security at PanCanada, and his curiosity and strict sense of duty would inevitably lead him here.

"Saw your performance on TV, missy. Convinced me to come here tonight and have a word with you. When I spoke to Beth she said you were expected."

"Pietr, it was stupid of me, but it was the middle of the night and it was Joanne."

"That woman gets you into altogether too much trouble. And now you've found another body. How did you manage that? No, don't answer. You'll have a good excuse. Just one thing, missy," he said as he encircled me with his huge arm, "stay away from this thing. Keep your nose out of it. I'm too busy these days to keep an eye on you."

"Busy at what?"

"I'm leavin'."

That was news, but not a surprise.

"Leaving Pancake or leaving Montreal?" There's been a lot of Anglo flight recently.

"Leavin' PanCanada. The new powers that be and I don't see eye to eye. Mainly, they want information I won't give 'em."

Pietr's one of the best in the world when it comes to airline security and had surely been a consideration when Pan-Canada was bought out. I could well understand their desire to pump him for everything he was worth. But they didn't know Pietr. He'd tell them everything he felt they were legally entitled to and not one word more. His experience and knowledge were his currency.

"What are you going to do?"

"Don't know for sure yet, but I got a few ideas and I don't want to move, so somethin' here. Keep you posted. Right now

I'm negotiatin' my departure. Financial security for information. Followin' your instructions."

He'd been contemplating this radical move for a while now, and had consulted with me on the best formula for the best results. I was flattered that he'd taken me up on my quasi-blackmail approach. He obviously had little respect for management, since he'd bridled at the mere mention of the idea when I had first broached it. That he'd resorted to those tactics reinforced the notion that things were not running smoothly at the airline, and it heartened my vindictive little soul.

"Babs, gotta run. Just dropped in to relay my condolences. Gonna be out of town for the next few days and might miss the funeral. Poor Wally. He was a good guy. Not enough of a shark for today, and sometimes a bottom feeder. I'll miss him at our Tuesday-night poker game. 'Bye."

He left before I could get another word in, which had probably been his plan, as he inched backward the whole time he delivered his parting speech. How such a big man could move so delicately was beyond me. He seemed to have some sort of internal radar as he sidestepped a table injudiciously placed in his path, never breaking reverse stride.

With Pietr gone I now set about the task of relaying my condolences to Beth. But she was nowhere in sight and neither was Beverly, so I went looking for food. All I found was a plate of gingersnap cookies set on the buffet piece that doubled as a bar. A very busy bar. Two bottles of scotch were empty and the third half-full. I peeked underneath and saw three more were in reserve. There was a Waterford cut-crystal bucket full of ice, and it wasn't moving; this crowd liked its scotch neat and plentiful. Gingersnaps aren't my favorite, but I was hungry, so I quickly scarfed down three and nearly choked from the dryness. They were a close approximation to the chalk that Joanne had once conned me into tasting when we were in kindergarten. I settled for a glass of water since there was nothing else nonalcoholic, and tossed in a slice of lemon to simulate vodka or gin. I didn't want to appear the teetotaler that I generally am in this well-oiled crowd.

Walter would not have been pleased. Every time I went to see him in his office, a plate of delicacies would be offered. He firmly believed in plying all comers with food, which he would mostly eat himself, since his visitors were generally too nervous to consume anything. A summons from the president can be an effective appetite suppressant. Those little goodies probably accounted for his avoirdupois—it didn't look as if Beth was interested in food.

I circled the room, scanning the crowd for a familiar, likable face. I'm not sure what I expected, probably some people from work, but the ones I knew hadn't been invited to this private gathering. I should have been flattered, but I was confused. Why had I been summoned? And where were Beth and Beverly? I wanted to say how sorry I was and get out of there before I starved to death.

As I stood near the door, an attractive man approached. He was around fifty-five and very well preserved, about six-two with abundant dark hair, graying attractively at the temples. The epitome of a captain of industry. And definitely pickled.

"Well, well, well, who have we here? A *friend* of Walter's? Old boy sure could pick them."

"I'm Barbara Simons. I used to work for Walter, and I'm a friend of Beth's." I let the inference slide, choosing not to point out the breach of good taste.

"Oh, the gal who found Wally. Sorry about the crack; I think I've had a little too much. I'm Winston Warfield, Beverly's husband."

I could have called it. We Canadians don't often have the double-barreled names that the English upper class is so fond of, so our families with lofty aspirations for their usually first-born male child elect alliteration to make a statement. This group boasted a Walter Whitestone and a Winston Warfield. And both had married women with similar-sounding names and the same first initials. Beth and Beverly. If there were any cousins around, I'd never sort this out.

"Where is Beverly?"

"Upstairs with Beth, going through some of Walter's stuff."

I wanted to ask him what stuff, but he reeled off to the bar for a refill.

Just then the door opened and a girl of about twenty entered, lugging a backpack crammed to the brim. She dropped it with a thud and looked around the room, surprised. As I was the nearest person, she glared at me and said, "Who the hell are all these people and what are they doing here? Where's Mummy? Is Kenneth home yet?"

Had to be the daughter. On Walter's office desk reposed a family photograph showing a handsome Walter, a passable Beth, a gorgeous daughter of about sixteen, and an acne-ridden son of about fifteen. Beth had delivered him one of each and then closed up shop. I never would have recognized this one. If memory served me, her name was Margaret and she was supposedly away at school somewhere. She was scruffy and dirty, and if she had flown in from an American school, I was sure she'd been hassled at customs. Which probably accounted for her snit. Her greasy hair straggled down her back, an unattractive mousy-brown split-ended mess. No makeup, eyebrows that seriously needed plucking, and the requisite torn jeans and flannel shirt. Very Seattle.

"I'm Barbara. You must be Margaret."

"Yeah, so?"

"Your mother is upstairs with your aunt; I don't think your brother has arrived yet. And these people were invited by your mother."

She looked at me suspiciously. "Did Uncle Winnie off him? Nah, he's too loaded all the time. How about dear, sweet Auntie Bevy? Why am I asking you? You're nobody. I'm out of here." With that, she picked up her backpack and trudged up the stairs, dragging the burden behind her. Maybe bumping that thing up the stairs repeatedly was the cause of the worn cabbage roses.

"Charmer, isn't she?" It was Winston again. He'd watched the whole interchange from nearby, looking remarkably sober. "She used to be such a nice young lady until she went away to school and found herself the obligatory useless boyfriend. All the usual palaver. He lives off her, doesn't work, drove Wally mad. Meg was always his little darling, but she's turned into an ugly little thing, always belligerent. To get her to disentangle herself from the boy Wally cut her off, but she's found enough money to live on somehow and we hear he's still mooching off her." He said all this without slurring a word, then lapsed. "Time for another drinkie-poo. Before her brother arrives."

As if on cue the door opened and a gorgeous young man strode in. Very Ivy League and blond. I suspected a little help in that direction since it was sun-streaked, and he had no tan. Maybe he used SPF 435. He wore well-cut, unripped Levi's that fit him like a second skin, accentuating his long legs, and a jeans shirt tucked in, with a white T-shirt peeking through the open neck. The urban cowboy at his best. The kid was drop-dead stunning.

As I was the only one near him—Winston had fled at the sound of the door and I seemed to have been elected head of the welcoming committee—he turned to me and beamed a huge smile full of very white teeth. "Hello, we haven't met before, have we? Although you do seem vaguely familiar. I'm sorry if I've forgotten your name. I'm Kenneth Whitestone, the son of the deceased."

Was everybody here nuts? This was not the kind of bereavement I was accustomed to. No keening and moaning or even keeping a stiff upper lip. Everyone was either drunk or saying very odd things.

"I'm Barbara Simons. I used to work for your father," I repeated. "Your sister's just arrived and is upstairs. So are your mother and your aunt."

"Ah, a little family confab. All accusing each other, I suppose. Comparing alibis. My money is on the chairman of the board at Pancake. Well, I guess I'll go up and add my two cents. Nice chatting. I expect I'll see you again soon."

Everybody was pointing fingers at everybody. And they were all related. And I was very confused. I spotted the aforementioned chairman coming out of the kitchen carrying a full bottle of scotch and shuddered. Here was the man who had personally fired me. All my years of service and devotion meant nothing in these leaner years where the word *downsizing* has come to be an accepted euphemism. This was the person who had figured largely in my violent fantasies for about two months after he did the deed. I hadn't thought about him for a while, reveling in my newfound freedom and all the perks associated with not being stressed out. All the old tension came rushing back, and I was ready to bolt out the door, when I caught myself. This was the new, calmer, wiser me. I could handle this. And maybe he did kill Walter and I could trick him into admitting it and all at PanCanada would be grateful and crown me king. Gender gets a little mixed up in my reveries.

I strode up to him purposefully and extended my hand, knowing he couldn't refuse to shake it. Also knowing that both his hands were full, one with a bottle and the other with a glass, and I might discomfit him. No way. He reached behind him and settled the bottle on the bar without even looking, then placed the glass on a small table beside him that held an empty ashtray. That was another thing; no one here smoked, although the ashtrays were plentiful and I was dying for a cigarette. I wasn't going to be the only one, and so, as often happens these days at nice upper-middle-class, upwardly mobile Anglophone gatherings, I abstained. Where were all those nice Francophones that I read about, the ones who still smoked like chimneys? This was a very English, white-bread crowd.

"How do you do," he said, as he grasped my hand in both of his. "I don't believe I've had the pleasure. My name is Harrison Harrison, a little peccadillo of my mother's, ha-ha."

The bastard didn't even recognize me. And I'd heard that stupid name joke a million times and still didn't see what was funny. I hoped he'd really killed Walter and would be put away for many years. Try that name out in prison.

"We have met. I'm Barbara Simons; you fired me." What the hell, I had nothing to lose. If he couldn't remember me, I couldn't very well ask him for a letter of recommendation.

"Ah, yes. We do miss you. Were you *close* to Walter?"

There it was again. That bad-taste innuendo. This time it wasn't going to be ignored.

"Excuse me? I don't understand."

"You know, *close*," he repeated, this time accompanied by a wink. I debated taking him down with one of the tricks Rick had taught me, but one of us had to be the adult here and I was the obvious choice.

"That's a very filthy mind you have, Harry," I said, knowing he hated the appellation. A company-wide memo to that effect had been circulated on his arrival—more a thinly veiled threat. "Walter Whitestone was my boss, a remarkable one at that. He cared for his employees and they cared for him. I, for one, will miss him. Perhaps you're envious of the effect he had on women? He was certainly the most attractive executive in the whole company—ask any of the secretaries."

I didn't dare tell him that he, conversely, looked like a toad, with bulging eyes and an angled receding hairline.

"You could be a little nicer to me if you want your job back. After all, now I'll be president and chairman and can call the shots. Home office isn't pleased with the job of your replacement—not seasoned enough in the market, and we've been discussing asking you back. So I'd show a little more respect, young lady."

I wasn't surprised the new guy was messing up. One of the things that PanCanada prided itself on was employee relations, and I'd been responsible for a good part of that. I'd always been seen to be fair, if a little tough, but never vindictive. I'd read in the paper (another no-no; the press should never have a hint of trouble) that relations were degenerating and a new contract with the pilots was due, as with the mechanics. I considered for a nanosecond reclaiming my position and decided I didn't want it. Especially if it meant working for this man. Things must be really untenable there if even Pietr was leaving. Harrison Harrison could keep his stupid job.

"Sorry, clean up your own mess. I'm not interested."

"Well, don't be too hasty. Maybe we can work out some other arrangement. I like you. You have spunk."

He exuded such slime, I felt like taking a bath. Or hosing him down, but he'd probably like that.

"Why are you here? As I recall, you and Walter were never on the best of terms. I know you tried to get rid of him but couldn't."

"Who told you that malicious lie?" The small amount of charm he'd displayed vanished, his eyes turning cold and mean. I'd finally gotten to him and was ecstatic.

Without sounding the least bit smug, I said, "I have my sources. Remember how well connected I am."

"Old Wally and I never disagreed, really. We saw the

direction of the firm differently, but it was never personal. Actually, I was rather fond of the guy." Really bad recovery, but at least the eyes went back to their normal bulging.

Fat chance. I had it from an excellent source, a secretary, of course, that these two loathed each other and Harrison was trying to convince the people at the head office in Memphis that he could do a better job and they could save a lot of money if they dumped Walter and gave Harry-Harry both jobs. A little more money for him, of course, but not the double salary they were now paying, was one of his rationales. Obviously head office hadn't seen it his way, since Walter maintained his control over the basic operations and decision making. The position of chairman was more a figurehead than anything else—someone from Memphis sent up to watch over the operation and report back. Harrison Harrison earned less money than Walter, which must have rankled; Canadian dollars, too, which put him at a disadvantage with his American colleagues and which he was lobbying to have changed to the same amount in U.S. funds. Another secretary told me that, but it was public information anyway.

Harry-Harry was making me ill, so I sidled away from him and went back to my post by the door. I took one last look at the crowd, saw absolutely no one that I wanted to talk to and no one I felt kindly toward, and let myself out. Once outside in the cool, fresh night I took a deep breath in an effort to cleanse myself of all the mean-spiritedness inside. A few months away from the rat race and I no longer had the stomach for it. Not delusional, I realized that I had probably been a lot like these people—always on the lookout for myself and how to improve my position. It was a horrible concept, fortunately now part of my past. At the moment all I wanted was to go home to bed. I'd sort out these strange people tomorrow.

6

A S   I   S T E P P E D   down the few stairs I heard, "Psst, Barbara." I looked around and could see no one. The door was firmly shut, so it hadn't come from there.

"Psst, Barbara, up here."

I looked up but saw nothing. "The corner window. To your right. Look."

Sure enough, there was Beth, her head sticking out the window, waving frantically. "Go around the back. I want to talk to you."

I couldn't fathom what she wanted to say, but it sounded intriguing. A secret rendezvous right under her family's nose. As I circled I noted the ground was still muddy from the spring thaw. It was soft and made a squelching sound under my feet. There was no delineated path to follow, or at least none that I could find in the dark. I tried to steer away from the barren bushes so as not to snag my clothes, trodding through unplanted flower beds, knowing my shoes would be filthy but, I hoped, not ruined. They were an integral part of the ensemble.

Around the back was a nice patio paved with multicolored stones. The regulation barbecue hadn't been unwrapped for the season and stood swathed in dirty plastic sheeting. The chairs and table were obviously still in the garage or basement or somewhere, since there was nothing else in sight. Not even Beth. I wanted to sit down in the worst way to inspect my shoes in the light spilling out from the kitchen window, but there was no place, so I stood and decided to count to twenty-five and then leave. I was at twenty-four and three-quarters when Beth rounded the corner—wearing rubber boots.

"I took the back stairs to the basement and came out the side door. I didn't want anyone to see me."

"Why not?"

"You've seen the lot. Would you want to talk to them?"

Okay. I wasn't going to respond to that. They were her relatives and friends, and I knew better than to get involved.

She grabbed my arm and held tightly, almost hysterically. She looked composed, sedately dressed in a simple dark gray suit with a white blouse, but the intensity with which she squeezed belied her calm.

"Ouch," I said, as I pulled away and began rubbing the spot. Another bruise.

"Sorry," she said, distracted, not really meaning it. I don't think she knew what she was apologizing for. "You must do something for me."

I'd already figured out that "why me?" would be a useless question. This was the determined, efficient Beth that I knew and not the taciturn, withdrawn doppelgänger of last night. Inevitably, I said, "What?"

"I want you to talk to *her*. I need to know what Walter's been up to lately. I've spoken with our accountant, and our finances are in a shambles. It seems that Walter has spent and invested unwisely, and besides his insurance policy there isn't very much. There had once been a substantial amount that is no longer there, which leads me to the question of how much of my money does she have?"

"Who's *she*?"

"Barbara, do not treat me as a child. The whole world knows about her. That you would think I'd be stupid enough not to know disappoints me. While I am aware of her, I will not stoop to confront her. I am a proud woman."

Beth was all the way back.

"Beth, I swear I just found out this morning. I never had a clue. Walter was very discreet. Anyway, I don't know who she is, and why do you want *me* to do this?"

"You're a capable woman. Walter was always fond of you and valued your input into things. Oh, yes, even with her around, we were still close. He talked a lot about his work, and I am well aware of his allies and his enemies, Harry-Harry being the prime one. You seem to me to be a take-charge kind of person, tempered with kindness and understanding. I'd like to thank you for last night; I couldn't have got through it without you. Please do this for me. I think the police suspect me, and I need to find out more before I begin accusing others. There is no use airing my dirty laundry in public if there is nothing to gain."

I noticed that she always called him Walter. I did, too, but he wasn't my husband and I'd often heard others addressing him as Wally. She's a very formal person, trained to be tight-lipped about family indiscretions, even if it meant being accused of murder. I would holler and point a finger in every direction, trumpeting my innocence and let the guilty hang, whoever it might be. I love my family dearly, but under no circumstances am I going to prison for any one of them. Family values are one thing; incarceration is a whole other one.

Unless, of course, Beth did it and was using me to build credibility. Or one of her obnoxious children or relatives did it and she wanted to lay the blame elsewhere.

"Beth, I don't even know who she is."

"Here," she said, as she thrust a piece of crumpled paper into my hand. "Put this in your purse and get on it tomorrow morning. Go home to bed now; you must be tired."

I *was* tired. We'd both been up most of the previous night. Meekly I obeyed her and shoved the paper into my bag. However, I had no intention of waiting until morning to check it out. I wanted to know the identity of this mystery woman whom everyone else seemed to know about, and I wanted to know now. Manners and obedience being very important to Beth, I nodded in agreement, impatient to get back to my car to inspect it.

Beth seemed satisfied that I would do her bidding and turned abruptly around, heading back the way she had come.

As I trudged through the mud toward my car I hoped I still had a rag in the trunk to wipe my feet off before ruining its carpets. I had stupidly taken the grimy winter floor mats out just two days before, revealing unsoiled, plush pale beige. Since Beth had just told me she had no money there was no sense even contemplating billing her for the carpeting and the shoes. I was tired and crabby and wanted my bed.

Rounding the last corner, I heard the front door close. I held back a moment, not wanting to be seen skulking around the perimeter of the house. Although Beth had summoned me, the person coming out wouldn't know that and I didn't want to attract attention and have to explain myself.

I peeked and saw Harry-Harry leaving. He headed directly for his car, which was farther up the block than mine and parked on the same side. His stride was purposeful, a bouncing gait that suggested he was in a hurry and had no interest in his surroundings.

Not in the least concerned about being spotted or accosted by Harry-Harry, I headed out toward my car and home. Still, I kept an eye on him. Kenneth had suggested he might have murdered Walter and he was a loathsome little man who bore careful watching at all times. We arrived at our respective cars at the same time. In the light, I decided my shoes weren't that bad and simply scraped them off on the edge of the sidewalk. I didn't bother wiping them, because I didn't think I had the time.

On the short walk to the car I had decided that it was imperative for me to follow Harry-Harry. I absolutely needed to know where he was going, sure that there was something nefarious afoot. The only excuse I can offer for this conviction is that I was very tired and I hated the man. The fantasy of catching him at something was too enticing to pass up.

I needn't have been concerned that my Mercedes might be too obtrusive a tail car, as Harry-Harry never looked back. He hardly looked at the road in front of him, often narrowly missing parked cars. As soon as he started up the engine he hit the phone. I could see he didn't have one of the hands-free kind that allows you to keep both hands on the steering wheel. He was using a regular pocket-sized cellular that was causing him difficulty. The overhead light in his car switched on as he tried dialing and driving at the same time. I guessed that he didn't have one of the newer models that light up, which was to my advantage in that I could keep a better eye on him.

He careened down the street, his attention still on the phone. Either he was getting a busy signal or he was a lousy dialer. Finally he made the connection, but conveniently neglected to switch off the light.

The next fifteen minutes was spent wandering through the side streets of Westmount, with Harry-Harry jabbering away. He was so engrossed with his conversation that I could keep the distance between us relatively short. I had no idea where we were going, or even in which direction we were headed, as he seemed to be driving up and down the streets with no fixed intention. Often we backtracked.

Finally we ended up on Cote St. Luc Road, at the top of the hill, heading downward. There was more traffic here, and Harry-Harry wisely decided to terminate his conversation before he got himself killed. We'd wasted a lot of time and a lot of gas getting here. I let a few cars slip between us on the busy street, as he'd remembered to switch off his light and was now paying attention. By this point I was convinced I was onto something, and would be let down if this escapade turned into nothing.

I nearly lost him at the Decarie intersection, because the light turned yellow just as I got there. I said a silent prayer and barreled right through it, eliciting only one angry honk.

At the corner of Harvard and Cote St. Luc he cut across two lanes of traffic and pulled into Provisoir, an all-night convenience store. I was seriously deflated. We'd come all this way for a lousy bottle of milk? Maybe I could catch him, Mr. Major-League Anti-Smoking, in the act of buying a package of cigarettes. I know I was clutching at straws, but something had to make this dumb trip worthwhile.

I pulled into a bus stop across the street, dousing my lights but with the motor still running. From this position I could see into the well-lit store and check out what he was buying. Only, he fooled me. Harry-Harry got out of his car, slammed the door, and walked right past the store entrance. After about five feet he suddenly got wary. I ducked as he furtively checked out his surroundings before proceeding. Why he chose this moment to become suspicious of someone watching or following him is beyond me. However, it confirmed the fact that I was onto something.

When I sat up and took stock of the situation, I figured out where he was headed. At the far corner of the building there was a public phone, the kind with the plastic bubble on top, open to the elements on all other sides. Perfect for eavesdropping.

If I got caught, so what? What could he do? Still, it would be better to be circumspect. Quickly checking it out, I saw the alley to the right of the store went around the back. With any luck it would completely encircle the store. I peeled across the street, lights still out, and drove down the lane. Sure enough, there was another lane in the back and one at the other end of the store. I hadn't been aware that it opened back up onto the parking lot, because a big Dumpster blocked the exit. It was perfect for my use.

Afraid that I might miss some vital bit of conversation, I jumped out of the car and scooted between the Dumpster and the building, able to get within three feet of him without much danger of being spotted. And I made it in time. Harry-Harry was still dialing as I reached my post. He must have had to look the number up somewhere.

I stood immobile, barely breathing since the stench was unbelievable. The Dumpster was full, and it smelled like today the store had thrown out absolutely everything that was beyond the expiration date. Things were rotting inside and smaller things were scurrying by my feet. It was horrible. My instinct was to kick out, but I didn't want to make any noise. Fortunately it was too dark in my hiding place to actually see what was scampering. It was either a large rat, a skunk, or a raccoon, none of which I wanted to confront. I turned my full attention to Harry-Harry, while taking shallow breaths.

He listened, punched in some numbers, listened again, and punched in some more. Obviously calling a company rather than a private home. Someone was working late or waiting for his call, even considering possible time zone changes. What puzzled me was that he had no compunction about using his cell phone in the car. Why did he now find it imperative to use a landline?

I had no time to consider that, as he finally reached a person.

"It's me." Silence. "Yeah, it's a secure line. A phone booth. Had to drive around a lot to find one I wasn't scared to stand in and had no one around."

That was a blatant lie. We'd passed many safe public phones on our trek over. He'd been busy on the phone talking to someone else.

"No. It's not scheduled yet. Are you sending anyone up? You don't have to, I can represent the company."

So he was talking to someone in Memphis, where the owners of PanCanada were located. I felt very clever and vindicated for being so suspicious. If only that scratching sound would go away. And the tugging at the hem of my skirt. I really wanted to scream.

"No one knows I was there that night. I told you. If I'd been seen you can bet I'd have already been questioned by the police. I know it's still early. Look, I told you, he was alive when I left. Sure we argued. Hell, it was a battle. I even threatened to expose his private life. Hey, you know who was there tonight? The Simons woman. Barbara, I think. You know, the one we let go before we understood the market. Do you think she could be another one of Whitestone's tootsies?"

The next time I came face-to-face with Harry-Harry I might possibly just kill him. Of all the nerve. I was so angry I almost sputtered out loud and nearly sprang from my hiding place to strangle him on the spot. Only the knowledge that a sudden move would result in a bite or a spray kept me immobile.

"I didn't do it, but I can't say I'm sorry. Somebody did me a big favor. You, too. You've got a better chance to land the president's job when it comes up in November now that Walter has no more say on the board and can't oppose you. Your little secret has gone to the grave with him. With your help—remember, I know it, too—I'm sure I can nail it up here and together we can run the whole thing."

The response wasn't what Harry-Harry expected, because he said, "Look, you fucker. When you sent me here to freeze my ass off you guaranteed it wouldn't take long. I waited six months and there was still no mention of Walter's being replaced. Now he's dead. If I'm not a lock for the job I'm going to expose everything, including the price fixing. I'm sure I'll look good on *60 Minutes*."

He listened for a short time. I wished I could see him to see if he looked as angry as he sounded.

"Yeah, I guess that is a threat. And, no, I'm not scared. Unless you guys arranged to have Wally knocked off, but you're such a bunch of chickenshits I can't believe you'd have the balls for it. A little skimming, a little white-collar crime is all you're capable of. Listen, I'm standing here talking to air, so I'm getting off. I'll expect to read an announcement in the papers in a week or so. If I don't I'll have me a chat with Morley Safer. He's another Canuck, and all these guys stick together. They may hit the big time, but they're still all backwater hicks as far as I'm concerned."

With that, he hung up and marched back to his car. He was pleased as punch with himself. I know this because he whistled dissonantly the whole way.

I was furious. He'd insulted me and all my compatriots. The hideous little toad thought he could manipulate us all. Not if I could help it.

I had no reason to follow him anymore. I'd learned a lot, but none of it useful. I even believed him innocent of Walter's murder, his tirade having convinced me. I was sorely disappointed.

The immediate problem was how to get out of there. Very slowly, with smooth, barely perceivable movements, I inched my way out from behind the Dumpster. The aroma came with me. After taking a few moments for some deep breathing, my nose aimed to the sky to avoid inhaling anything that wafted off me, I was sure Harry-Harry was gone. Then I went into the store to buy a can of room deodorizer for me and my car. I really did stink; the cashier wrinkled her nose as she took my money. She continued staring at me as long as I was in her sight lines, looking confused. After all, I'm sure she didn't often come across someone that well dressed who smelled as if she'd been Dumpster diving.

I sprayed everything. Me, my car, my hair, my purse. I drove home quickly with the windows wide open. Once in the reasonably secure garage I sprayed the cloth roof again and put it down, leaving the car open. Better to risk it being stolen than have to endure the stench for the next few months.

I had a passing moment of sympathy for the next occupant of the elevator as I alit.

Once home, I took every single article of clothing off and crammed it all into a plastic bag, which I sealed tightly. I'd discuss their possible redemption with Mme Jacqueline, my wizard who knows everything about cleaning. Then came a long hot shower and lots of shampoo. By the time I got to bed I smelled delicious.

All this unexpected activity had made me completely forget about the note Beth had forced on me.

7

AFTER A RESTFUL night during which I had wonderful dreams about the mortification and/or death of Harry-Harry, I woke up Wednesday in a great mood. Morning ablutions complete, I was at the kitchen table by seven-thirty reading about Walter in the paper. The eulogies were glowing; the only discordant note was a sidebar about the takeover and his reluctant participation. What I hadn't known was that he had agreed to a five-year contract, which had been insisted upon by the parent company, much to Harry-Harry's dismay. The cancellation of this document must have been what Harry-Harry had been trying to extort from Walter when he went to see him that night. The *Gazette* went on about the rivalry at length, speculating on whether Harrison Harrison would now don Walter's mantle.

As I pondered how to find out more about this, trying to calculate which secretary would be the best source of information, the phone rang.

"Where were you? Robert is very upset." Susan seemed to have given up saying hello this week.

"Oh, God. I forgot. I'm so sorry. Poor Robert. He must be furious."

"I tried to cover for you as best I could. I told him something very important must have come up, because you wouldn't stand him up like that. He says he'll give you another chance tonight, but after that, forget it."

"Susan, I'm really sorry. I have an excuse of sorts, but it really isn't good enough."

"And what is it?"

I told her about my finding Walter and the gathering at Beth's last night. It worked. I was excused my oversight on the condition I keep her posted on every single little detail and show up for dinner tonight so Robert could ask me his special question. Try as hard as I could, she wouldn't give it up, and so I still had no inkling of what could be so important to an almost nine-year-old boy. The one thing I was sure of was that I would be there. The prospect of a future without Robert was cold indeed.

"Are you working this week?" I asked. Susan had recently landed a terrific job as the local representative of an international art dealer. With so many people fleeing the province for calmer territory, there seemed to be some good pickin's available and an astute Swiss man had decided that there was a fortune to be made. Susan was perfect for the job; rooting around in other people's treasures suited her just fine. She had a good eye and a knowledge of value in art. The two years working at a reputable gallery before her marriage, coupled with a six-week crash course at Sotheby's in New York, furnished her the necessary credentials. It offered a decent wage and plenty of free time, which as a single parent she needed.

"Not much. The Barkleys have asked me over to see their collection. They want to sell the Manet, but I have my eye on the little Matisse that's in the front hall. I'm not sure when they want me, but that's about all I have to do this week. Why?"

"I may need you for something. I haven't figured out what it is yet, but I'll let you know. Anyway, I'll see you this evening. Please, please persuade Robert not to be angry with me; you know how that upsets me."

"It's not that bad. I exaggerated a little." Which was about par for the course and to be expected, but when it comes to Robert my sense of balance goes out of kilter and I'm prone to believe anything. I love him that much.

I hung up, went to the kitchen for a fresh Diet Coke, and went back to the *Gazette*. I scanned the front page, stopping to read about the pyramid operation that had imploded, but realized within a few seconds that I was retaining nothing. Last night was very much on my mind; the whole thing had been so bizarre. The kids were spoiled little brats, Winston wasn't as sloshed as he pretended to be, Beverly had never made an appearance, and Beth had directed me to talk to the mystery mistress. Harry-Harry had topped it all off with his strange and infuriating phone conversation. I was still furious every time I thought about it, which was pretty much all the time. I had to do something, but what?

After finally deciding who would be my best source, I dialed.

"Pietr Korlinski's office. How may I help you?" In English, which I'm not sure is exactly legal.

"Hi, Jennifer. It's Barbara Simons, and it's you I want to talk to."

"Hi, Ms. Simons. What's up? Aside from Mr. Whitestone, that is. Wasn't that terrible?"

"Firstly, call me Barbara. I am no longer your corporate senior to whom you must pay reverent respect. You're above me now, since you're at least gainfully employed."

She giggled. Jennifer has a gregarious, outgoing personality, which makes her popular and easy to get along with. Everyone in the company loves her and many have tried to woo her from Pietr by offering extra perks, but she'd never leave him. She counterbalances his absentminded gruffness and they make a good team. Mostly he treats her as a valuable asset and partner, which she is.

"Thanks. I'll try, but it'll take some getting used to. Ms. Simons trips off my tongue."

"And is starting to make me feel old."

"You know Mr. Korlinski is planning to leave? I hope you haven't called to ask me to try to talk him out of it, because I think it's a great idea. He's happier than he's been in ages, and best of all, he's promised to take me with him. He hasn't told me where yet, but I figure I should be able to break him down within a week or so."

"No, nothing like that. I saw him at the Whitestones' last night and he looked great, though he wouldn't tell me what was up his sleeve, either. Which brings me to my question."

I hesitated. Jennifer liked me well enough, but would she think gossiping about the president disloyal? Well, it couldn't hurt to try.

"Jennifer, this may be a sensitive topic, but I'll just blunder on in. Last night, at the Whitestones', somebody made reference to a mistress. Do you know anything about it?"

"Sure. Which one?"

"What?"

"Don't tell me you didn't know. Every secretary in the building knows about it."

"Did Leeanne know?" Leeanne had been my secretary, and I'd always thought we had a good relationship. I would have called her instead of Jennifer, but she left when I did. My glowing letter of recommendation and international connections had landed her a job in Brussels, where she was now happily ensconced and to where I was plotting to write anonymous, damaging, and embarrassing but untrue letters if I discovered she'd been holding back. This was a juicy bit of information, and it upset me that I was so out of the loop that I knew nothing about it.

"Don't be mad at her. We underlings have a powerful network, and no matter how nice the boss is, it's still the boss."

"I assume Pietr knows."

"Mr. Korlinski knows everything. But don't bother asking him, he'd never talk. You know that."

"Yes, I do. Which is why I called you, and since I'm no longer the boss, give." That came out more petulantly than I would have liked, but it elicited a giggle, so I knew she'd tell.

"Okay. First I'd like to say that none of us care about Mr. Whitestone's private life—we all liked him and he was a good president. Until the buyout, that is. Since then it's been hellish around here. Mr. Whitestone and Harry-Harry have been at each other from day one, and it's filtered down through the ranks and everyone has taken sides."

I knew just which side she was on. Walter Whitestone was Mr. and Harrison Harrison was Harry-Harry.

"I feel like a traitor telling you all this, but Mr. Korlinski loves and trusts you, so I will too. The first mistress is Luce Richer."

"No shit!" Well, it was better than "what!" I know Luce. She's a high-profile woman in the business community, an enormous success story. She had taken over her father's small leather goods business and turned it on its ear and now owns a whole slew of related companies, the largest of which supplies the automotive industry, selling to all the Big Three and even the Japanese. Her strange product, for which only she had figured out the potential, is leather-wrapped steering wheels. All luxury cars seem to have them these days, but she developed the best and cheapest way to do it. The head office was here in Montreal, but there was a string of *maquilladoros*, huge factories in Mexico, right across the border from Texas. Lately she had expanded into leather seat coverings and made another gazillion dollars.

And she's gorgeous, which I'm sure doesn't hurt in her negotiations. At the age of fifty or so, she's still a stunner, deliciously plump and always beautifully turned out in the kind of clothes I love but sadly no longer need. I still sit on a couple of boards with her and see her for lunch infrequently. I was completely stunned by this news. I knew she had never married, but then neither had I, so I never gave it a second thought. I've always regarded her as a role model, if not a mentor. On thinking about it, Walter had been my mentor, and in all the time we spent together discussing all kinds of things, I now realized we'd never spoken of personal things. I'd known nothing of this liaison and was a little miffed.

"Jennifer, I'm flabbergasted. I know her reasonably well and never had a clue. How long had this been going on?"

"Ages, as far as I know. I've been here for seven years, and it was old news before I got here."

"I don't know what shocks me more—the affair or the fact that I knew nothing of it. It sure doesn't do much for my self-image. I always thought I was so well informed. Leeanne used to tell me lots of juicy bits of secretary gossip, since she knew I'd never repeat it. But I never had an inkling. . . ."

"Oh, Ms.—Barbara," she said tentatively, enjoying the newfound informality. I was glad I had opened the conversation in this fashion, since it put us on a friendlier level and might thus induce her to tell me more stuff that I should have already known in the first place. I wondered how many other deep dark secrets she knew and if any of them were mine. I was too chicken to ask.

"This was the biggest secret. No one told. It was nothing personal."

"I'm going to try to accept that, but now you're going to atone for the sin of keeping me, Miss Needs-to-Know-It-All, in the dark." She giggled some more; I was glad someone was amused. "You said 'which one' when I first asked. You mean there's more than Luce?'"

"Yes. And no one was keeping it from you since it's relatively new, about two months. I don't know much about her except that she's in the music world. A singer or something. Jazz, I think, but I'm not positive. I say that because Mr. Whitestone loved jazz and went to all the clubs and concerts. No one knows much about her, but the buzz around here is that she did it. Offed Mr. Whitestone, I mean. Oops, sorry, that was really insensitive of me, knowing how close the two of you were."

"Couldn't have been that close, since I knew nothing about this." I was harping, but I truly was seriously pissed off. It was a total offense to my inquisitive being, which reflected badly on my character, which bothered me even more. If I didn't get off the phone soon this could spiral into a full-fledged snit, or worse, depression.

"Thanks, Jennifer. I owe you a big one. Maybe we could have lunch one day? Not as payment, but just maybe, since we're now equals of sorts, although you're employed and I'm not, which gives you the upper hand which I usually don't like but this time—" Her giggling cut me short. "You're right. I'm babbling. Lunch next week?"

"Sure. I'll even tell you more secrets."

"I don't know if I can take it, but I'll try. Thanks again."

I rang off and thought about what she had told me. Walter had been a philanderer, and I should have disliked him for that. But I couldn't. He'd been so kind and helpful to me and such a good leader. Maybe he had an evil twin that surfaced after hours; the nice Walter went to work and the bad Walter went to play. Or two personalities that vied for attention. I couldn't figure it out, and it was giving me a headache.

I suddenly remembered the slip of paper Beth had stuffed into my hand the previous evening. Harry-Harry had distracted me last night, and by the time I got home and disinfected and deodorized myself, I completely forgot about it. Definitely a new me.

I dug it out and it emerged from the pit all crumpled. After smoothing it out I saw it was a heavy piece of personalized stationery, cream colored, with deckled edges and the words *Mrs. Elizabeth Whitestone* engraved in navy blue script across the top. This must be her informal paper; the formal would say Mrs. Walter Whitestone. It was very Beth.

Sure enough, in matching blue fountain pen, were the block-printed words LUCE RICHER. No phone number, no address. And only the single name, which led me to believe that Beth was unaware of the second mistress.

Instead of recrumpling it, I carefully folded the missive and tucked it away in a drawer. Should the worst prove true, that Beth had indeed killed Walter, it might come in handy as evidence of sorts. I didn't know what it could prove, but it was in Beth's hand and might have some import. Mostly I was astonished I had forgotten about it and so accorded it more importance than it deserved.

I glanced at the clock and saw that it was already nearly ten. My cleaning lady should have been there by now, would probably be arriving any second, and I hoped I could get out of there before she caught me. She talks a mile a minute in very bad French, and my head was too full of Walter, his family, his mistresses, to absorb any more. Her conversations are generally one-sided, running to long sagas about her family, which surpasses any I have ever known relative to dysfunction. I had been caught up in the continuing tale of her ex-nun-turned-biker daughter of late, but today there was too much else to ponder.

I got dressed and collected my things in record time, managing to get out of there safely. I went to the gym, where I wouldn't have to think about anything for an hour and twenty minutes of sweat and another forty-five minutes of cleaning up.

In the shower, after a satisfying workout, I thought about Luce for a few seconds but washed her away with shampoo. She could wait. After drying my hair with the provided hair dryer and slathering my body with the free cream, I felt a lot better, almost cheery. I wondered if Luce was a member here. I know I come at odd hours, hoping to avoid the masses, but still, I must have seen everyone who's a member there at one time or another and I'd never run into her. Also, the place is pretty Anglophone and there are only a handful of Francophones there to the best of my knowledge. As I reflected on that, I once again cursed the government for turning us all into such racists. We're all alike, yet lines have been drawn and we cross them infrequently in our personal lives. We're like my new opinion of Walter: By day we pretend we get along fabulously and work and break bread together, by night we gather our tents and stick to our own. I guess I wasn't as cheery as I had thought.

Since I had an actual business appointment, I had brought some dress-for-success clothes to change into. A good opportunity to take some of the expensive clothes out of my closet and give them a public airing. I had selected a navy blue, short-skirted Versace suit with a fitted jacket. A blush pink lacy camisole peeked out of the neckline. It had been designed to wear with nothing underneath, but I wasn't brave enough to do that in the middle of the day. I'm not completely averse to flashing them from time to time, but an appointment with the accountant wasn't one of those times. Now that winter was finally over, I was no longer burdened with cumbersome overshoes and slipped into a comfortable pair of Robert Clergerie pumps. I twisted my hair into a knot that was now in style again, applied minimal makeup, and gave myself a final going-over in the full-length mirror at the end of the row of lockers. Damned if I didn't look successful. I felt great and confident and ready for the corporate world.

IT WAS GOOD that the office building that housed my accounting firm provided indoor parking. It was even better when it turned out they temporarily had valet parking since they were redoing the lower levels and had to cram all the cars into half the space. Normally I am loath to cede my precious little Mercedes to a car jockey, but on the short walk from the locker room to my car I had learned that I had lost the ability to walk in high-heeled shoes. I teetered precariously, and my toes hurt. Men didn't have to suffer the pain and indignity of fashionable shoes, and I was surprised to find that I no longer resented them for this, I was just jealous. Boy, had I ever mellowed.

I sat cooling my sore heels in the elegant lobby, inspecting the artwork that my retainer subsidized. I waited a good ten minutes before someone came to fetch me.

"Mr. Sideman will see you now, Ms. Simons. Please follow me." The secretary led me down a series of corridors to the farthest corner. I wobbled along behind her, willing her to slow down.

I was ushered into a small conference room that was empty save for an ice bucket in which resided a not too elegant one-liter bottle of Diet Coke, with a lone crystal tumbler beside it. These guys might be expensive, but they did pay attention to detail. I'd always wondered how anything was accomplished in that room. It was a corner office on a high floor with sweeping wall-to-wall windows that afforded a breathtaking view of the city. On a clear day you could see all the way to the Green Mountains of Vermont.

Martin Sideman strode into the conference room first, followed by a clone. Both wore paisley bow ties and small, round tortoiseshell glasses. They were dressed in almost identical navy blue suits with white shirts and black tassled loafers. With all the navy in that room we looked like flight attendants waiting to board. They also had no idea how silly it was that we all paid so much attention to our clothing. I may do it, but at least I know it's dumb. Furthering the notion that they were duplicates, Martin Sideman introduced the other man as Marvin Seedman. I burst out laughing.

"I warned you she had a strange sense of humor," said Sideman.

"I'm sure we'll get along just fine," said Seedman.

I reached for some Diet Coke and hoped I wouldn't explode again and cause it to dribble out of my nose. The tone had been set, and I was going to adore working with Frick and Frack.

Seedman was the reason I was here. After finishing my taxes for the previous year, Sideman had discussed with me the possibility of having a professional investment counselor handle my portfolio. I had done fairly well on my own, but there was room for improvement and if I didn't find another job I needed good planning. I was mildly upset at the lack of confidence he seemed to display about my future employment possibilities, but I got over it and decided he was right. If I could make more money this way, it made sense. Thus this meeting had been initiated.

We spent the next half hour discussing my needs. I made dozens of, to me, quite funny comments, but they never noticed. Not a smile. This was definitely a hard room. Seedman finally said he'd get back to me with a concrete plan and left, smiling for the first time. Sure, he was getting all my money and I was paying him to take it, so there was reason to smile. I was exhausted from having tried so hard.

Left alone with Sideman, we discussed my least favorite subject (taxes) for a bit and I again considered the possibility of joining the Anglo flight from the province, which was galloping along at unprecedented rates. Being the highest-taxed place in North America was not one of Montreal's more attractive attributes. Since the government does so little for me, I see no reason to give them such a large chunk of my much-needed money. And don't say I deserve the government I voted in. I don't. In the last provincial election not only had I voted but I had campaigned fervently for the other side. But the current political parties in Quebec were a lot like Sideman and Seedman, virtually indistinguishable. After he told me what installments I needed to make for the rest of the year since I was no longer deducted at source, my heart sank. Not earning visible money was one thing, forking over savings another.

While he was droning on about shelters and deferments that both of us knew I couldn't afford but made him look good, I had a thought.

"You're Walter Whitestone's accountant, aren't you?"

"Not me personally, but the firm handles all of the family's affairs."

"Even the Warfields'?"

"And both the children's. We administer the trust fund. And, of course, the elderly Mrs. Whitestone also." He preened; his tiny little chest puffed out, straining against his shirt. He was indeed a very important clone; I half expected his bow tie to spin around like a little rotor so he could levitate to show his superiority. I sure had made his day.

"So what financial shape are they in?" I asked, trying to sound nonchalant.

"Barbara," he huffed, "I certainly cannot comment on our clients. It would be highly unprofessional."

Usually tenacious when I want to know something, I let this one go. I had recently discovered how to get the true dirt in any large corporation, and ever the student, I waited patiently through ten minutes of financial jargon of which I heard not a word, but I must have nodded at the appropriate times, because I kept getting nods of approval in return. All the while I was plotting the best plan to test my lessons.

When Sideman excused himself to answer the phone, I took the opportunity to wave good-bye and leave. First taxes and then paying him for the privilege of speaking to someone else and the double billing that the meeting engendered didn't do anything for my frugal soul. For a fleeting moment I thought I should have listened more attentively; there was the possibility that I had nodded my way into financial ruin. Probably not, he was too buttoned down to be shifty, I told myself hopefully. I couldn't give it any more time, because there were pressing things that needed my attention.

On the way out, I passed Sideman's secretary's desk and stopped for a second to say good-bye. I hoped I looked innocent and open.

She had lots to say. "Ms. Simons, I saw you on TV last night." Rats. I'd almost forgotten about that. I have the uncanny knack of instantly forgetting all my embarrassing moments only to remember them in the middle of the night when they come back to torture me into sleeplessness. There are usually two solutions to this problem. Either don't drink in the first place or turn on the air conditioner. But maybe this was the opening I needed.

"Me too. Did I look okay?" When speaking to someone who is no more than twenty-two years old, has hennaed hair, dangerously long fingernails, and a cute little miniskirt that barely covers her pert little bum, that is not as superficial an approach as it may seem.

"Nah, you looked great. Like, I love that red jacket. Actually I didn't recognize you at first. You looked, like, so much younger."

If I hit her now I'd never get anything out of her, so I shut up, but my eyes must have betrayed me.

"Oops, I didn't mean that the way it sounded. It's just that, like, I don't usually see you dressed so cool."

Which goes to prove that money can't buy style. The Armanis cost thousands, the "cool stuff" a fraction of the price. I chided myself for not having taped the bit so that I could further inspect it to see exactly what was so great about the way I had looked. Maybe Joanne could make me a dupe.

My new fashion consultant continued. "Did you really see Mr. Whitestone? Like, dead, I mean?"

"Yes, I did, and it was really icky. There was lots of gooey blood." I looked around to see if anyone could overhear me talking like this. I'd be mortified.

"Eeuuw!"

"Who handles the Whitestone account here?" I asked, switching topics abruptly, hoping she'd follow me.

"Mr. Adams does. Addison Adams."

I should have guessed. Everyone associated with this family seemed to have double initials. Also, Addison Adams was the most pedigreed partner in the firm. I'd wasted a lot of time talking like a teenager instead of using my brain. Just as I was about to leave and try to figure out what to do with this new information, she spoke again.

"Mr. Adams is out of town until tomorrow, but, like, maybe I can help you?" From the look on her face she really meant it and it was not an empty brush-off statement. It didn't hurt to try.

"Mrs. Whitestone told me that there were financial difficulties. I thought I'd try to find out more about it before I offered assistance." This made me out to be a very nice person if you were idiot enough to believe that I was close enough to the Whitestones for any of them to ask for my help about something I obviously knew nothing about. Maybe she thought I'd lend them some money. The idea that she was well aware of both our financial statuses, and that I might have more money than they did, was making me uncomfortable but had no effect on her.

"Well," she started hesitantly, looking around to see if anyone was coming. She gave me a conspiratorial grin. "I always thought they had lots of money—I type up the tax returns, so I know how much they make—but lately Mr. Adams has been meeting with Mr. Whitestone quite a few times. And all the files have been removed to his office, so something must be up. I know he had a new will drawn up recently, because the lawyer had it sent over here for him to sign and I witnessed it. Couldn't see anything, though, just signed it. Something was going on, but now with him dead I'll have to wait for Mr. Adams to come back and settle his affairs. Something's up, though. The police called this morning and scheduled a meeting for tomorrow morning, as soon as he gets back."

"The police! Wow!" I might as well stay in character. I shifted to insider mode and asked, "Is it okay if I call you tomorrow to find out what happened? It's kinda exciting."

"Sure. Just don't tell anyone."

If she were my secretary I'd fire her in a second. The idea that she might be handing out information about me with the same ease was a little disconcerting, but for now that had to be placed on a back burner. For as long as this nitwit held on to her job, she could be a great source for me.

Deeply into her drama, she whispered, "You'd better go now. Like, I don't want anyone to get suspicious."

8

WHEN I GOT home the message button was flashing frantically. The counter read fourteen. I don't usually get that many calls in a week, much less a couple of hours. I'd been on the screen for only a few seconds, but obviously plenty of people had seen me. I checked my watch and saw I had plenty of time before I had to go to Susan's, so I thought I'd better get it over with now or there'd be more when I came home. I got a piece of paper and a pen in case one of the messages was important and needed noting, all the while knowing none of them would be. Just my friends and acquaintances passing editorial judgment on my performance.

Diet Coke and cigarette in hand, I began to play the tape, listening with one ear while I did the crossword puzzle from the newspaper. Didn't get past clue #3 before I heard something interesting. Rick called—just being friendly, call him back when I got a chance. He left a phone number, which I dutifully copied down. He didn't mention my television gaffe, so I decided I'd return his call. Either he hadn't seen it or he was very polite. Either way it earned him points.

My mother called to ask why I hadn't informed her I'd be on television. She and my father saw it during dinner, and she wanted to know what I was doing gallivanting about at that time of night. Please call her. It was an order, not a request. Martin Sideman must have called the minute I left his office. He apologized for not saying good-bye properly and wanted to know my impression of Marvin Seedman. Just the thought of the two of them made me smile. I figured if I saw them separately and not in tandem I could muster the serious demeanor appropriate to the relationship. I'd call him tomorrow and praise his choice.

Really interesting was the call from Jennifer, Pietr's secretary. She said she'd dug up some info on Mistress #2. Definitely call her back.

Very strange and surprising was the call from Luce Richer, purported Mistress #1. I was still having trouble picturing the straitlaced Walter that I thought I knew as master of a harem. Luce asked if she could have lunch with me. Absolutely!

And then Detective-Sergreant Gregory Allard. He wanted to speak to me but said he'd call back. No number. I wasn't sure if this was good or bad and decided I'd leave it in abeyance. There were lots of interesting things to learn just by returning some phone calls, and I wasn't going to upset myself by trying to invent a relationship with Greg that obviously did not exist except when he considered me a suspect. I decided he wasn't even attractive. My mind works very well when it's put in the denial mode and makes my daily existence simpler.

First I called my mother back. The good thing about calling her is that she's one of the few people left on earth who don't have call waiting, so I knew I could get it over with quickly without interruptions and without thinking I was somehow second class when I got dumped for the next caller. And people lie so blatantly when they dismiss you. It's always the excuse of a doctor or dentist or long distance. Three-quarters of the time it's just someone with better gossip. I do it, too, so I can't complain.

My mother wanted to know why I hadn't been wearing a scarf, since I was so susceptible to colds. I don't know who she was talking about, since I haven't had a cold in years. She told me I looked very pretty (I can always count on her as being my biggest booster) and wanted to know why Joanne hadn't given me more time. Not a question about the murder. My health was more important. She told me my father had passed his driver's renewal test, which shocked me. Thirty years ago the man drove like a maniac, and age hadn't improved the situation. None of his three children would get in the car with him behind the wheel, but my mother went blindly. He never had accidents, but often left a wake of fender benders in his trail, when he'd decide to stop quickly to look at something or change lanes with no consideration to other drivers. The car directly behind him usually could anticipate the situation and gave him wide berth, but the cars following didn't and plowed into the first driver while my father blithely drove on. The government must be harder up for money than I thought if they issued him a new license. They cost a bundle here because of the no-fault insurance that is built in.

I congratulated her on his achievement, saying it was wonderful, long ago having learned there was no sense arguing. Anything my father did was perfect in her eyes. I wondered when she'd last seen an ophthalmologist but kept my mouth shut. This was a duty call; the interesting ones were to come, and I had no intention of exhausting and frustrating myself, as is often the outcome of our conversations. She never notices. After promising to bundle up in the future, I said good-bye and dialed Jennifer before she left the office.

"Hi, Barbara," she said conspiratorially. She had good scoop and couldn't wait to tell me.

"Okay, come on, it sounds intriguing."

"I'm not going to tell you who told me, but I heard about Mr. Whitestone's other mistress. I don't know how he had time for all these women. He worked long hours and had a full schedule. Anyway, all I know is her name is Cassie, and I was right, she's a singer with a jazz band. They're the house band at Truffles, in Old Montreal. That's really all I know for now, but I'll try to find out more."

"Jennifer, thanks. But don't get yourself into trouble on my account. You're still on the payroll there and have to protect your job."

"Not for long. Mr. Korlinski is getting ready to leave real soon. Oh, don't tell him I told you this. You know how he feels about gossip. But this isn't really gossip, it's a fact, and if it can help you find the murderer I don't mind passing it along. Oops, here comes someone. Bye, now."

Me find the murderer? Wait a minute. I thought I was doing this because I was nosy and Beth had asked me to. I had no intention of facing another killer ever again. But a little snooping couldn't hurt, and I could pass on what I learned to Detective-Sergeant Allard on a professional basis. He'd owe me then, and that might even out the scales and he might talk to me as a human being, maybe even an attractive human being. I might even get dinner out of it.

I had to stop this. I was mooning like a teenager. I've never had problems with men finding me attractive. Joanne does better, but she's famous and has professionals to do her makeup and hair. However, it does bother the hell out of me when available attractive men ignore me. And that's what Greg was doing. Obviously and pointedly. To me, at least.

I dialed Luce. It took a receptionist and a private secretary to get through to her, but she came on at last.

"Barbara, I'm so glad you called back. You looked wonderful on television the other night."

There had to be more to it than this. I hadn't spoken to Luce in months, and our relationship, while friendly, had always been formal.

"Thank you. I hadn't planned on airtime, and when I saw it I was glad it was mercifully short."

"You're friends with Joanne Cowan, aren't you?"

"Yes . . ."

"And I seem to recall that you know the detectives involved with Walter's case."

"Yes . . ." I was hesitant because I had no idea where this was leading. Was she going to confess to having stabbed Walter in the hope that I'd relay the message after she'd skipped town? No, if that were the case she'd already be gone, or not. This was making me dizzy. Particularly the reference to Greg.

"Joanne and I are old friends and I have had some professional dealings with Detective-Sergeants Allard and Boucherville. How do you know that? My name has never been publicly linked with either of them."

"I remember Walter telling me about the case." Pietr must have told Walter, which now nullified his interdictions against gossip and left me a wide-open field.

"Luce, I don't understand any of this. What is it that you want from me?" I was getting a little peeved. People were talking about me behind my back, and whereas I probably do it to them, I think they should have better breeding than to do it to me. I seem to think I have a monopoly on the right to rumor.

"Lunch. I'd like to take you to lunch and explain some things. Then you think about it and decide what to do with the information, or counsel me on what I should do."

"Why me?" This was a familiar plaint. "You're surrounded by professionals who can surely offer better advice. That's what you pay them for."

"Barbara, please. Just hear me out."

"Okay."

"Then tomorrow at one at Il Cortile. If it's warm, the terrace will be open."

"Okay."

"See you then."

Not a word had been mentioned about her close relationship with Walter. I didn't even know if I was supposed to know about it. If this was going to be her big revelation, it was old news. And back to the question of why me? I'd find out tomorrow.

I had time for one more call before getting ready for Susan's. I expected an answering machine but got a curt "Hello."

"Hi, Rick, it's Barbara."

"Hang on a second, I'll be right back. The other line." I preened. Someone was getting dumped for me. I wondered what kind of important excuse I was. Couldn't ask, though. Everyone thinks they're the only one who does it, so it isn't fair to burst the bubble, because then you'd have to admit to doing it yourself and therefore could never do it again for fear of losing all your friends. It's a friendly little illusion.

"Hi, I'm back. Sorry."

"So how was the date? Call to tell me all about it in exacting detail?"

"You know, for an adult you're very immature. No, I did not call to *dish* and I will not tell you about my date. I did, however, catch your brief appearance on television. It surprised me. I'd always thought you more together than that."

"I know. It was a huge embarrassment. Joanne Cowan is my friend, and when we're together we seem to revert to the behavior of our childhood, with its attendant vocabulary. Mercifully it was short. Did you call to critique my performance? I'm facing a long list of people who did and whom I have no intention of calling back, so if that's the reason, I'm hanging up."

"No, actually I called to ask you to dinner. But now that you're a star, I don't know if you'll have the time."

"I'm going to let that pass and suggest we start this conversation all over again. I've decided to try to be nicer and less inquisitive while demanding that my friends be less critical. It won't work, but with some effort it might help."

"Okay, I accept. Will you have dinner with me?"

"Sure. When?"

"Tomorrow?"

"Sure, but wait, I have a great idea. I was planning to check out an act at Truffles tomorrow night, but I hate going to those places alone. Can we eat and then go there?"

"I never pegged you for a jazz enthusiast."

"I'm not. I'll explain over dinner."

We talked for a few more minutes, and after forming concrete plans, hung up. I was delighted. Rick was fun to be with. I didn't feel any sexual tension or energy since he was younger than I, just the comfortable feeling of being with a person you like. He'd seen me at my worst and heard most of the foul words I knew when he knocked me repeatedly to the mat, so there was no need to impress.

IT WAS TIME to go see my favorite child in the world.

When I arrived I wasn't disappointed. He was waiting in the hall when the elevator doors opened on his floor and bounded into my arms, giving me a tight squeeze. For a moment I was sad. These displays of affection wouldn't last much longer. He was eight now, going to be nine next month, and soon all this hugging and enthusiasm would disappear. But now it was wonderful and I hugged him tightly back, returning his ever-growing and starting-to-get-too-heavy body to the floor, and ruffled his hair. I just loved this kid.

"I'm not mad, Auntie Barbara. My mom told me how sorry you were you couldn't come last night. But next time your car breaks down, call CAA. We're members, and you can use our number. We won't mind."

So Susan had evoked a breakdown as my cover. She was standing in the doorway, and I mouthed "thanks" in her direction and she nodded in understanding. We both tacitly agree that keeping Robert happy is of prime importance. He'd been through a lot recently, and it was wonderful to see that all his zest for life had returned. Susan has great mothering skills and a softness that she hides from most.

"Hi," she said, a great grin on her face. This was all so warm and welcoming. All thoughts of police and Luce and murder vanished as I was enveloped in a cloud of comfort. Even though it wasn't, this truly felt like family.

"Mom saw you on television, but you were gone by the time I got there. She says you were terrific."

"Thanks," I said, nodding at Susan. I was going to owe her big for this, but now was not the time to fret.

"Let's eat. I'm starved." Robert said that, but it could have been me. We went into the dining room of her spacious apartment in Westmount Square, another building that needed no street address, and sat down. Although she wasn't on a very high floor, the view was still attractive. To the north, the Westmount slope looks a little like the south of France near Cannes from this angle, with rooftops peeking out through the trees. Well, in a few weeks when all the leaves were out it would. We sat at the table and Susan brought out the pizza, accompanied by a salad so we could have some semblance of a balanced meal. I kept waiting for the major question, but Robert just prattled on about school and especially his science teacher, on whom he had a major crush. As is common in these casual days, the teacher was on a first-name basis with the students and Robert referred to Ashley, the perfect private school name, so I never figured out if it was a man or a woman. Either way it was of no import. The bigger the crush, the more science he would learn. Susan smiled benevolently throughout the monologue, obviously not listening, having probably heard the whole thing a thousand times. I thought it was adorable and listened to every word attentively, my eyes glued to his face. This was my duty, the price I had to pay for the honorific "Auntie" and all those hugs.

When it came time for dessert I'd had enough. Not pizza, though I'd had plenty, but science and the wonderful Ashley. It was time to find out why I'd been summoned.

"Okay, Robert, ask me whatever it is you want. I can't wait any longer."

"Mom told me to make you wait for dessert before I ask. She said it would be good for you, and when I asked why, she said to just do it. Why, Auntie Barbara?"

I cracked up. Susan is even nosier and more impatient than I, and she knew I would be sitting on tenterhooks until I knew the reason for my being here. She knew I would patiently listen to Robert's prattling until I could stand it no longer. This was payback.

"I don't know why either, Robert," I lied. "Well, what is it?" I would deal with Susan later. If no one was going to tell me soon I was leaving. I had enough conundrums on my plate without this.

"As soon as school is over in June, my mom and me are going to Disney World. We want you to come. We'll pay for your ticket and everything, so it won't cost you anything. Can you come? Please?"

Now, how can you turn down a request like that from an almost nine-year-old? I couldn't.

"I'd love to come. It's so nice of you to ask me. I can't wait." I hugged him hard. One day I'm going to squish all the air out of the poor kid, but he never complains. Just wriggles out as fast as is polite.

"I'm going to phone my friend Joshua and tell him. May I be excused, Mom? I can eat dessert later."

Susan smiled at him and nodded. She'd said virtually nothing since I had arrived. I wondered if she had laryngitis for a second, but she looked too healthy to be sick. Her streaked blond hair was tied back and she wore little makeup, just the ubiquitous lip liner and lipstick for which she is famous. She keeps the manufacturer of both products in business by virtue of her constant applications and therefore consumption. The day Susan eschews these implements the Revlon stock will drop at least two points.

"Where did you get the money for Disney World? I know you're doing okay now, what with your new job, but it costs a fortune. And I like how you offered to pay my airfare in front of Robert to make you look good."

Everyone I know well knows that I can fly anywhere I want to free of charge. First class, too. It was one of the perks I successfully negotiated in my humbling and humiliating severance package. I hadn't used it as yet, but was planning to get my money's worth soon, and this looked like a great opportunity.

"You know, I still have some connections there and I might be able to get you and Robert a pass, too. I can't guarantee anything, but I can try." Pietr Korlinski was my best bet. He could never refuse me much, but he was leaving soon and I didn't know if he could still swing it. I'd see.

"Even so, this is going to cost a fortune."

Susan sneered, so I knew she was going to talk about her not-too-dearly-departed husband, Frank. She always gets that look on her face when she brings him up, which is not very often. Frank had been murdered a few months back. Susan had been a suspect, and I had meddled too much for my own good. They'd been separated for a long time, and it had not been amicable and he was an all-around rat and loser, so it was no great loss. Frank never had much money that didn't rightfully belong to someone else, and I remember that even though he had left everything to Robert in his will, there had been nothing to leave. The cost of his burial had mostly come out of Susan's sparse account, and she was devastated. Now she was back on her feet, with a job she loved and no worry of interference or dunning from creditors. It suited her well, and she looked happy and rested. The bags under her eyes, which I had thought permanent since we were both on the wrong side of forty, were gone, I noticed. Had I not spoken to her on an almost daily basis I would have suspected the work of a plastic surgeon. Getting rid of Frank was an elixir for her.

As I expected, her next sentence began with the "F" word.

"Frank's lawyer called me a few days ago. It seems they located an insurance policy, with me as the beneficiary. I didn't know he had it and couldn't believe he'd kept up the payments on it. I vaguely remember him telling me he'd done it when we first got married, but I guess I didn't believe him and I forgot all about it. It's only for a hundred thousand dollars but since he got murdered it's paying off double. I've put it aside for Robert's education, but I felt he needed a treat after all he's been through. He's the one who asked if you could come along, by the way. It was his idea."

"That's great news." And almost unbelievable if you knew Frank. "Maybe I can help you with the investment part." I proceeded to tell her about my meeting with Seedman and Sideman, and soon we were both laughing loudly. Robert came out to tell us to keep it down: Joshua thought we were crazy through the phone, and he'd tell all the other kids. Peer embarrassment over one's parents had set in, a sure sign he was growing up.

I brought Susan up to date on the Whitestone affairs. She wasn't all that surprised, the recent events having bestowed her with a greater cynicism than ever. Her respect for men in general had all but disappeared, which was something she would have to work out with a therapist if she wanted Robert to be any better than Frank. I didn't say this to her, our relationship having taken a nurturing turn, which I hoped we would pass through. I tended to think of her as fragile these days, and was careful not to upset her. I missed our old bantering. She still had a lot of bite in our conversations, but I censored my words. It was tiresome, and I was starting to get frustrated by this lopsided association. It was my problem and I'd better get over it soon, since she was getting suspicious, and a suspicious Susan is not a friend one would want since she's pretty good at harassment. It's similar to my dealings with Joanne, yet these two, while not exactly disliking each other, weren't friends. I think they recognized too much of themselves in the other. I loved them both but didn't often bring them together.

As I was leaving I thought to ask, "Do you know anything about Beth Whitestone or Beverly Warfield? Anything good, I mean?"

"Not, really. But Winston Warfield was the one who held Frank's insurance policy. Frank probably went to him to impress me. Winston's one of those insipid Anglophiles, always trying to be more English than the queen. It's probably good that he was Frank's broker, since I think he's the only person in the city Frank didn't screw. Too embarrassed to. I hear he drinks a lot, but then they all do."

It was unkind stereotyping and sweepingly untrue, but you could have fooled even me, if the offerings at Walter's wake were any indication.

"I've never met Beth, but I have seen Beverly around. A friend of a friend sort of thing. I once saw her buying just about everything at Holt Renfrew, but it was before Christmas, so maybe it was for gifts. I'd like to be on her list; she dropped a bundle. That's it. Sorry."

"I'm surprised you know that much. I can't understand the shopping, though. Beverly's clothes all look old."

"Not old, dear, matronly. Look carefully and you'll see that each piece of her little-old-lady attire is expensive."

"You're right. On reflection, I can see that the tailoring is excellent and the fabric good. Even those ugly oxfords are expensive. I just assumed that because her clothes are so dowdy, they're cheap. I, of all people, should know better."

"Yes, Barbara. Not only fashionable clothes are expensive."

Properly chastised, I said nothing in retort. And there was certainly no arguing the point with her, since Susan is one of the best all-time shoppers around and can tell you the price and make of any article of clothing from fifty paces.

We said our good nights, kissed each other on both cheeks, and I departed in a burst of well-being and happiness. Driving home, I was very close to opening all the windows and yelling out to the world in general "I'm going to Disney World." But this was Westmount and I might get arrested for disturbing the peace, and I never wanted to go back to that station house again. Unless Greg was there. Even with my head full of pleasant fantasies, some of them unprintable, I managed to get my car into my garage and myself into bed without incident.

THURSDAY I WAS awakened by a loud thunderclap. That old saying about April showers is more applicable to early May in Montreal. Lightning flashed and every digital clock in the house went blank. The power was off. I sprinted into the shower, determined to get there before the last of the hot water disappeared. It was kind of romantic in there, the only light coming from the scented candle that is there for atmosphere and hardly ever gets used. It didn't smell at all anymore, as it was over three years old. All it did was remind me how single life was not all it was cracked up to be and that I hadn't had a serious local relationship for a very long time.

I threw on my very favorite pink flannel duster, my comfort attire, the kind of clothes that you hide at the back of your closet and hope no one ever sees. You can only get the really good ones in Kmart or Wal-Mart, which was good since it ensured I wouldn't run into anyone I knew when I shopped for them. I sneak in a lot of wardrobe choices in those kinds of stores. Carefully selected and mixed with the good stuff, it passes easily. And saves a bundle. White cotton shirts are a particularly good bet.

When I opened the front door to collect the morning paper I came face-to-face with my across-the-hall neighbor. I can't stand her; I think she spends the greater part of her life spying on me and passing judgment on our rare encounters. I try to stay out of her way, but I'm convinced she listens for the snick of my lock to confront me. I wasn't embarrassed at having been caught in my duster, as she was similarly attired. Mine was prettier.

"A terrible thing, Barbara," she said. It screamed for an answer or a question or something, but I wouldn't bite. The auxiliary emergency lighting in the hall cast somber shadows, and she looked scarier than ever with her thin white hair flying about as she stooped for her paper.

"A terrible thing," she repeated.

It was better to get it over with quickly. After all, she was an old, lonely lady and perhaps scared in the dark, although the windows in our apartments are generous and the gray daylight ample.

"What's terrible?" Politesse was not called for, just a response.

"Why, this power failure. One would think with all the taxes we pay they could manage to keep the power on."

In a way she was right. The power had been out quite often lately, sometimes for no apparent reason. It usually happened during the day, and as I was often out I never noticed, except for the flashing 12:00 that greeted me from every clock on my arrival. And I have clocks everywhere. I never wear a watch and am a punctual person, so I need to be reminded at every turn. The death of the battery in my watch and the end of my career happened almost simultaneously, and for some reason that I choose not to delve into, I haven't replaced either as yet.

"I don't think it's the city this time," I said. "I looked out the window and saw that the people across the street still have power. Their kitchen lights are on."

"Well, I shall certainly take this up with the condo board. It's a disgrace."

I smiled at her and retreated to my gloomy space without another word, happy that she had another cause besides me. She complains to the condo board about me quite regularly in long handwritten letters. Since I sit on this board I do not find it at all amusing. Her complaints usually run to too much noise, often caused by Joanne, who begins talking in a very loud voice as soon as she exits the elevator, on purpose. And typically, Joanne's soliloquy is an invented story, designed to shock, that turns off automatically as soon as my door closes behind her. This is all accompanied by an enormous smirk. Mrs. Brooks transcribes all these speeches—she must have a tape recorder at the ready—and sends the transcript to the board. They used to stare at me in shock at the beginning, but now they look forward to her missives, and Joanne has gained a loyal following.

A new biker bombing filled the headlines. Two gangs have been vying for control of the drug trade for about two years now, and they have been busily blowing each other up with regularity. It's so common these days that it only makes page three, so an innocent passerby must have been blasted for it to have made it back to page one. Sure enough, an elderly couple had been blown to smithereens as they were out for their afternoon constitutional. I wondered how many of their faculties they had retained prior to their sudden demise. No way you would find me walking by one of those establishments, even at two o'clock in the afternoon. I read the papers and watch the news enough to know they're dangerous places. Besides, I'm too much of a snob to be caught dead in those neighborhoods. And there was always a good chance of just that.

I turned to the obits to look for Walter Whitestone. There was a short entry listing all family members, most with stupid alliterative names. I was pleased to see Walter and Beth had not repeated this silly convention on the advent of their off-spring. I bet there had been huge family fights at the time, but sanity had ruled. The funeral had been set for Friday, eleven A.M., at the Anglican cathedral. The bishop himself would officiate. This must be a big deal, since they saw fit to print the information in the two inches allotted. I made a mental note to get there early, as I expected a large turnout and the cathedral is on Ste. Catherine Street, in the heart of downtown on the main shopping drag. Parking would be difficult.

It was getting darker and darker outside. Although it was only ten o'clock in the morning it looked like dusk, and even by the window, reading was difficult. I took the candles off the dining-room table and brought them into the kitchen, putting two on the table and two on the counters. It didn't help much, but I labored on, reading the rest of the slim paper but not hazarding the crossword puzzle because the type was very small and I hadn't as yet given in to reading glasses.

After puttering around in the dark for a while, it was time to get dressed. I hung up all of yesterday's clothes, which for me was very unusual—I generally leave them piled on a chair for my cleaning lady to put back. But I couldn't access my computer, and there was nothing much else to do in the morning gloom.

I dressed and made up by candlelight and indeed looked great when I checked out the results in the full-length mirror. Now, if only the restaurant had similar lighting I could pull the illusion off all day. I'd elected a smudgy taupe pantsuit with a white shirt to reflect the colors of the day. No tight, short skirts and uncomfortable shoes anymore if I could help it. Luce could handle the executive look today.

Just as I was ready to leave, the power popped on, setting off two televisions and three radios. It must have been a powerful jolt, for that had never happened before. As I made a tour of the house, switching everything off, I feared for my computer, hoping the surge protector worked as well as the salesman had promised.

With all the lights back on it was an unfretful elevator trip to the garage. I had been debating taking the stairs, since I wasn't quite confident about the emergency power situation after three hours of use. Did it take batteries, and how long did they last and how often were they changed? Another question for the next condo board meeting.

The garage was well populated. Angry residents were lined up in their cars at the door, engines running, emitting no end of foul fumes. It seems the door had jammed. Something had given when the first volts returned. Above the odor of exhaust was the faint smell of burning, so I presumed the motor was shot. The janitor and superintendent were hard at work trying to haul the thing up manually. I noticed none of them helped; they sat in their cars and seethed. I was about to offer my services to prove I was a better person, when I was saved by the arrival of the doorman. The three of them grunted and huffed, and the door rose. Cars moved immediately, almost knocking them down. I could see the workmen taking tally of the passengers, no doubt planning some revenge, as the cars drove through without even a thank-you. I was boxed in by the line, and when it cleared, I made my way to the exit smiling and waving hello. I'd had enough problems in this building and had been trying for the past three months to make myself as invisible and likable as possible. I knew I would be redeemed only at Christmas when I stuffed a larger number of bills than usual into their envelopes. Apartment buildings are very political places where one must have allies to ensure that all the services contractually agreed on at purchase are provided. Naively, I had once thought a smile would do it. In reality, cold hard cash delivered.

It was still pouring as I drove down the hill to Sherbrooke Street. Fat rainsnakes slithered down the car windows, the wipers barely able to keep up. There were few pedestrians. Those brave enough to face the elements were bundled into themselves, their umbrellas useless in the gusts of wind. Originally, I had planned to walk the few blocks to the restaurant, but one look out the window had changed that and saved me the torture of walking back up the hill. Mountain Street is the steepest ascent of all the neighboring blocks and offers a spectacular view of the river and bridges, over downtown high-rise office buildings. One would think that with all my working out and hours logged at the gym I wouldn't find it such a trial, but no machine that I know of has been invented to simulate and train for the Mountain Street climb. I tend to go to far places so I can drive and not be obliged to tackle the hill.

The walking idea had also been born of the knowledge that there is little parking space available around Il Cortile. It's tucked into the bottom back floor of a series of elegant graystone houses that have been converted to commercial use, near the museum and on a main thoroughfare where delivery trucks double-park and drivers jam quarters and loonies every few hours into the meters they have luckily found. There is little turnover in the few spaces available, and the side streets aren't much better. Concordia University is just around the corner, and the students get there early and snatch up all the nonmetered spaces. Which is why I don't eat there that often.

The horrendous weather must have kept others at home, and after performing an illegal U-turn, I found a place right in front. God must have mistaken me for Joanne today. It was only about twenty feet to the door that led to the passage that led to the restaurant, but I was still soaked by the time I got in. I shook my coat and scarf out in the passage as others had done, evidenced by the puddle just inside the door, then entered the restaurant in surprisingly good humor. The place was crowded. Tables had been placed in a friendly manner, which meant you got to know your neighbors well and there was no privacy. The restaurant boasts a beautiful outdoor terrace, snuggled behind and between the historic houses, laden with flowers and tables placed at discreet intervals, but the inclement weather had forced all patrons inside. The combination of Italian cuisine aroma and wet wool odor clashed violently on entrance, but then settled into background fragrance, which while not unpleasant nobody would ever think to bottle.

Luce Richer was already seated in a far corner, a waiter's station between her and the next table. It's the bad table in the place, the one where they put poorly dressed tourists and suspicious single women. Luce's reputation rated her front and center, but she had obviously chosen this; the maître d' would have been fired for seating her there of his own volition.

We exchanged polite and formal hellos as I handed my wet coat to a waiting waiter and settled myself. Oh good. This rotten table was in the smoking section, with a pretty ceramic ashtray placed between us. And smoke I would, after lunch, of course, since I'm not that barbaric, and I know Luce doesn't. But she'd picked the place and the table, and I was entitled to the perks.

"I hope you don't mind this table. It offers the most privacy. I had hoped we could sit outside, but I should have known. It's only early May." She sighed deeply as she looked out the sliding glass doors to the sodden seats of her choice. I wasn't that disappointed. Early May can be tricky, the bright sunshine—when it appears—belying the frigid temperatures. Everyone is so happy to be out after the long winter that they sit outside anywhere, pretending they're on some warm island, long sleeves hiding the gooseflesh beneath.

"Nope, it suits me fine. What would you like to drink?" I asked, preempting the waiter, who hovered. If Luce Richer decided to sit at a rotten table, that was one thing, but she wouldn't be subjected to the attendant lousy service.

"A glass of red wine would be wonderful. The house wine will be fine." She flashed the waiter a big smile, and her eyes twinkled. Luce Richer was a flirt, I remembered, and any man, any age, was her target. Surprisingly, I found this very endearing and an effective talent. I have been known to resort to such tactics when I want something from someon,e but had started to tone down, thinking I was getting too old for it. Luce was some years older than I and it worked for her, so I'd have to rethink the whole thing.

"Yes, ma'am. And you, madame?" he asked, reluctantly looking into my nonsmiling face. I sure couldn't beat her, and I had no intention of joining her.

"Diet Coke, no ice, please." As he turned away I said to Luce, "Betcha I get ice. Fifty bucks."

"Oh, Barbara, don't be silly," she said in faintly accented English. She didn't, however, take my bet.

We made small talk until the drinks came, hers perfect and mine loaded with ice. When Luce brought this oversight to the attention of the waiter, her eyes still all atwinkle, he was mortified and exchanged it immediately, never once glancing in my direction. I felt invisible but amused. Lunch was ordered. Luce nodded a greeting to a few people who came in, but I had my back to the door and my face to a wall, so for all I could see of the beautiful people, we were alone. The view was boring and the conversation stultifying. She seemed slightly interested in how I was managing to survive on an emotional plane without a challenging job. I stressed how happy I was, but she seemed so doubtful I was beginning to question myself.

Something was different about her. I decided to take inventory to figure out what. She was as beautiful as ever, larger than the current fashion decreed. Nobody could ever accuse Luce of being waiflike; she was juicy and sexy in her extra poundage. Rubens would have gone mad for her. Her luminescent skin was set off by green eyes that I suspected were lens enhanced, and her generous lips attractively swathed in bright red lipstick. She was dressed in the regulation power suit, hunter green double-breasted jacket with gold buttons, a cream silk shirt caught at the neck with a small gold pin set with tiny seed pearls, and twelve-millimeter pearls circling her neck. Real pearls. Expensive pearls.

Finally I noticed the anomaly. On the fourth finger of her left hand sat a whopping great diamond ring. In any kind of light it would flash brilliantly.

It's a good thing I gave up playing poker years ago, because I have difficulty hiding anything. My nonchalant look resembles a pinch-lipped biddy who has just hacked her grandmother to pieces. Luce looked at me strangely, then noticed the target of my grimace.

"Yes, that's part of the reason I wanted to have lunch with you. But maybe it's best if I start at the beginning."

"Good idea." It would give me the chance to eat. My linguine had arrived, and it looked delicious. I noticed Luce had ordered a salad. I prayed she wasn't on a diet and giving in to them all. She looked wonderful at her size. Also, if I was manipulating pasta strings, trying not to let any of the dangerously red tomato sauce ruin my white shirt (even if it did come from Kmart), my face would not betray any of the surprise I might feel at her tale.

"I assume you know of my relationship with Walter. It's been ongoing for seventeen years. Longer still, if you count the college years."

To my credit I didn't sputter and spray my spaghetti or say "what?" I just twirled the fork faster and faster, inspecting the resultant glob and trying to figure out how to get it into my mouth. I've often been told I have a big mouth, but I didn't think this was what people meant. Impossible. Have to start all over. I slid it off the fork and finally looked up at her.

"You didn't know? I'm surprised. You were so close to Walter, I assumed he had mentioned it. The vanity of the mistress, I guess."

Now, that didn't sound very loving. And she didn't seem broken up by his demise, either.

"No, he never said anything about his private life. That long, huh?" I was truly shocked. No one I knew ever mentioned it. How can you keep such a good, gossipy secret for so long? In such a small city? I didn't say any of this.

"Walter and I were in university together, l'Université de Montréal. Walter comes from a very proper and somewhat egalitarian family, so they thought it would be good for him to begin making connections in the French community at an early age. Networking, it's called nowadays. They were strong believers in bilingualism and the opportunities it would afford in later years. He was one of only a handful of Anglophones in the place and thus, with his good looks and good breeding, stood out from the crowd. We were so intellectual in those days. We were all going to be filmmakers or writers or something in the social sciences. Walter was the only one who said he wanted to go into business with a capital B, which made him a lesser, coarser being to the rest of us.

"But I was captivated by this attractive, ambitious boy, and we started seeing each other. It was not appropriate. Neither family was happy, and after a while we just started to sneak around together, to ease the tensions at home. In those days, religious lines were not crossed by good families, and mine was very Catholic. That was also part of the attraction, knowing that the nuns who had been responsible for my schooling until then would not approve. I don't think I took Communion or went to confession once during those years. Not that there would have been that much to confess. Ever the good, guilty, Catholic girl, I wouldn't sleep with him. I knew I had to save myself for my husband, who couldn't be Walter as long as our parents were alive. We were very immature and sheltered in those days.

"We were passionate about each other, and think we loved each other very much. But we were basically conformist, obedient children and after university went our own ways. After getting his degree in business administration at Harvard, Walter returned to Montreal, started working at Maple Leaf Airlines, which was what PanCanada was called then, and married the very appropriate Elizabeth Calders, Beth as she has always been known. I cried for days when I read the announcement."

Luce finally took a bite of her salad, lost in the reverie of days long gone. My linguine was cooling rapidly, but I had no thought of further tackling it out of consideration for my clothing bill. I was mesmerized by this tale. So deep was she in her memories, it was necessary to prompt her into continued vocal recounting. The best I could come up with, without upsetting the fragile intimacy we had constructed, was "And?"

"Oh," she said, startled by the interruption to her thoughts. It was as if she were telling this one last time, or maybe the very first time, to be filed and parceled away forever after. "I went into my father's business, since they couldn't find me a suitable husband that I would accept. I suppose I felt nobody could measure up to Walter, although in retrospect most of my suitors have turned out quite well, with large families and older-than-their-years-looking wives.

"I was an early success in the business. My parents had no sons, so it was acceptable for me to work there, better than working for strangers while I continued my search for the right husband. They had no idea I would eventually take over. It would have been unthinkable."

It was weird. This woman who was worried about pleasing her parents and being conventional had carried on an illicit affair for seventeen years. And headed an international organization. The pieces didn't fit with the soft, gentle-looking woman who sat opposite me. I waited for more.

"Quite a few years later, I ran into Walter in New York, when we were both there on business and staying at the same hotel. One thing led to another and we began seeing each other again."

All of each other, I thought, still unable to accept what I thought to be an immoral breach of good behavior. This whole tale bothered me. If she was so good and pure, how could she continue for seventeen years? And if she was so soft and pliable, how could she head up a megacorporation? It was possible that Luce Richer could add good actress to the list of her talents.

"It went on forever. He wasn't happy at home, or so he told me, and I believed him because I wanted to. It satisfied me on all kinds of levels for a long time. There was the romance of the danger, the excitement of sneaking around, the lavish gifts. At first, I think I really believed that we would eventually live out the rest of our days together."

"It sounds like the thrill eventually wore off," I said. Indeed the timbre of her voice had changed. The moony tone had changed to something harder, more the sound of the Luce I expected.

"It did, but I continued out of habit and nothing else to do. My business was expanding at a rapid rate, and I had no time to date. Walter satisfied all my needs, or so I told myself."

She returned to eating as though that were the end of it, but I wasn't buying. She'd dragged me out in the pouring rain to the worst table, where I faced the wall and couldn't people-watch. She'd have to be more entertaining than that.

"None of this accounts for the ring. What about that?" I asked, wanting to know where it came from. Actually I wanted to ask her if it was real, not a cubic zirconia that she had ordered from the Shopping Channel. It was at least two carats, maybe closer to three. If it was genuine it had cost big bucks.

"Last year I met somebody, a lawyer from Chicago. Again on a business trip; I have few opportunities to meet men here in Montreal. I seem to know them all."

Which was exactly how I felt. Certain parallels were beginning to emerge that made me decidedly uncomfortable. I'd sort it out later; there was the rest of the story to hear.

"I fell in love. I loved Walter, but I don't think either of us was 'in love' anymore. He, not Walter, asked me to marry him, and I accepted, surprising myself but quite happy about the decision. My parents are still alive, and he's worse than Protestant in their eyes, he's Jewish. But I'm over fifty, and the time has come for me to enter a new stage in my life. I want the next years to be full of fun and not all work."

"What about your business?" She'd been so active and so successful, I couldn't picture her giving it all up for a man. I didn't know what kind of perks he could offer, although judging by the size of the rock, plenty.

"I'm retiring. It hasn't been publicized yet; I only decided finally last week. I've built up a good management team and have chosen a successor. I'm sure he'll do an excellent job. It's really mostly coordinating all the division heads these days."

I wondered what this announcement would do to the stock price. I'd better call Marvin Seedman when I got home and make sure he hadn't bought me any. This bit of insider knowl-edge was probably illegal, but I had no intention of profiting, just not losing, so I doubted if I would go to jail in any event.

"What did Walter think about all this?"

"He didn't know. I planned to tell him last week, at our regular Wednesday lunch."

So they were down to nooners. That couldn't be very romantic. And she had continued seeing Walter after meeting this other guy. Not quite the good Catholic girl she thought she was. With as full and rich a fantasy life as mine. We were both given to self-delusion, and that niggly feeling persisted.

"And what happened?" Now that we were getting down to it she wasn't as forthcoming. I still didn't know why she was telling me all this, but I wanted to hear every last detail. Joanne would love this story if I decided to tell her.

"Wednesday, Walter broke up with me. Before I had a chance to say anything, he terminated the affair. Just like that. After seventeen years."

"Any reason?"

"Yes. He said Beth was getting suspicious and his mother was ill and he couldn't cope anymore. I was taking too much of his time. Once or twice a week for a few hours was suddenly too much time. His mother has been failing for four years, so that wasn't anything new. And I've always suspected that Beth knew about this and went along with it, not wanting to rock the boat. He broke off with *me!*"

She was indignant. There she'd gone, to tell Walter the heartbreaking news that she was marrying someone else, and he'd preempted her. If it had been me, I would have been furious. How angry had Luce been?

"What did you do?" I asked, taking a sip of my drink so she wouldn't see my smirk.

"I was flabbergasted. And very angry. How dare he? I stomped out of there and—"

"Where there?"

"What? Oh, the Ritz. We always ordered room service for lunch. The past few weeks that's all we'd been doing. Having lunch."

In a convoluted, totally male way, Walter had been faithful to his new mistress. It was laughable.

"Sorry I interrupted. What happened next?"

"Oh, nothing," she answered, all innocent.

Sure. A woman scorned and all that. Not a satisfying end at all, particularly when Luce had felt she'd have the upper hand.

"What do you mean, nothing?"

"Nothing. I stormed out of there and never saw him again. Then I heard about his death. And saw you on television, which prompted me to ask you to lunch to explain myself. I was sure you knew." She fumbled with her wineglass and drained it. "Will the police want to speak to me? I can't get involved with them. It could damage the value of my company, and though I'm leaving I still hold a lot of stock."

It still didn't explain what I was doing there. Although I'd admired her and modeled some of my professional behavior on hers, she didn't know that. I was suspicious of this whole encounter. She obviously wanted something from me, but I couldn't figure out what. She hadn't shown up just to give me an inverse stock tip.

"I don't know. It depends on what they hear from everyone else they interrogate."

"Interrogate!"

"No, I meant ask. It's just that one of the detectives always sounds like he's carrying on an interrogation, even when he says hello. Maybe it's because I'm English, but I sense he doesn't like me. I'm sure you'd get along much better with him." I wasn't sure at all, but it seemed like a comforting thing to say, although why I should want to comfort her I didn't know. This was a woman who was getting out of the rat race, had found herself a wonderful man with whom she wanted to live happily ever after and it seemed vice versa, and was sporting a gigantic rock on the fourth finger of her left hand.

She should be trying to comfort me. Dangerous signs of feeling sorry for myself were cropping up, plus that teaser at the back of my head. It was time to deal with the situation at hand.

"I certainly never mentioned you. I never knew you had anything to do with Walter in the first place." Not until Beth sicced me on her, that is. Which validated her supposition that Beth was onto the affair but not that she had delivered any sort of ultimatum to cause Walter to cease immediately. "Where were you on Monday night, anyway? It's none of my business and it may not matter, but in case they ask."

Like Detective-Sergeant Fernand Boucherville would ever ask my opinion about anything. Greg might, though. And I wanted to know.

She fell for it. Maybe she wasn't as smart as I had thought. Or maybe much smarter.

"Look, I know I don't have a good alibi and I'm the scorned mistress, if anyone knows that we broke up. I've only told you and another person, whom I will not implicate."

Everyone has to tell someone. There is no such thing as a real secret. Human nature takes care of that. I was just miffed that I hadn't known this one.

"I was at home, watching television. What I do most nights when I don't have a meeting. I did a little work while watching, and went to bed early. I can tell you what was on."

Which meant nothing even if it was true, since I figured Walter had been killed sometime after midnight, the time she claimed she was asleep. Even if it had happened earlier—I just assumed that he had been killed shortly before our arrival; it might have been earlier—television wasn't a good defense in these days of VCR-equipped homes. If she watched a lot of television as she claimed, she would know that.

"I'm sure there's nothing to worry about," I lied again. I'm good at that when it doesn't affect me personally, which makes me an excellent, if not totally ethical, negotiator. But then they lie back to me. My face only betrays me when it comes to something personal. "Go about your life as if this never happened and maybe they'll never approach you." Fat chance. The police seem to be able to ferret out everyone's dirty little secrets. Which is why I planned to keep my distance.

Luce seemed reassured. I can't understand why. Essentially, I had no sway over the police, couldn't pull any strings for her, didn't believe her entire story to boot. After seventeen years you don't just storm out and never speak to the guy again. No closure there after such an investment. She was either omitting large chunks of the story or trying to manipulate me. But I couldn't figure out the reason for either scenario.

It was all over. The bill arrived and she paid, so at least I got a free lunch along with the perplexity. When I stood and turned around to face the room, I recognized a lot of people. Luce busied herself nodding to quite a few and spent some moments with others, while I donned my still-soggy coat and made my way to the door, pausing to steal a handful of packets of matches. I somehow felt exploited and used. Luce had planned a private lunch in a very public place where she would be known and placed by quite a few people, judging by the number of stops she made. I watched and recognized a professional room worker. She pointed to me on a number of occasions, as though setting up a clear memory for the people she spoke to. I was decidedly uncomfortable with the obviousness of it all.

As we finally left, she kissed me warmly on both cheeks while I aimed for air. I didn't think I liked her very much anymore and would have to do a lot of thinking about why this event had been orchestrated.

There *was* one more thing.

"Luce, how big is it?"

A broad grin replaced the initial incomprehension. Every last inch of her smiled as she answered, "Three point two carats, brilliant white, emerald cut. The surrounding stones weigh in at another two point six for a total count of five point eight carats."

Wow!

10

OUTSIDE, IT HAD stopped pouring and had settled into a relentless, steady drizzle, so I regained my car, while not sopping wet, decidedly damp. I was only a few blocks from home but needed some driving time to try to figure things out. I love my old 560 SL Mercedes, especially in the summer when I can put the top down and don a stupid cap, my latest favorite being a silly thing with Mickey Mouse perched on the crown, topped by a propeller that spins in the wind and makes me feel like I'm part of a large cartoon world where no one can hurt me. Fifteen minutes or so of just cruisin' rights the world and revitalizes me.

And I badly needed some invigorating now. Lunch with Luce combined with the dreadful weather threatened to depress me, and it was time to evaluate the realities.

Okay, it wasn't Luce Richer and her tall tale that upset me. She'd presented the facts as she'd decided I should view them. I didn't quite believe most of what she'd told me, but would deal with that at another time. It was the backstory that got to me. That niggly feeling of unease that had plagued me throughout the meal, of which I ate very little, thus saving my clothing but causing even more dissatisfaction.

What bothered me was that I judged her. I thought her immoral and Walter disloyal. Which was entirely unfair of me, since there were just too many parallels in our lives. I had to wonder if she knew about my own little not-so-well-kept secret. I'd tried almost successfully not to think about it for a while now, but it was finally time to face up and make some decisions. I could kill Luce for forcing me into this. Introspection is not one of my favorite things or anything that I am at all good at. I prefer to sail along in a state of acceptance or denial as the case presents itself, to be as superficial as possible when it comes to dealing with my own emotions.

I'm a happy sort of person, given to depression only irregularly and not deeply. I have a highly developed sense of the ridiculous, which allows me to handle most situations with equanimity. And I spend a lot of time involved in and settling the lives of others, be they personal or professional, which makes me a busybody, which I deny. I have good friends who don't seem to mind this character flaw, often even seeking my input, which I offer generously, and sometimes amusingly. It works for me.

I continued straight east along Sherbrooke Street, past the Art Deco building of Holt Renfrew, which has been known to garner large chunks of my paycheck when the sales are on, past the stately Ritz Carlton Hotel where blue-haired ladies were undoubtedly sipping tea at the very moment, past the upstart Westin Hotel, which had stolen a lot of the Ritz's thunder in the game of "classy hotel with snotty service," past the wrought-iron Roddick Gates with the clock that in my memory has never worked, even back in the days when I alighted the bus across the street and proceeded through to my classes at McGill University. I was blocks beyond my turnoff, but this was the longest street in the city and if I just kept going straight I would get to the eastern tip of the island, down near the oil refineries and the smelly air. This was my serious thinking route. Generally by the time I got to the Olympic Stadium, which was built for the '76 Olympics, shaped like a flying saucer in a B movie and still costing me tax dollars annually, I'd have the problem sorted out and would turn around and go home.

Even in my own head, with nobody around to own up to, I skirted the issue until I had passed the stadium. I'd better get on with it or I'd run out of island soon and find myself on the way to Quebec City. The continuous rain and annoying flapping of the windshield wipers did nothing to improve my mood.

The problem was Sam. Sam Levine is my sometimes, out-of-town, somewhat taken, boyfriend. Well, boyfriend stretches the point. We've been conducting an off-again mostly on-again affair for twelve years, which makes me almost as bad as Luce but not quite, since he isn't married although he does live with someone. He lives in Connecticut, which until this year suited me just fine since I was always so busy. We'd see each other every few weeks in a neutral third place, out of town, away from everyone we knew and any sense of reality. He's a nice man: kind, intelligent, funny, and though I'm not sure I ever loved him (I revise that often), I like him an awful lot (I revise that not so often). We're too different in temperament to consider a full-time commitment; one of us would have to change too much, and the one thing we do have in common is that we're both pigheaded.

Now that I had more time, the relationship had begun to feel onerous even to me. Joanne, one of the few people aware of him, has always maintained that I would never allow myself to be involved with anyone else if I kept him around as a crutch. I was beginning to realize that she was probably right.

He's all of the above-mentioned things plus another

doozie: insensitive. Or at least, *I* think so. A few months back he had called announcing his incipient arrival in Montreal. Here, on my turf, where everyone I knew lived, without even asking for permission. And his timing couldn't have been worse. It was while I was embroiled in a series of stupid adventures, which was how I met Detective-Sergeants Allard and Boucherville in the first place. I was out busy nearly getting myself killed and Sam was coming to Montreal. That's way too much for one person.

In the two or three days I had to consider his impending arrival, I had convinced myself that he was the love of my life, and he was coming to break up with me. In the meantime, I was flirting with Gregory Allard while he decided whether he should have me arrested or not. Luce Richer appeared as a specter, sitting beside me in the passenger seat, laughing her head off. I knew it was my fertile imagination, but I could picture her sitting and smugly saying, "And you had the gall to judge *me!*"

She'd be right. I had no business deciding what was appropriate behavior in others if I couldn't control my own. It's just so easy to be moralistic and pontificate. Real life sometimes gets complicated.

I had fretted and worried and constructed all kinds of horrible scenarios, the most dramatic of which ended with me throwing myself off the Champlain bridge. I gave that one up when I realized the St. Lawrence River was frozen over and I would seriously disfigure myself. I couldn't bear being a flattened corpse.

In desperation, I had sought Joanne's counsel about the prospective breakup, which I was sure would signal the end of life as I knew it. While her deportment in matters of the heart is not exemplary, she can usually be relied on to give good advice. She has the ability to tell you what she thinks within the framework of your own comprehension and acceptance levels. So do I, except when it comes to myself. I had worked myself into such a tizzy I could hardly articulate as I pleaded my case. And I wasn't at all amusing, which signaled to her how deeply I felt about this. She told me he couldn't be coming to break up with me since men were big cowards and he wouldn't want to face me as he delivered the news. Men never travel to dump you; they just let the whole thing dwindle away in inertia.

I should have listened to her; it would have saved me a great deal of heartache.

All had come to naught, and it was a huge letdown. He'd called me three hours before his due arrival time and announced he'd solved his problem and therefore wasn't coming. He had entered into discussions with a Canadian attorney about a copyright infringement suit and he'd settled the whole thing by fax. I never let on how angry I was about his insensitivity, angrier at myself for having so overreacted.

He redeemed himself somewhat by substituting a long weekend in the Bahamas. I was expected to pack up and leave the next day. Against my better judgment, I did. In the end, white sand sure beats gray snow in dreary February. I'll admit he must have felt a little guilty, since he uncharacteristically bought me a nice piece of jewelry, a fabulous amethyst necklace whose price I cajoled from the jeweler while Sam was doing his laps in the pool. A hefty chunk of cash that mollified me to a degree. What had been most upsetting was the realization of how much of me I had vested in this affair, and I knew it wasn't healthy. I'd been trying to wean myself from him and hadn't seen him since that minivacation, although I still spoke to him regularly. He had no idea all this was happening in my head.

The question was, did I confront him and end it face-to-face? Travel to break up with him? Or just do the "guy" thing and let inertia take over, which was the direction I was headed in.

Checking out the window, I discovered I was way past the Quebec City turnoff. In the gloomy haze of drizzle the sight before me was otherplanetary. Enormous chimneys blew white smoke all around me, pipes created confusing, three-story-high mazes on either side of the road, which had narrowed considerably from the wide boulevard of downtown. Every here and there a stack was topped with an open flame, causing the drizzle around to sparkle and shimmer in a halo effect. It was very pretty and very eerie, and I was much too far east to be driving around alone in a Mercedes. The place was desolate, megastructures, mile-long pipes snaking in and out and over and around, everything belching substances that were surely toxic, judging by the odor that permeated the car, even through the tightly sealed windows, and not a person or vehicle to be seen. It was likely perfectly safe, but so foreboding I made another illegal U-turn and headed back.

The idea of Sam seemed comforting in this bleak landscape, and that was not good. I needed to see people and life to return him to his proper place. I didn't solve anything, really—just gave myself a good talking-to and cautioning. I think in the end I adopted the inertia idea—to have faced him with my decision would entail the risk of backing down. I like him a lot and he excites me on many levels. Our times together have been filled with fantasy that I was trying to convince myself was just that. I kept summoning Luce to mind. She'd given up her illusion and had found herself a nice man for a husband and was going to live happily ever after. I repeated this over and over, almost like a mantra, so as not to drive my car through the huge holes in her whole story. Anyway, did I want to get married? I was over forty, self-supporting in a style I had no desire to give up, surrounded by friends I loved, and rarely bored or lonely. Could I live with someone? Share space and a cleaning lady with another person on a long-term basis? That thought was scarier than the idea of spending the rest of my life alone. Either way, the future was not exactly looking rosy.

The snick-snack of the windshield wipers kept time with my yo-yo-ing thoughts. I couldn't come to a concrete decision, because I didn't want to. That was it. I wasn't as yet strong enough to give up Sam, or even men in general. I like company and I like sex, though I get the latter so rarely. Hmmm, a husband could ameliorate that situation.

Even I could see this was going nowhere. By the time I drove into the garage, I was no longer depressed, just confused. Soul-searching does that to me, which is why I do it so infrequently.

When I got to the mailboxes, I saw Mrs. Brooks, my across-the-hall neighbor, in deep discussion with the doorman. Either I was developing the new trait of paranoia or they were talking about me. As soon as the doorman spotted me, he cut her off with a few words I couldn't hear and they both turned to me and smiled. He smiled, she grimaced.

"Hello, Ms. Simons. I have a package for you."

I went over to retrieve and sign for it. Mrs. Brooks was intrigued, snooping over my shoulder to see what it was. A very official manila envelope. At first I thought I really had won the grand prize in the never-entered sweepstakes, but cursory inspection showed it came from Marvin Seedman, my new investment broker.

"That frightful boy on the bicycle tracked in a lot of mud when he brought this. You must do something about that, Barbara. It's just not acceptable." She sniffed the air, checking to see if I had caused further pollution to her environment. I was suddenly sorry I hadn't thought to knock on her door when I had come home reeking of eau de Dumpster the other night. This time I think she was angry that I wouldn't let her see my envelope. I cradled it like a precious gift, smiling down at it. Which further got up her nose.

The doorman started to say something, but she interrupted. "The police were here again, looking for you. Barbara, this is not that kind of building. We can no longer be subjected to these visits."

They'd come to see me, not her, and I hadn't been around, so she didn't know why. Must have driven her crazy.

"I can't stop people from coming to consult with me," This effectively changed the visit from an inquisition, with me subsequently being led away in handcuffs to her great delight, to a consultation, where they sought my input. That should get her.

"Well, it must stop." She turned and stomped down the hall, in the wrong direction, away from the elevators and her apartment. She'd be too embarrassed to come back, having made her dramatic exit, and I peeked down the corridor to find her taking the emergency stairs to another floor. If I timed it right I could get in the elevator and meet her, but I disliked her too much to even bother. Jousting is only fun if the adversary is worthy. I turned back to the doorman.

"Who was here?"

"Two detectives. The same ones as last time. She must have recognized them, because they were in plainclothes, not uniforms. Don't let her bother you, she complains about everyone."

"Not just me?"

"No, but mostly you. I never write it in the log. I would have brought you your package, but your car was out, so I knew you weren't home. Figured I'd catch you on the way in."

This was the same doorman who had probably saved my life a few months ago. He had adopted the Chinese philosophy that he was now responsible for me forever, and was always helpful and gracious and hand-delivered anything that arrived for me, contrary to the building rules that stated everyone must come to the front desk and get whatever has arrived, as the doorman must never leave his post. Mrs. Brooks obviously didn't like the special treatment.

I collected the mail and rode uneventfully up to my floor. Mme Jacqueline, the cleaning lady, was gone. She had left a note in fractured French attached to the plastic bag that contained my smelly clothes. It was a profuse apology for not being able to do anything about them; they were beyond redemption.

At least my apartment was crisp and clean and odorless. This was the way I loved it but didn't seem capable of maintaining without outside input. Every time I tried, when she or one of her kids got sick or needed an operation, which in a family that size turned out to be more often than I liked, the place disintegrated, my small efforts buried under the rigors of daily life. And now that I was at home more, it was worse. When I knew she was coming regularly, I managed to keep some semblance of order between visits, had even improved my comportment. But when she missed more than two visits in a row my apartment transformed itself into a place where a small bomb had exploded or which had been professionally tossed. In this instance, I am a very dependent person.

The rumblings of my stomach reminded me that I hadn't eaten much at lunch, so before opening the package, which would surely be dull if it were anything like its dispatcher, I scoured the refrigerator. I settled on a container of peach yogurt and sat down to inspect the contents of the envelope.

One for Marvin Seedman. On the top left-hand corner of the covering letter was a small caricature of himself, bow tie and all. I decided we'd get along just fine. Before I settled down to peruse the attached documentation I decided I had enough time to learn a little about what would later ensue. I flicked on the radio and hunted for the all-jazz FM station. Normally I am given to AM talk shows, to further enlighten me about the latest silliness of the government, dissected to the ends of the earth by the callers. On a good day this can be entertaining and hilarious. I would have to forgo the pleasure today and listen to some music.

I don't *hear* music. I find it hard to differentiate the sounds. I like songs where I can distinguish the words and follow along, but my knowledge is basic enough to be considered nonexistent. I don't go to symphony concerts, because when they turn down the lights and begin playing the soothing sounds, I fall asleep. I have been known to snore on these occasions, so I eschew the pleasure if I can. Too bad, because I sleep so well there.

Jazz is a whole other thing. I know that Walter was passionate about it, which was how I knew about the existence of this particular radio frequency in the first place; it always played softly in the background in his office. When I first walked in, I would notice the, to me, discordant sounds but could tune them out after a few moments, and by the end probably swear Walter and I spoke to a silent background. If I was going to a jazz club tonight I didn't want to appear a complete idiot, so I would see what I could learn in a couple of hours. I just hoped it wasn't uninterrupted music, that some deejay would break in with explanatory expositions.

He wasn't all that chatty. Two hours later I knew not much more. I learned that Thelonious Monk had written "Round Midnight" and everyone played some version of it. Often. Even I would be able to recognize it in any of its incarnations. I discovered I had an affinity for the blues, especially the numbers that the deejay called tunes, with words. I wasn't so fond of scat, liked bebop, and hated that electronic fusion stuff. None of which made me a maven.

Rick called to say he would pick me up at seven-thirty. I was surprised at how much I was looking forward to the evening. It wasn't just Rick. Yes, he was attractive and bright and young, but it was the idea of doing something different, going somewhere I had never been before. A foray into the unknown. I wasn't sure what I would say to Mistress #2 when I met her, and meet her I would surely engineer, but I had time to think about it. I was curious to see whom Walter had dumped the luscious Luce for. And this one was an even bigger secret, since I was sure Beth wasn't aware of her.

Just as I was thinking about that, the phone rang again. This time it was Beverly Warfield.

"Barbara, I'm so glad I found you in. I've called before, but you've been out."

It sounded accusatory. "Well," I fudged, not understanding the necessity to report all my comings and goings to Beverly, "I've been busy."

"I hope you're looking into things for Beth. I so wanted to speak to you the other night, to impress on you that we must find out who did this terrible thing. It's just that we were busy getting his clothes ready for the Goodwill."

Walter hadn't been dead for twenty-four hours and they were giving his clothes away. Poor people were having a good week between my closet clean-out and Walter's demise.

"Can you tell me what you've found out?" Beverly asked.

"No, I don't think so. I think I should clear it with Beth first."

"My dear, you can tell me, it's family."

The imperious tone made me cringe. I was back in the third grade, being interrogated about Joanne's and my latest misadventure. Teachers always knew it was easier to get information from me than her. That poker face.

But this was the telephone, and I was older and tougher. "Thanks anyway, Beverly. I understand your trying to spare her." Like hell, I did. "There isn't much to say, and I'll speak to her tomorrow after the funeral if I get a minute alone with her."

"You'll come back to the house afterward. The immediate

family and a few good friends are invited. I do hope you can join us. We can have a little powwow. Just us girls." She sounded positively tickled at the thought. She was the one who belonged in the third grade. Maybe I didn't like her.

"Beverly, where were you on Monday night?"

"Oh dear, this sounds like the police. I was at home. Winston and I spent the evening at home alone. We went to bed at around eleven. It was quite uneventful until Beth's phone call."

"Didn't mean to upset you."

"You didn't upset me. It's that I hate to be reminded of the police. They're so intrusive, and we're a close-knit family."

Who really hate it when the world at large learns that they are human and not perfect, I didn't say.

"Okay, then, see you tomorrow. Bye."

I wondered if Beth had put Beverly up to calling me. Or if she had done it on her own to find out what Beth wouldn't tell her. Or to cover her own ass.

Time to get dressed.

11

WHAT TO WEAR? A question that never fails to tantalize me. For tonight's foray into the romantic smoky jazz den of my imagination I selected a matching smoky gray pantsuit, the long jacket effectively hiding what I considered my worst asset. Under the jacket went a gray-and-white-striped man-tailored shirt. Gray suede, ankle-length, lace-up boots that I rarely get to wear because of the long messy winters completed the ensemble. I left my hair loose to nullify the androgynous look that faced me in the mirror and that I had latterly discovered. With my new, kinder, softer persona, I had begun to notice that most of my clothes ran to tightly constructed, almost masculine suits. They no longer felt comfortable, but I had a closetful and was too frugal to exchange them for replacement ones to suit my new lifestyle.

A different doorman was on duty when I arrived at the front door to await Rick.

"It's chilly outside tonight. You should take a coat, Ms. Simons."

Just what I needed, another mother. If you're single in

this coupled world, people seem to think they have the right to tell you how to live; they presume you're incapable of taking care of yourself. This particular doorman always reminded me to bundle up, cautioned that I wasn't wearing heavy enough boots in winter, warned me about the chill of air-conditioning in cars in summer. I think he was very upset that his confrere had saved my life, not him. Until that episode I had lived blithely ignored and happy about it. Now they all seemed to think it was their moral obligation to look out for my welfare, as if something terrible would happen to me again at any second. It was tiresome but sweet, and they always took my side in the continuing battle with meddling Mrs. Brooks.

"It's okay. I'm not planning to do much walking." I never plan to do much walking when I go out. I figure the gym sessions take care of my physical fitness, and living at the top of a steep hill contributes to the laziness.

At that moment a car pulled up, bearing Rick, resplendent in a scarlet ribbon adorning his ponytail. He wore a heavy charcoal-gray tweed overcoat flecked with bright colors, in contrast to my lightweight topper, a reminder that the Chateau Apartments where he lived was one of the few buildings in the city with no indoor parking, which meant facing the elements every time. Strike that one from the list of places I might like to live.

The doorman saw me to the car, held the door for me, and checked Rick out carefully. He had never seen Rick before and felt it was his duty to take note. I wouldn't be surprised if he wrote down the license number, in case. If Mrs. Brooks knew he had left his post for me, she'd have a further fit and I'd be in trouble again. With a backward wave at the doorman, who had indeed taken out a piece of paper and was dutifully writing something, we drove off.

"That's a suspicious man," Rick said. "Do they always vet your dates so carefully?"

I had no intention of going into the reasons behind the suspicion, so I opted for deflection. "This is a date?"

"No, not really. But he doesn't know that."

"True. Where are we going?"

"I made a reservation at les Caprices de Nicolas. I hope you don't mind."

Très chic. Very expensive. I hadn't been there since I'd relinquished my expense account. Rick must be making a bundle if he could afford to take a nondate there. For a moment I panicked. Since this wasn't a date and I didn't know Rick's habits, what if I was expected to pay for my half? Or even treat him? Well, I always had plastic for such emergencies even if it meant cutting back in the future. I no longer allowed myself such extravagances but could always manage in a pinch, as long as I had enough left for Diet Coke and cigarettes.

Rick let me off at the door while he looked for parking. I relaxed. This felt like a date, so he'd probably pay.

Although the night was clear, the rain having finally ceased, it was as damp and chilly as the doorman had forewarned, so I went inside. The maître d' greeted me effusively; it was nice to be remembered. We made small talk until Rick arrived, whereupon he was greeted even more effusively. The man continued to surprise me.

Les Caprices de Nicolas is populated by politicians on expense accounts, high-priced lawyers on the accounts of their clients, and people with altogether too much inherited money. It's a place where the women dress to the nines, and I felt a little dowdy in my gray attire. The food is scrumptious, adhering to the new fashion of tall food. I never could figure out why that came into style, but these days all your food is mounded in the middle of the plate into a lofty pile, with some sort of herb sticking up like a mast. And here the platters were truly high. The waiters carried them in one at a time, not daring to balance more. At the back is an atrium room that was once a courtyard in this graystone renovation, which even in the dead of winter evokes the feeling of dining in a garden. A fountain trickles softly at the rear, and I always toss in a coin and make a wish before I leave. The setting is almost worth the prices.

Rick ordered an expensive bottle of wine, though I had warned him that I didn't drink. We chose our dinners and made small talk until the food arrived. Rick complimented me on my newly polished, clear lacquered nails. I just hoped I would never have to use them. I tried to find out more about his dating habits, but to no avail. If we were going to be friends he would have to learn to be more forthcoming. I figured I could train him.

I did learn that he was self-educated, a high school drop-out who had succeeded on his own. The product of a modest background, he had looked around and seen that there were a lot of perks life had to offer, if one had the money, so he proceeded to read everything in sight until he could figure out what to do to earn such an income. Stealing was out of the question, because he knew if he got caught, he wouldn't last more than a day in jail. He was too pretty. His words, not mine, though he really was. He had an inclination toward mathematics, could always figure out percentages and odds, and considered becoming a professional gambler. But that would have entailed a life on the road, which didn't appeal to him, so he went into gambling on his own, big time. After successful forays into the stock market he became interested in commodities, figuring the wins would be greater. He called himself a commodities broker to the world at large, but in truth he was his only client. He must be very good at it, judging by his address and selection of restaurant.

I polished off my *poisson de petite pêche annoncé de vive voix, arrivage du marché*, which is much classier than the

English "orally announced fish from small fishing, arrival from the market," which sounds dreadful. It turned out to be salmon, piled high as expected, with chives aiming skyward. It took nerve to topple, but once demolished, was delicious. I declined dessert, but Rick ordered a warmed chocolate concoction that I found myself sharing against my better judgment.

As I licked my spoon, Rick finally returned to the question of where we were going afterward and why. I filled him in about Walter's demise, skipping quickly over the image of him in supplication on the carpet. In retrospect, it was disturbing. In the recounting, everyone seemed suspicious. I wasn't certain about motives, although I could invent hundreds and everyone I'd inquired about so far had come forth with an alibi that wouldn't hold up. How did the police sort it all out? I was at least as smart as they were and should be able to produce a culprit. Maybe later this evening we could rule out Mistress #2 and reduce the field. I sincerely hoped she had been out in a very public place, on view to hundreds at the time.

"Do you like jazz?" I asked. "I dragged you into this without even asking. You're a good sport to come. I have no idea what kind of music they play, or if I would recognize the style, since I'm a neophyte to the field. Just about everything I know I learned on the radio this afternoon, so it can't be comprehensive."

"I like the old Miles Davis stuff. Fifties period, before he went all fusion. Before he plugged in and started sounding more like rock and roll."

"You're a jazz snob. I love it. That's a great line that says virtually nothing but makes you sound so knowledgeable. You should look down your nose more when you intone it, look snootier. I'll make it easier: Who do you hate?"

"Pat Metheny. More of the fusion sound. I like my sounds acoustic."

"Aahh, a purist."

"You're making fun of me. So what do you like, young lady?"

A good-looking, younger man called me young lady. With no hint of sarcasm. The night was looking up, and it hadn't been bad so far. Rick was definitely going on my "favorite people" list.

"It was easier to figure out what I didn't like, which is why I asked you. I tend to agree with you. I like my sounds harmonious and mellifluous, not cacophonous."

"Who's the elitist now? That's three big words in one sentence. Are you testing me?"

Rick and I were going to get along just fine.

After Rick paid the hefty bill—I sneaked a look at it, having developed the skill of reading upside down a long time ago—with a platinum American Express card no less, we headed back to the car. This time I took notice. I'm really bad at identifying makes and models, but a Range Rover stands out. The affluent boomer's response to a Jeep. Joanne would love this guy. Young, cute, tight buns, and rich. I'd have to keep them apart or have a stern cautionary talk with her.

"I thought you said you drove a Lexus," I said as I climbed in as gracefully as the car would allow.

"I did and I do. This is my other car; the one I use mostly in the winter."

That's not as frivolous as it sounds. In this city, the winter months can be grueling to a car. The streets are liberally doused with salt, and when it gets too cold for that to work, gravel is strewn on top. Little indented pings are to be seen around the front and sides at the end of the season, the tiny stones having done their work efficiently. Also, as we have an abundance of snow and hills, four-wheel drive ensures one's destination. Although I love my little Mercedes there are days when it barely makes it to the top of my street, in spite of the most expensive snow tires available. Just before my parting with my livelihood, I had been considering a second car. With that no longer in the offing, I'd take taxis next winter and save my darling.

We headed toward Old Montreal, down near the old port. It's a historical neighborhood, the narrow streets lined with cut-stone buildings that were once warehouses and offices. The financial district used to be here and the old bank buildings still stand imperiously, their magnificence impaired by the small space allotted them. Defunct names are carved over entrances, most of them illegally English. The Tongue Troopers have not tackled that problem as yet, and it would be a sad day when they got around to it and defaced the edifices.

In the winter, it's a cold lonely place despite all the renovations of warehouse space into condo units. The thick stone traps the cold, while in the summer it always seems hotter than elsewhere. It's a prime tourist attraction, and most of the boutiques and bars on the wide cobblestone avenue of Place Jacques Cartier, the main drag, cater to them. Here and there, tucked into the side streets, were expensive restaurants that had converted to cheaper restaurants since the locals aren't as fond of the neighborhood, with no parking available.

Calèche drivers tended to their horses, as they awaited the next fare.

There were bundled-up people milling about the streets even on this chilly evening, recognizably tourists by their footwear. Tourists always wear sneakers. I do when I'm one. The theory is "I don't know anyone here, so it doesn't matter what I look like." Locals wear proper shoes. They had on all the clothes they had brought from their warmer climes, which made it look like a convention for the overweight. Their number so early in the season boded well for the municipal coffers.

Again Rick dropped me off, this time at the bright red door marked "Truffles" in contrasting green neon. I didn't want to go in without him, as I wasn't quite so secure and familiar with my surroundings. Fortunately, there was a boutique next door that sold all kinds of souvenirs and Canadiana where I could shop and keep warm. I picked up a genuine sealskin stuffed seal with an explanatory tag identifying it as such, and attributing it to some Inuit tribe. The price tag said $29.95, which seemed to me an inordinate amount even if it was a native craft. I turned it over and saw that the bottom said "Made in Taiwan." So much for Canadiana.

Rick found me perusing the birthday cards and virtually had to drag me out of there. I love cards; I buy the most outrageous ones and hope my target has a sense of humor. I carry a large stock but run out of stamps all the time, so mostly they just sit there, in case. That's one of the things I miss most about not working, the free postage, or more the availability of it.

We ducked through the low doorway. I'm sure it would have accommodated my height, but it was narrower and lower than present regulations dictate and the crouch was instinctive. We entered the anteroom, an unattended coat-check cubicle to the left, the salt-stained colorless carpeting screaming for a good cleaning. There were a couple of broken chairs stacked in the corner. I had been expecting a den but got a dive. I liked it.

A weight lifter dressed in an ill-fitting tuxedo, the cheap kind that shines, ushered us to a teeny table no bigger than a dinner plate in the main room near the stage. There were four chairs around it, but I couldn't imagine four people seated in such a small space. Rick ordered scotch and they had only Diet Pepsi, so, ever the purist, I requested Perrier water, which I don't like but prefer to Pepsi. I asked for a lot of lemon. Piped-in music provided the background.

I estimated that the room could hold about 150 people at best. The smoke I expected was there in abundance; it clung to the walls and permeated everything. I could feel it infecting me as I sat there, and would have to send the suit I was wearing to the cleaners. The crowd was small for a Thursday night and ran mostly to tourists at the tables, and what I presumed to be regulars gathered around the bar that was to our left. The barflies were solitary, not talking to one another but drinking steadily, making no eye contact. It looked lonely but appropriate.

A pretty waitress, who didn't look old enough to be there and whose fresh-scrubbed look was marred by a tarnished silver nose ring, brought us our drinks. I was surprised to find mine as ordered, loaded with fresh lemon, which I proceeded to macerate with the plastic straw in an effort to make lemonade. Rick watched and tried almost successfully not to laugh.

"Again the accuser shows her fallibility."

"What are you talking about now?" I asked crossly. I sort of knew, but maybe I was wrong.

"Miss Diet Coke won't drink Pepsi. And tries to make lemonade. Trying to turn a sow into a silk purse."

"Mind your own business."

At that point, when it looked like we might be having our first fight, the burly guy who had shown us to our table took the stage. He spoke rapidly in very bad French, and from the perplexed looks on the other patrons, I could tell virtually no one in the room understood him. It's a local problem. We spend big bucks targeting Americans to come visit quaint, friendly, safe Montreal and then proceed to behave unintelligibly. The owners must know their clientele; they could get someone who could speak English. But they rarely do; the sight of confused tourists is a regular one throughout the summer months. I wonder if they ever come back. And Rick thought *I* was the elitist.

My French is fluent, and I could hardly understand a word. He was obviously introducing the band, and I heard the name Cassandre Cartier, who I assumed was the singer. She'd caught the disease and had selected an alliterative name, and a stupid one at that. She couldn't have been born with it and had probably seen it on a storefront where she longed to shop and was sure she would once her career took off. I had to stop empathizing; I already felt sorry for her and hadn't as yet laid eyes on her. And she might have murdered Walter.

A quartet took the stage and began playing.

"Oh, no," Rick groaned.

"What's the matter?"

" 'Round Midnight' by Thelonious Monk. The de rigueur, standard opening number. It makes me want to stomp on all the instruments."

"It's probably one of the only tunes I'd recognize. Everyone does it. It must be easy."

The band, which consisted of a drummer, a bass, a sax, and a piano, segued into "Willow Weep for Me."

"Hey, I know this one," I said, inordinately proud of myself as I rattled off the title for him. "It's one of Dinah Washington's," I added, beaming. It was the only one I knew, but I was still proud; I had digested and learned a lot during my afternoon crash course.

"Everyone knows that," he retorted. He'd have to be trained to be more generous with his comments. I thought I was brilliant.

While the band executed the instrumental, a beautiful black girl took the stage to a smattering of applause. Cassandre Cartier at last. She was breathtaking, and for a split second I could understand Walter's infatuation. Only average height, she had regal bearing that made her look inches taller. Her skin was the color of dark chocolate and she looked just as delicious. Hundreds and hundreds of tiny braids were pulled back to expose her flawless face, and trailed halfway down her back.

As I get older I have trouble gauging people's ages; I tend to lump them into young, medium, and old. Black people afford further problems, as they don't show the ravages of age as fast as we white folk. Cassandre could have been in her twenties or possibly thirties, but I couldn't pin it down further. Nothing sagged, and her ample breasts, well displayed in a slinky low-cut black dress, looked real, so she was probably in the twenties bracket. I glanced at Rick, who was entranced.

Cassandre smiled knowingly at the audience, took the microphone in her hands, effectively displaying long, intricately appliquéd nails, and began to sing the song that Dinah Washington had made famous and beloved. Big mistake. She was atrocious. Sounded more like George might than Dinah. Although her backup quartet was good if not great, I couldn't figure out how she came to be the headliner. Her voice cracked as she reached for the high notes, and she was too young to carry off the melodramatic phrasing she had adopted. If she didn't find a new trade or a sugar daddy she'd never be able to shop in her namesake.

I glanced back at Rick and saw the spell of her beauty had been broken and he was staring at her incredulously. He caught my eye, which was a big mistake, because we spent the rest of the song trying to stifle giggles. When it was over, the audience gave her an enthusiastic hand, probably out of pity, giving her points for trying. The female sax player, who in my opinion was excellent, shook her head, closed her eyes, and looked as if she had a headache.

The next number was "Lullaby of Birdland," which I also proudly recognized, and was equally dreadful. Rick signaled me, silently asking me, or maybe begging, if I wanted to leave. I answered no. I was totally intrigued by this girl, so beautiful yet so terrible.

The payoff finally came. She sang two or three more tunes through which I daydreamed and speculated about her life, and Beth Whitestone's and Luce Richer's. The time passed quickly, as there was much material to mine. I had no idea what Rick was thinking about, but he didn't seem to be there either. The next and closing number was "It Don't Mean a Thing if It Ain't Got That Swing." Rick told me that later, as I couldn't identify it. Mercifully, it was an instrumental number, designed to show off the individual talents of the band. Cassandre kept the stage, swaying sensually along to the music. The sax player was as good as I thought, judging from the enthusiastic nods emanating from Rick and some of the others in the audience. All the members acquitted themselves well, and the band would have been great if they didn't have Cassandre's vocals as a liability.

Cassandre went to the side of the stage for a moment and came back with a violin, no less. I was terrified at the prospects when I saw it was plugged in. But she was wonderful, a magician on her instrument, her fingers tripping over the strings and the bow sawing wildly as she went through her energetic paces. The sound was electric in all its meanings, and electrifying. All the senses were engaged as she played on, her thousand braids flying around her like whirling dervishes. Her energy made you want to gasp. Rick looked as stunned as I. They finished up to thunderous applause, and I realized that she was indeed very talented, only it was misplaced. Someone had to have a serious talk with this woman, but it wouldn't be me. My newer self was no longer so bossy, and I had ceded the role of know-it-all to Joanne. Though maybe I could get her some airtime with my connections. I was still in my daydreaming mode. Her fiddling was so good that I had momentarily forgotten what an awful singer she was.

As the band left the stage I asked Rick, "Was her playing

as good as her voice was bad? Or do I have a lot more to learn before I offer an opinion?"

"No, you're right. She's a helluva fiddler. Unbelievable. I never expected that." He looked genuinely impressed, almost reverential. "I'd like to know where she got her training. That was intricate fingerwork and delicate bowing."

It didn't look delicate to me. It was more like mad sawing, but it had produced the most incredible sounds. Rick seemed to know what he was talking about, so I said nothing. He excused himself and left me alone for a few moments. Rick doesn't smoke and I'm a polite guest, so I hadn't had a cigarette in hours. A lot of secondhand smoke, but it wasn't the same. I didn't think he'd notice if I lit up; this place hadn't been aired out in years. I was happily puffing away when he returned, much too soon for my taste, as I was only a third of the way through the offender. I was about to butt it out when he further endeared himself to me.

"Don't bother. I don't mind. I don't smoke like you don't drink."

A perceptive man. I was beginning to wish he were older. Not that there's anything wrong with the woman being older than the man—both Susan and Joanne seemed to specialize in the practice. It's my particular problem. It always makes me feel uncomfortable. This would soon become a big obstacle, since guys who were my senior were starting to look old, whereas I never aged. A little Dorian Gray trick that I had begun to develop since my fortieth birthday and would no doubt cultivate over the next years.

"You've been very well mannered all evening. When we first walked in I was sure you'd light up immediately, the smell being so pervasive. I'm impressed by your discipline."

He would be. He was very much in control of his own life, seeming to have compartmentalized all the different parts. I wondered how long it would take me to unlock all the doors.

He may be controlled, but I am tenacious. All I knew was that the more I unearthed, the fonder of him I was becoming.

Rick rose suddenly, smiling to or at something behind me. I swiveled my head to see Cassandre standing there, looking at him as though confused, her face still beautiful, although her eyes were scrunched up. Myopia. Probably with an astigmatism severe enough to negate the use of contact lenses.

"François said y'all wanted to meet me?"

So that was where Rick had disappeared to. Not the bathroom. I wouldn't have ventured into the ladies' in a place like this, so I could imagine what the men's looked, or rather smelled, like. I'm sure Rick could, too. He'd gone to see Mr. Muscles, whose name was obviously François, and requested an audience with Cassandre. I wondered how much it had cost him. Must have been a decent amount, judging by the generous smile she bestowed on him.

"Welcome. Please have a seat for a moment. I'm Rick Fogarty and this is Barbara Simons. You play the violin like the devil incarnate, and we're honored to meet you."

Comparing someone to the devil didn't seem like a compliment to me, but she fluttered her eyelashes in pleasure and sat down. She examined me at close range, the puzzlement clearing from her countenance after a few long seconds. Close scrutiny is not one of the things I am overly fond of.

"Hey, didn't I see y'all on the TV the other day? On the news?"

My five seconds of infamy sure had a long shelf life. She had a very good memory and a fake southern accent no better than her singing voice. How did she play the violin so well?

"Yes," I muttered, still not proud of my performance.

"You're the one who found Wally's body." It came out more as an incredulous question than a statement. "You discovered him. I know. I saw you."

Not exactly, but this seemed as good a starting point as any.

"Well, yes—"

"Were you sleeping with him, too?"

A lot of people had asked me that lately. Rather than take exception to it on this occasion, I was somewhat flattered. She was divine, and she put me in the same category as herself. Before I let my vanity sweep me away I thought it prudent to right the record.

"No, I was not sleeping with him. I worked for him."

"So what were y'all doin' there in the middle of the night?" she asked, not believing me but remembering her accent. It seemed to switch off when she wasn't paying attention.

It wasn't worth a whole explanation that I doubted she could follow. So far she hadn't shown a lot of brainpower, and if she wasn't aware of how bad her voice was, how smart could she be?

"It's a complicated story."

"Yeah, I bet."

This wasn't going well. She didn't like me at all. It was flattering to be considered a rival, but it wasn't going to help.

Rick jumped in to save me. "Have you had classical training?" he asked.

"Yep. I take three lessons a week from a real singing teacher. He used to be an opera singer, so I guess that's classical."

I was right. She was dumb.

"I meant on the violin."

"Nah. My daddy taught me to play when I was very little. It's very popular on Prince Edward Island. I come from a small town, but I did shows with the family band all over the island and that's what made me want to go into show business. So I came to Montreal, because there's more opportunity here."

They might possibly have been the only black family on the whole island. I wondered how that must have felt and how they got there in the first place, but couldn't figure out how to phrase it without causing offense. I had the feeling that she would find most of what I said offensive. Rick didn't have the same problem. Her deep brown eyes stared into his blue ones in such a personal manner that they negated everyone else in the room. We all disappeared as they continued their private conversation. Fortunately Rick was on my side.

"How did you meet Mr. Whitestone?" he asked, as though knowing him somehow bestowed something special on her. He was very good and had probably broken a lot of hearts in his thirty-six years.

"Wally came in here a few months ago. When we just started. He liked me and we became friendly. He's the one who suggested the singing teacher."

A point for Walter. He may have been smitten, but he wasn't deaf.

"He even paid for it. And he helped me change my name. My real one is Ethel Burnsides. Awful, isn't it? Not a good name for a headliner. Actually, the new name was sort of my idea, but he helped. Wally and I were in Paris, France, and we went to this store so he could buy me a present. See," she said, thrusting her hand out. Rick nearly got clipped by her nails.

Jewelry always interests me, so I leaned forward to examine the proffered digit. She was so proud of it she didn't mind my interest. On the fourth finger of her right hand sat a Cartier roller ring. I have one too, but hers had six bands, two each of white, yellow, and red-gold, while I had settled for three. Her bands were also wider than mine. I stuck my hand in my pocket, not wanting her to see my puny specimen. That ring had cost Walter plenty, in addition to the trip to Paris.

"I liked the name of the store, Cartier it was, and adopted

it. Wally suggested Cassandra because he said she was very beautiful, just like me, and she could see into the future but nobody would believe her. I never heard that before and I'm not sure it's right, but I liked it. It's me. I know I'm gonna be a big star, but nobody believes me. They'll see. I dropped the *a* at the end and made it an *e* so it would be more French. And Cassandre Cartier was born. Neat, eh?"

Definitely in her twenties. She smiled at Rick as though he were the last and only man on the planet. I felt I should throw him a life preserver or he would drown in her gaze but wisely kept my mouth shut.

"It's a beautiful name for a beautiful woman," Rick said in all seriousness. I nearly choked.

"Thanks. Wally liked it. I'll miss him. Hey, do you think he left me some money in his will? For my lessons, you know?"

"I have no idea. I'm sure the family lawyer will be in touch with you if there is something. So you were quite close . . ." Rick said, with great empathy, further closing the magic circle around them. I may as well have stayed home. I felt ignored and neglected, which prompted me to do something stupid, which was open my mouth.

"Where were you on Monday night?" As soon as I said it I knew I had made a big mistake. I'd broken the spell of intimacy and aroused her suspicions. She may have been dumb, but I was sure she was street smart enough to be self-protective. As beautiful as she was, I was sure she'd developed a lot of defensive mechanisms.

"Why do you wanna know? What business is it of yours?"

"Ignore her," Rick interjected. It was insulting to me, but I realized he was trying to be helpful, attempting to cover my mistake.

"No," she said, belligerence turning her ugly. It was an overreaction to a simple if undiplomatic question, and she no longer found Rick as enthralling. She shut down.

"I'm sorry if I offended you. I'm just upset by Walter's death and trying to find some reason for it. Anyway, the police will ask you the same question, if they haven't already." I was trying to get her to say something incriminating or at least elucidating, but she wasn't buying it.

"You did offend me. You insulted me. You *were* sleeping with Walter, weren't you? He told me I was the only one, but I didn't believe him; a rich guy like that. I recognize the ring, but mine's bigger."

I never should have taken my hand out of my pocket.

"No, I wasn't. I wouldn't."

"Yeah, you were. I can tell."

I was about to ask how when I realized it would be pointless. She wouldn't hear a word I said. I wondered what made her so sure Walter had another mistress. Was there a third one floating around?

"Look, I don't wanna talk to you anymore. I don't care how much you paid François. I'm outta here."

She stood up to leave as Rick interjected, "Cassie, please—"

"Don't call me that. My name is Cassandre. You're cute, but you're with her."

"I'm really sorry if I offended you," I said and meant it, although I couldn't figure out what I had said that was so bad. "If you'd give me a chance—"

Her hand shot out and stopped in front of my face, about two inches from my nose, palm out.

"Talk to my hand, because my face don't wanna hear it." With that, she stomped off to the bar into the waiting arms of a tall black man. I watched the performance with interest as he enveloped her in his arms and cooed sympathetically into her ear. I nudged Rick to get him to watch, but he already was. Cassandre said a few words and the man's eyes alit on the two of us, anger shining all the way across the room.

"I think we'd better get out of here," Rick said.

We gathered our things, Rick paid the bill, and we headed out. The souvenir store next door was closed and I didn't want to wait there alone, a little afraid that Cassandre's boyfriend might come after me and the evening would further degenerate with the possibility of my finishing it up in the emergency room of some hospital, so I tagged along with Rick in search of his car. It had started raining again.

Two soaking blocks later we reached the car, my boots making squishing sounds. The paving stones trapped puddles between each block, and I found all of them. We hadn't said a word to each other on the way, the inclement weather forcing us to concentrate on each footstep. I learned about three seconds into our trek that wet cobblestone streets are slippery. Rick caught me as I was on the way to a big splat, wrenching my arm but saving my clothes. It was a fair trade-off. The rain came down in sheets, accompanied by a strong wind, and we were the only people on the street. I hated every second of the five minutes it took and was cranky as hell by the time we reached the car.

Once seated, I was about to launch into a diatribe about something or other when Rick looked at me and said, "Cassandre Cartier. Can you believe that name?"

I looked at him and cracked up.

"She'll probably name her daughter Tiffany."

"And her son Bulgari."

"A houseful of jewelers."

We chuckled at our cleverness as Rick pulled out into the sodden street.

"Did you see those nails? That must take hours to have done. And those million braids must have taken forever. I know they're extensions, but they still mean a huge investment in time. She must be one patient lady," I said in admiration, I think.

"She is gorgeous, though. Your boss had a good eye."

"I don't think his wife knows about her. I can't say the same for Luce Richer, but this one I'm sure was a secret. He took her to Paris, bought her gifts, probably rented expensive hotel rooms for their trysts—not the Ritz; he took Luce there so would opt for somewhere else. He must have spent a fortune on her."

"That guy in the back looked like her boyfriend. I wonder what he thought about her affair, and I wonder where he was on Monday night. Could have been jealous and decided to do something about it."

The idea was interesting. "But would Walter have let him in? There were no signs of forced entry. I know, I looked. It did look like the room may have been demolished in anger, which would fit the profile, but I can't figure out why Walter would have welcomed him into his home. I might even understand his meeting him elsewhere, and Beth was due at any minute, so he wouldn't bring Cassandre's world into his own house."

"But Beth didn't come home early, did she? You say she was driving around looking at gardens. Sounds fishy to me. Maybe Walter knew exactly where she was and what time she would be home. We have to find out more."

"We?"

"Well, you're obviously sticking your nose in, and I might be able to help. It, and particularly Cassandre, intrigues me."

"I wonder how it would feel to be the only black family on P.E.I?" I mused.

"Don't wonder, because it didn't happen."

"What do you mean?" Note the string of words following "what." I was showing signs of improvement.

"There were others. Not that many, but some. According to the 1961 census, which would be a little before Ethel/Cassandre's birth but still applicable, there were forty-eight blacks inhabiting the region, up from the previous count of forty-three in 1921. No mention of the intervening years."

"How do you know that?"

"I like figures. I always remember numbers, and I read census reports avidly. It helps in my business."

I was about to ask how when I noticed that his eyes, although locked to the road, were slightly out of focus. Rick had disappeared to a world I knew nothing about. If I asked I might be subjected to a lecture on the machinations of the commodities market, and unlike Rick, my love of numbers extends only to the ones involved in my financial security. Some things are best left unasked.

I was silent for a while, returning to the puzzle of the Whitestones. Rick navigated carefully; the windshield wipers needed replacing, and it was difficult to see through the sheets of rain. It was past midnight on a dreary night and the city looked bereft, the skyscrapers disappearing into the low clouds, the leafless tree branches whipping about in the stiff wind.

"When's the funeral?"

"Tomorrow, at eleven. Why?"

"Where?"

"The Christchurch Cathedral. Why?"

"I have nothing to do tomorrow at that time. I think I'll attend."

"If you want to come with me, I've been invited back to Beth's afterward."

"That sounds interesting. I'll pick you up at ten-thirty. We want good seats, and it'll be packed."

It was comforting that Rick would be going with me. I'd have to face a lot of people from the airline, my redundancy a still-sensitive subject. This way I wouldn't have to sit alone and would have someone to listen to my disparaging remarks. And keep me away from Harry-Harry. It sounded like a wonderful plan.

"Thanks. Until you mentioned it I hadn't realized how much I've been dreading the event. I liked Walter. He was kind and supportive to me, and now I'm surrounded by all these people who may have killed him and who all wanted something from him. He had a busy business schedule, and his private life was even more cluttered. I'm surprised he didn't just die from exhaustion. I'll miss him, and not for the gifts and money like Cassandre, the social position like Beth, the annoyance of not being able to get the last word in like Luce, and all the malevolence of the rest of the gang. I'll miss him because he was my friend, and that's something to be cherished."

We'd reached my front door by then, and there was nothing more to say. The doorman scurried out of the building with a wide umbrella, and came right to the car door to escort me in. Faced with the competition, Rick wisely elected to stay inside; we were both wet enough as it was. I waved good-bye as he drove off, sadness about Walter finally settling in and having to be dealt with.

The doorman bade me good night and I went up to my apartment and the coziness of my own bed, tears trickling down my cheeks.

12

FRIDAY MORNING DAWNED sunny and warm. I know because I forgot to pull the blinds and the sun streaming in woke me up very early. Looking out the window, I noted that the world around me had changed almost magically. Yesterday's rain had turned the lawns green overnight; the tulips in the garden at the front of the building across the way had opened, their bright reds and yellows a cheery sight. The radio forecast a beautiful day, more appropriate for June than early May, with the temperatures expected to reach an unseasonal seventy-five degrees. A great day in the offing.

It would be warm in the church, as our bodies had not learned to acclimatize so early in the season. The nice thing about Montreal is that we have four distinct seasons, although the long winter often makes us forget. Spring is short, with seesawing temperatures, fall is accompanied by brilliant colors in this city laden with maple trees, summer is hot and humid, and winter is unbearable. Today was gorgeous.

Mme Jacqueline arrived unexpectedly at nine. When she left the day before, she'd forgotten to collect the money I had left stuck to the refrigerator with a broom-shaped magnet. She insisted she could only stay a moment as she had another household to tend to. Yeah, sure. Once she had me she wasn't going to let me go, and there was no good excuse to escape, because the funeral was at eleven and there was not enough time to go to the gym or even do some shopping. The better stores don't open until ten and I didn't feel like driving all the way out to Wal-Mart. I had plenty of white blouses.

Sure enough there were problems in her family. Her eldest son's daughter had been tossed out of school, the third one in two years, and had been blackballed by the entire Catholic school board. Schools here are run on the confessional lines, with most Anglophones going to Protestant schools, and Francophones to Catholic. The debate rages as to whether to change to linguistic boards. So far there had been a lot of talk—about twenty years' worth—and no action. Jews, Muslims, and all other groups go to Protestant schools, depending on how long they have been here. In order to qualify for an English education, one of the two parents has to be able to prove that he or she has been educated in English in the province of Quebec. A certificate of authorization is necessary to register a child. Which is a good reason why we don't get many American or British or, for that matter, many English-speaking immigrants to our fair province. It's sad, because it's a great place to live, especially if you're deaf and can't read so you can ignore the insanity.

As she recounted her sad story, Mme Jacqueline wrung her hands along with the dish towel she was using to dry the newly washed dirty glasses I had left on the counter. The poor little ten-year-old was simply misunderstood; she hadn't meant to set fire to the whole school, only the girls' bathroom where she had been caught smoking the previous week. She'd just returned from her three-day suspension and should surely be given another chance. How could she get an education if they kept tossing her out? It was only the second fire she'd set, and the first one this term. I knew better than to offer an opinion about the budding pyromaniac. I'd never get out of there and she wouldn't leave, so I kept my mouth shut and listened inattentively while I thought about my plan for the day and she polished glasses and chattered on.

I was curious about the finances of the Whitestone family. I had the idea of calling my new friend, the secretary of Addison Adams, the family accountant, but didn't think it would get me anywhere. The immediacy of my "cool" presence dispelled, she'd likely remember her position and not reveal anything, or worse, tell Mr. Adams that I had been snooping. It was bad enough they were burying Walter today; I didn't need an upbraiding, either public or private, by an accountant at a funeral.

Finally, it was over and Mme Jacqueline went on her way, with me making all the appropriate supportive noises that her monologue called for. I care about her a lot; she takes great pride in managing my household life and feels needed, which she desperately is since I seem incapable of managing on my own. I can cook well enough, I just can't manage to clean up the mess left behind.

Because it was going to be so warm I had to rethink my planned wardrobe, settling on a black crepe suit with a bright tulip-yellow camisole peeking out at the neckline to add some color and in celebration of the new flowers. The shoes were a big problem, high heels having proven themselves to be uncomfortable and possibly dangerous of late. I found a nice pair of medium-height pumps that I thought I might be able to manage without too much pain. The idea of going the Gregory Allard route and wearing comfortable sneakers crossed my mind, but it wouldn't be appropriate. This was going to be a very dignified crowd.

Rick arrived punctually, this time driving the Lexus,

which my doorman obviously approved of, because he didn't
note down the license number. He was spiffily dressed in a
charcoal-gray suit, nearly but not quite black. A white shirt
and a blue-and-gray paisley tie transformed him into someone I had never seen before. He still looked like a baby, the
blond hair tied back with a black ribbon in recognition of the
solemnity of the occasion. I wanted to pinch his cheeks but
refrained.

"Do you think Cassandre and her boyfriend will have the
gall to show up?" he asked.

"We don't know he's her boyfriend. It could be her
brother or something. However, I'll admit they did look very
friendly. This morning I had some time to kill and decided
to look her up in the phone book, see if I could find her, but
expecting nothing, which was what I got since she'd said she
hadn't been here very long. But a search on the Internet
yielded interesting results. As I thought, there was no Cassandre Cartier, but when I checked Ethel Burnsides, there
she was. If he is indeed her boyfriend and they live together,
the phone's listed in her name, which strikes me as unusual.
Maybe he has something to hide."

"It could be for any number of reasons."

"True. But I tend to think the worst of people who don't
like me, and she sure didn't, so by extension, neither did he.
I'd like to know more about these two and their activities.
Even if they had nothing to do with Walter's death, which I'm
not convinced of, they're up to no good."

Rick started to laugh. "Just because some people don't
fall for your charms is no reason to suspect them of nefarious
activities."

"Maybe. Seems a good enough reason to me. Getting back
to your question, no, I don't think she'll show her face today.
I think she'd be too intimidated by the size of the event. She's
a small-town girl newly arrived in the big city, and I can see

her making a scene at an intimate gathering, but a conclave of the captains of industry would put her off. Remember, she's from Prince Edward Island and didn't seem that confident to me. Except when it came to her worst asset, her voice."

We pulled up to the front of the church about twenty minutes before the service was scheduled to begin. People were arriving in great numbers, chauffeur-driven cars dropping them at the door. A great deal of fancy machinery filled the short block; it made our polished Lexus look positively dowdy.

"Save me a seat. I'll go hunt down a parking space," Rick said when he saw there was nothing available in the immediate vicinity. With great difficulty the police were trying to keep the cars and buses on the crowded street moving, only one lane of traffic being available to the general public.

Christchurch Cathedral is located on the busiest shopping street, on its own block, between the city's two biggest department stores. The sidewalks were cluttered with gawkers, trying to catch sight of someone famous. Unless it was a politician or they read the financial pages of the newspapers they would have difficulty recognizing anybody. The power brokers I knew would be present in abundance were low-profile people, thinking all undue publicity unseemly. Since there was no one good to stare at, most of the attention was focused on the cars.

In front of the church, the only patch of grass to be found for many surrounding blocks had also turned green after yesterday's rain. I was pleased at my camisole choice when I noticed that I matched the daffodils and tulips that edged the building. It was too beautiful a day for a funeral, and indeed, everyone seemed to be smiling.

I'd never been there before. The cathedral has been a landmark in the center of the city for many years, attracting thousands of tourists every year, but I'd always taken it for granted and had never visited. I should have. As I took note of my sumptuous surroundings I promised myself a lengthy visit soon.

Even the entrance warranted further attention. Three vaulted oak doors with wrought-iron detailing beckoned. The Gothic arches carried the theme through, as did the gargoyles perched above. They were not at all menacing, more resembling frolicking puppies. Inside were the requisite dark wood pews with red leather upholstered kneelers. The intricate stained-glass windows depicting saints I didn't recognize fragmented the entering light into staggered rainbows. Empty, this place must be stunning; full as it was today, it was warm and welcoming. Not at all suitable for a funeral, in my opinion; more a jubilant wedding, with the colored light dancing over the bride's white dress. If I could keep up my relationship with Beth (if she didn't get put away for murder) and her daughter saw the light of day and ditched the boyfriend, returned to the fold, and married a young scion, I might get the opportunity. It would be something to look forward to on all counts.

After calculating the sight lines I took a seat near the aisle on the left, three-quarters of the way down. It was a long aisle, and halfway would be too far back to note expressions. None of the family was evident, so I assumed they were in a back room somewhere, grieving in private. Everyone else was there, though. I wondered who was minding PanCanada, since it seemed the entire staff was present. Fortunately it was a funeral and called for some decorum, so I didn't have to smile and wave brightly at my ex-coworkers. Harrison Harrison strode down the center aisle like the guest of honor and took a seat in the first row, not bothering to acknowledge his many minions on the way. The vice presidents sat together in the fourth row, all in a line, without me. The entire Anglo elite was present along with a great number of Francophones. To me he was simply Walter, the head of my firm, a man I cared for and respected, and it took this gathering to make me understand the power he wielded. Even the presidents of competitive airlines were present, and PanCanada's head office in Memphis had sent up a contingent, in direct contradiction to Harry-Harry's suggestion, which had to have pissed him off. I could tell who they were because these were the only people Harry-Harry would deign recognize, offering them a grimace that he tried to pass off as a smile.

I had been worried and disturbed at the prospect of an open coffin. I had already seen Walter dead and would not like to repeat the experience, no matter how well the mortuary people had prepared him. Fortunately, I was spared the sight. Walter lay mercifully ensconced in a beautiful brass-trimmed mahogany casket, adorned with a simple spray of white roses. It was dignified and fitting, the lonely focal point at the front of the church. I said my silent good-byes.

Rick made it about three minutes before the service began—punctually, as befitted the buttoned-up atmosphere. All the smiling on the street had been replaced by sober faces as the somber atmosphere reminded the assembly of its mission.

"Boy, traffic is a mess. I parked three blocks away in a crammed garage. Next time you take me to something like this, remind me to get a driver."

When Rick decided to climb his way out of his background he sure decided to climb high.

"The whole financial community is here," he said, looking around. "And the men outnumber the women six to one." I remembered Rick was a mathematical wizard so didn't accuse him of hyperbole. And it looked about right to me. I guess they were mostly business acquaintances whose schedules had to be rewritten to accommodate the event. They would leave their grateful wives at home for this.

The assembly hushed when the bishop made his entrance, all decked out in beautiful robes. And people accuse me of being into clothes; I'd consider the job just for that costume. The family filed in and sat quietly in the front row, Beth looking very dramatic in a black hat with a veil. Beverly wore a black beret and even daughter Margaret had a black straw boater atop her now glossy, newly trimmed hair. She'd cleaned up well and resembled the photograph on Walter's desk. I wouldn't have recognized her without the entourage.

Looking around, I noticed that a great majority of the women present wore hats. I was annoyed at myself for not having inquired about the dress code in advance, as I love hats and have a small collection that I never wear because they make me feel stupid and conspicuous. Susan, the arbiter of what is proper dress, should have warned me.

The bishop went on at great length about Walter's achievements, which were legion, and made reference to his parentage. I hadn't known that Walter's father had been the president of one of Canada's leading financial institutions, and was impressed. He got his good breeding and learned his manners at home, unlike Rick, who could fool most people if he wanted to. A sad mention was made of Mother Whitestone—no first name—still clinging to a life that only she recognized and thus unable to attend. We were asked to remember the matron that was. Kenneth, the son, said a few words on a more personal level, which reduced most of the audience to tears. White handkerchiefs emerged from breast pockets to dab surreptitiously at eyes. Not having one, I blinked furiously until Rick handed me a tissue.

They went in for the whole kit and kaboodle. High mass, a million psalms sung by a full choir, lots of kneeling. During these periods I sneaked a peek to see who else was trying to be unobtrusive as they held their seats; there was a surprising number of us. My mind wandered back to the beautiful day outside, and I promised myself a walk on the mountain over the weekend to see what else was sprouting.

Finally it was over. The body would be interred at Mount Royal Cemetery, nestled into the side of the similarly named "mountain" so I could knock off my weekend resolution immediately if I chose to. I didn't.

As the cortege, led by twenty-six real and honorary pallbearers, solemnly filed down the center aisle, Rick poked me and whispered, "Are we going to the cemetery?" It was asked in a way that prayed for a negative answer, and I obliged.

"No. We can have a cup of coffee while waiting for the traffic to clear and then go to the house. I don't want to see Walter put in the ground, and we weren't suitably close anyway. It might cause more speculation about our relationship, and I've had enough of that. Remember, I don't work there anymore."

I had no time to see if he was relieved, since I was busy checking out the family as they followed the coffin out. Beverly was stone faced, not a single emotion displayed on her face, as befitted her upbringing. Her husband, Winston, didn't look too steady on his feet and was sweating profusely. I wondered how much he'd had to drink so early in the day. Kenneth nodded to the assembled, obviously feeling he had acquitted himself well with his eulogy. Margaret looked beautiful, radiant in her new haircut and artfully applied makeup. Tiny tears glistened at the corner of her eyes, transforming her into a graceful belle.

Beth walked alone, directly behind the assembly of pallbearers and the bishop. She was as serene as ever, her eyes dry, with only her clenched mouth betraying any feeling. The epitome of proper behavior, she acknowledged the gathered mourners and celebrants of her husband's life with the tilt of an eyebrow. I marveled at the control.

I searched the crowd for Luce Richer or, better, Cassandre Cartier but could find neither. Which didn't mean they weren't there, as it was difficult to effectively scan the more than one thousand people in attendance. Walter had received the elegant funeral he merited: a full service, flower bedecked, presided over by the bishop himself, attended by the prime minister of Canada and premier of Quebec along with Ontario and Alberta, full to overflowing congregation. And a lot of sad faces on people who looked as if they would genuinely miss him. I was touched and proud of our association. The person who did this had deprived us of him and should be put away forever. I temporarily forgot about all the seedy things I had recently learned about him and concentrated on the man I respected.

It was nice to get outside again. People were amassed at the front of the church, filling the pavement and spilling onto the grass, which would have to be reseeded after such a trampling. I hoped they were being careful about the flowers; they're such an unusual and rare commodity in downtown Montreal. We stood silently and reverently as we watched the hearse and following cars head out. The police had now cordoned off the entire block, allowing no traffic to get through, and blaring car horns could be heard, dirgelike, in the distance.

Rick and I went to the cafeteria at The Bay, the department store flanking the east side of the church, to await the return of the normal flow of traffic. Others had the same idea, and the assemblage was probably the best-dressed, highest-profile crowd the place had ever seen. We gathered inquisitive looks from lunchtime shoppers as we passed through the self-service line.

We were lucky to find an uninhabited table for two and settled down to eat, a Danish and coffee for Rick and a slice of pizza and Diet Coke for me. Rick had sneered at the culinary offerings, not finding anything worthy of his delicate palate. I told him not to be such a snob and cautioned him about the likely dearth of anything edible at Beth's. He selected the Danish condescendingly, but I did notice that he enjoyed it, picking up every single last crumb.

"Lots of media present," Rick said, as he happily munched away, proving that everyone, no matter how great the aesthete, loves junk food. "All the television stations, press, and even radio. I didn't see your friend Joanne."

"No, she wouldn't be the one assigned to cover this. She mostly does the crime beat, but I'm sure when the final story breaks she'll include some of the footage. Pomp and ceremony attended by lots of rich people makes for good television. She must be busy at something, though. She didn't call me this morning, and if she were free she would have shown up as a private person. She liked Walter and she would have come just to pay her respects. Something's abrewin'. Film at six and eleven."

"I'm looking forward to meeting her. Sounds like quite a character."

I didn't respond. I wasn't sure how I felt about the coupling of Rick and Joanne. I sort of wanted to keep him all to myself—hoard him, as it were.

So I changed the subject. "Look, we're going to be conspicuous at Beth's. Your hair is all that's necessary in that crowd, and I'm an ex-employee and the finder of the body. Well, not quite, but that's how it's going to be perceived. So be prepared to be stared at. What I'd like you to do is speak to the kids. I didn't get off to a brilliant start with Margaret, and Kenneth leers a little too much for me. A lot of people seem to be asking me if I was sleeping with Walter, and if he insinuates it too I'll bop him one, which would be undignified. And dignity seems to be the operative word with these people. It always amazes me that good manners can excuse serious character flaws. We're so taken in by appearances."

"This from someone who labors about the right thing to wear to any given occasion."

"Shut up, you're worse than me. Those fancy ribbons."

After politely clearing our dishes and dumping them on another empty table when we couldn't figure out where they were supposed to go, we took the escalators down and wandered out into the street to collect the car. I did experience longing pains as we passed the fashion floor, but now was not the appropriate time, so I quashed them. A rust beaded evening jacket haunted me all the way to the bottom.

Rick had parked three blocks away. Normally I would have sent him to get the car while I sneaked back up and purchased the jacket, but I calculated that he would spot the bag and I would be in for a frivolity lecture, and it was such a beautiful day that I abandoned all acquisitive thoughts and strode along happily beside him. The temperature had soared, and it was glorious. Lunchtime strollers were out en masse in celebration of the day, smiling and nodding to each other as though they single-handedly had pulled off this wonderful occurrence. A few convertibles drove by with their tops down, which made me long to rush home to drive mine. The idea of going back to Beth's, to a room full of people dressed in black, to not enough food and too much alcohol, was anathema.

Rick seemed to be of the same mind.

"Can we play hooky?" he asked. "Get some delicious food and have a picnic on the mountain?"

"Sounds wonderful, but no. I'm not ruining this suit by sitting on the ground, and we have work to do. Shape up," I answered, more in response to my own thoughts than his words.

"Yes, dear. You're so bossy."

I think he said that affectionately.

13

WE DESCENDED BELMONT Avenue in Westmount and found a parking space easily. The family had obviously returned from the cemetery, because there were cars already parked near the house, fewer than I would have expected until I remembered that the main participants had been limousined around for the morning, eliminating the need for some. Once more I noted the newly blossoming flowers; it seemed to be the theme for the day. Tulips and daffodils along with snowdrops and irises dotted the front gardens of all the neighboring houses. The traditional impatiens borders that line so many walkways and edge lawns in Montreal hadn't been planted yet, but the new splash of color coupled with the recently verdant lawns was exciting, if sparse.

"Nice homes around here," Rick said. "I've never been on this street before."

"It backs onto Murray Hill Park, and all good rich people like to live here so they can let their golden retrievers out the back door to run. Or used to. With the leash laws and designated "doggie runs" they can't do it anymore, and I'm sure there's all sorts of people who now live here, some of them not particularly top-drawer, but it's an illusion I like to evoke. Sometimes I like my notion of the old aristocracy better than the present-day meritocracy. So much more genteel."

Rick laughed and didn't call me a snob, even knowing that in the old system he wouldn't have the lifestyle he had earned.

"Which house?" he asked, having followed my barked instruction of "park here" without comment or question.

"The gray fieldstone one across the street. You can recognize it by the black crepe bow hung on the door. I didn't know people did that anymore."

"I never knew they ever did it."

"You should read more."

He didn't get a chance to respond; we had already reached the front door and were about to make our entrance.

A gentleman's gentleman attended to the arrivals. I'd never seen him before and didn't think he was a permanent fixture, more likely a daily rental, since I remembered Joanne's mentioning that there were no servants. Beth may have to clean and scrub on a daily basis, but on this, her day of grief, when her home was open to public view, it wouldn't do to be short-staffed. Since it was sunny and warm we had no coats or hats to hand him. He looked bored.

"The family will be receiving in the living room," he intoned, for want of something better to do, I guess. This was not a huge house with a tremendous choice of reception rooms. He sounded like a pompous idiot, but it wasn't my job to tell him, or the agency that sent him.

We adjourned to the instructed room. Thirty or so people were already gathered, chatting as though at a dull cocktail party. More were arriving behind us. It was a larger group than that on Tuesday previous, again mostly attended by men.

There was a stir as the prime minister entered, flanked

by two RCMP security officers who hung back at the entryway and tried to look unobtrusive. He went directly to Beth, perched primly on the edge of a long couch that flanked the south side of the room. Everyone in the room stopped talking the moment he entered, so we could all hear him offer his condolences in the accented English that has become his trademark. He must have known Walter well, as he addressed Beth by her first name and took a moment to speak to each of her two children, who had instantly appeared at their mother's side. Beverly was seated beside Beth, and he said some personal words to her, very quietly, when he realized his was the only voice to be heard in the room. It was an elegant if uncomfortable performance, and he departed immediately thereafter, whereupon everyone started to talk at once. Beth may be the height of good breeding in her stoic impassivity, but the rest of the assemblage was duly impressed by the visit, judging by the gushing comments uttered all around us. After the initial outburst, everyone resumed their quiet conversations and all returned to as before. It was like a magician's trick, these placid people suddenly behaving like animated marionettes and then having their string all slackened at once and returning to their placid worlds.

Rick and I were met with a few stares, but most of these people were too polite for that. We generated more sidelong glances than overt scanning.

"I'm heading for the bar," Rick said. "That's where most of the action seems to be, and I see the two kids are over there. We'll reconnoiter later." He was getting into the spirit of things. A man with a mission.

Which left me to Beth and Beverly. Although I had done it before, and due to the circumstances it was totally unnecessary, it would be noticed if I didn't offer my formal condolences to the bereaved. Noticed and speculated about. What surprised me was that I knew more people here than expected. And not from business, from my social life. I was impressed that I ran with such a fancy crowd.

Girding my loins as though off to do battle or, more accurately, running the gauntlet, I strode purposefully across the room toward Beth, garnering my fair share of glances. Those who knew me wondered why I was there (I could tell by the gesticulating). I wasn't a member of the Whitestone inner circle, and those who had no idea of who I was in this place where everyone knew everyone, speculated about me. I kept my head high and had nearly reached my destination, when I was accosted—in almost the literal, street sense of the word since it was by Harry-Harry and every exchange with him felt slimy and indecent. He didn't let me down.

"Ah, the acolyte returns to the scene of the crime," he said too loudly, eliciting open stares. At least he had a good vocabulary.

"Yes, sir," I answered, tugging at my forelock and with as much volume. Once again everyone stopped talking and tried not to stare. Good stuff was in the offing, and it would be a hot topic on the gossip circuit for days to come.

"Came to see the widow about continuing the child-support payments. Mr. Whitestone was very generous with us. After all, you didn't respond to your court order and little Harry-Harry Harrison misses you so much. I have to remind him daily that you're just another deadbeat dad, featured in last week's *National Enquirer* series, but we're praying that someday you'll find God and do the right thing by your unacknowledged family. It's sad to relate the story of how I slept with you to keep my job and then you fired me anyway when I got pregnant. Little HHH just cries his heart out when Little Wally gets toys from his dad and he gets nothing. It's so hard to support a family on welfare these days." I don't know what got into me, but he started it. I know the time frame was also out of whack, but it was effect, not veracity, that I was aiming for.

I would have loved to hear the answer, but suddenly Beth was at my side, grasping my arm in apparent affection yet a little too hard for my taste.

"Barbara, you're such a kidder," she said, smiling for the first time since Walter's death. "Come along, I have so much to tell you."

Boy, she was good. She had turned a potentially nasty situation—possibly violent if Harry-Harry had continued and I'd been forced to take him down with one of Rick's tricks—and changed it into a little insider joke. People started speaking again as she led me off, likely discussing the possible truth of my declaration.

Beth steered me to the kitchen, her fingers digging into my arms. Thank heavens her nails were short or I'd have needed stitches. Fingerprints would be evident. The kitchen was deserted, no maids about busily preparing platters of food. I had noted that the buffet table held a few trays of assorted packaged lunch meats and some cake platters. It was a boring offering; didn't these people know anything about food and its wonderful capacity to dissipate all ills, especially grief? Wrong religion.

"And what was that all about? It was not in good taste, Barbara."

"I know, and I'm sorry." I actually hung my head. I felt as if I'd been caught shoplifting or exposing myself in public. "He just brings out the worst in me. He's so sleazy, he makes me feel like washing."

"That's no reason to descend to his level. I thought you had better manners."

Would the scolding ever end. So few words, but such great effect. I truly felt chagrined and remorseful.

"I'm really sorry," I repeated. "What can I do to make it up?" I asked, in hope of being able to redeem myself. I hated her being angry with me. She made me feel so small. She was very, very good at this, her disapproving face betraying more emotion than I had thought her capable of. No wonder the kids chose schools out of town. Beth's wrath was not a pretty sight.

In an instant she composed herself, her visage cleared, and she said evenly, "Ignore it. I'm sure there's no damage done. Although I am well aware of the man's shortcomings and constant bad behavior, please try not to let it happen again, no matter how great the provocation."

Please?

"Now, to get back to the business at hand. I've not had the chance to speak to you since the other night, what with making all the arrangements and getting ready for today. I called you last night when I had a free moment, but you weren't there and I dislike speaking to machines, so I did not leave a message. Therefore, I have not been able to ask you for the results of the little task I set you to."

Everything she said sounded like a proclamation. I liked it. Maybe I'd try to learn how to do it. You could get anyone to do what you wanted with that tone of voice, and it didn't even sound bossy. Almost regal.

"Now, Barbara, tell me about this *Luce Richer.*" She made the name sound like a dirty swearword. Also, she just assumed I'd done her bidding. And I had, which annoyed me.

"Beth, I don't know much more about her than you probably do. You know who she is and what she does. Everyone knows that; she's a prominent member of the business community. One thing of interest, though. She's getting married. To a man from out of town. Soon." I couldn't get the words out fast enough.

"Did Walter know about this turn of affairs?" Strange choice of words for someone in her position.

"No, I don't think so. At least she said he didn't."

"So, Barbara, while Walter knew I would be absent, she

could have arranged with him to come here to tell him and somehow it might have escalated into an altercation and she could have stabbed him. With his own knife."

My sentiments exactly. Not my choice of words; a little formal for such a nasty deed. She'd sized up the situation immediately, whereas it had taken me a couple of days to finally decide that Luce wanted to have lunch with me to tell me the story of her impending nuptials so if the police ever asked, I could corroborate the fact that Walter hadn't known about it. That she'd never gotten around to telling him. No other reason made sense, although my agreeing with her was only hearsay, since she was the source of the story. I couldn't dwell on this at the moment, because Beth had said something interesting that bore following up.

"Your knife? From your kitchen?"

"Pay attention, Barbara." I wished she'd stop using my name in every sentence. It made me feel so belittled. "No, not my knife. I said Walter's. Not from the kitchen, but from the desk in the bedroom. Three years ago it was given to Walter by a tribal leader in Brazil when he was there inaugurating a new route. He was fond of the sharp blade and used it as a letter opener for the mail. I always leave the morning's post on the desk for him to peruse, and he opened his personal letters with it. I never liked it, but Walter thought it was a delightful artifact. I think it made him feel dangerous. He would wave it around while we discussed the bills."

Ever the dutiful wife, Beth didn't open her husband's mail. It would have been an impossible temptation for me to resist, and I marveled at her discipline. And he liked to brandish his knife to punctuate sentences. And they discussed the family expenditures, which meant he didn't trust her to spend wisely. And she did all the washing and ironing and cleaning. Didn't even have a dishwasher, I noticed. She sounded more like an indentured servant than a wife. I realized that I really didn't know Walter the husband and lover at all, just Walter the president. I felt cheated and deceived.

It had to have been a crime of passion and not a planned hit. The tossing of the premises would have been done to cover up. I'd always suspected this, and now Beth's mention of the accessibility of the weapon coupled with the set-scene mess further strengthened the theory. I wondered if the police agreed but couldn't ask Beth if they had mentioned anything of the sort. Evoking the constabulary at such an occasion would be more bad behavior, and I'd already been upbraided enough.

"Now you say she's getting married. To a man of substance?"

"I don't know. I've never met him."

"Don't be obtuse, Barbara. Does he have any money to speak of? You would have ascertained that information."

Why did she intimidate me so much? I wasn't *that* insecure. I was a woman of talent and merit. And I dressed a hell of a lot better than she did. Her last inference was worthy of me walking out on her, or asking exactly what she meant by it. Instead, like a meek sheep following the shepherd even without his threatening staff, I answered, "Yes, I think he's loaded. She's sporting a really big diamond and has plans to retire and travel."

Beth looked at the small but tasteful adornment of the fourth finger of her left hand. A week ago I would have said it was quite large, but after seeing Luce's offering I had rethought my grading system. More to aspire to.

"Then she's in no need of money. Maybe I could speak to her about it. Or you could."

More trouble here. Go do her dirty work and then get insulted. No more. No way. But before I declined the task I had to find out what she meant.

"Need money? Why?"

Beth sighed. A great big heaving sigh that had me feeling sorry for her and on her side in a second. "This family has suffered some financial setbacks of late, and there's not much money left. The airline held Key Man insurance on Walter, but we had none privately. We used to both have policies on each other, but Walter canceled them without consulting me. What did surface of value was that unbeknownst to me Walter held quite a lot of stock in that woman's company. He left it to her in his will. Kenneth should have inherited the bulk of the estate, with a proviso that I be provided with continued support until my death. Margaret should have received an appropriate legacy, as was the custom in the Whitestone family. The document states all this very clearly, but there's virtually nothing to disperse. Fortunately we hold the house outright, with no liens or mortgage, so I can sell it and raise some capital. I won't get all that much for it, the political situation being what it is in Quebec, but it will help. I can live simply."

When normally closemouthed Beth spoke, she said volumes. I was completely stunned. Okay, I had noticed the house was slightly shabby when I had ascended to the second floor the other night, but virtually penniless? Walter earned an enormous amount of money and his family lived reasonably well. I know he spent a lot on Cassandre, and a weekly or biweekly tryst at the Ritz with Luce had to have cost plenty, but there should still be enough left over to satisfy a family of twelve in another neighborhood. Another mystery.

This time I stood my ground. "No, Beth," I said, using her name but not noticing any effect. I'd need practice. "I won't go groveling to Luce for you. I don't know her that well. However, I think she may be open to a discussion with you. She seems very happy with her new life and might be sympathetic to your plight. You'll have to talk to her yourself. Don't have your lawyer do it, it'll get her back up. She's a proud woman, but I don't think a vindictive one, and you might just have a shot at it."

"You're right, my dear." That sounded a whole lot friendlier than "Barbara." "I apologize for asking you. It wouldn't be right for you to do it. Crow has never been my favorite dish, but I shall have to eat some. I'll do it Monday. I'm glad that's settled; now we must return to the living room. Smile."

With that, she grabbed my arm again in exactly the same spot, plastered the semblance of a smile onto her face, and virtually dragged me out. By the time it got warm enough for short sleeves the black-and-blue marks should be faded. Beth regained her perch on the couch, and Beverly immediately took her hand and patted it. Beverly said a few quiet words to her and Beth shook her head in response. Beverly glared at me. Now the other one was mad at me for I don't know what. No one remotely sane could have expected me to ask Luce Richer to hand over her legacy. It was none of my business and I had no intention of making it so, but the more I saw of this family the loonier they seemed to get.

I spent the next few minutes chatting with some people I knew, being pumped for information, as they had seen my command performance on television. Would that never go away? One woman ventured that Harrison-Harrison was an abomination and I'd done what she wished she could, which made me feel a lot better. It seems that after Beth had commandeered me to the kitchen, Harry-Harry had headed straight for the bar, muttering something about crazy people and their delusions. He was red-faced enough that some people probably believed my tale of woe. I didn't mind, and we had a quiet giggle at his discomfiture. It would not do to laugh out loud here.

After half an hour or so I was getting very tired of all this good behavior. It was such a trial to have to watch every word and talk to a lot of people about nothing. In keeping with my theme of the day, gardens and flowers were the main topic of conversation among the women. The stock market figured highly with the men. I could have made a few points by telling them of Luce's departure, initiating a run on her stock, but thought better of it. Dealing with Beth was enough punishment for her having subjected me to that awful seat in the restaurant.

I looked around for Rick and saw he was engrossed in conversation with Kenneth and Margaret, so I decided not to interrupt. I went to get something to eat, as the pizza I had consumed earlier was by now thoroughly digested and I was hungry again. Although the offerings were meager there was more than enough, since no one except me showed any interest. Can't say the same thing about action at the bar. Traffic there was good.

And there, smack in the middle of the table, was my second-favorite food. On a footed cake plate decorated with tiny pink roses, a matching cake cutter alongside, sat a white cake with white icing. No nutritional value, loaded with calories, probably a little dry, and totally irresistible. I cut myself a large slice and polished it off quickly, carefully dabbing my lips and then whisking the crumbs off the front of my suit with a white monogrammed napkin. It was delicious. When I was a child I looked forward to birthday parties with great excitement for just such a cake. This was even better, since there was no danger of getting a piece dotted with melted candle.

When I finished cleaning myself off I turned around to find Winston Warfield, Beverly's husband, watching me. Or looking in my general direction, as his eyes were so unfocused I couldn't pinpoint the exact location of choice.

"No drinkie?"

"No drinkie."

"Come on. Have a snort with me." More like a snootful.

"No, thanks. I don't drink."

"Oh, I understand. Tried the program once m'self. Too many dreary people whining about their problems. Very boring. Couldn't relate."

It took a few beats to realize he was talking about Alcoholics Anonymous. It wasn't worth denying and having to launch into an explanation about how I simply didn't like the taste of liquor; he wouldn't believe me in any event. So I nodded solemnly. Another tidbit for the rumor mill. I was doing a good job of it in a short period of time. I wondered how long it would take for today's performance to get back to me.

"Well, I'm going to get m'self another, as this glass unfortunately seems to be empty. Ta-ta."

Yes, the whole family was definitely bonkers.

Winston teetered off in the general direction of the bar, completely soused. I had never seen him so drunk before. He had the reputation of being a voluminous consumer. I'd never seen him without a drink in his hand, but neither had I ever seen him so out of control. I guess we all deal with loss differently; falling-down drunk would never be my choice. Before I could become a pontificator of the first order, I went off in search of Rick again.

I found him engaged in conversation with a man I didn't recognize. We were introduced, spent a few minutes in small talk, then Rick looked at his expensive, gauche-for-this-crowd, gold Rolex and said we had to leave because he had an appointment. I didn't believe him for a second but was delighted by his invention. Although we'd only been there for a little over an hour, it felt like months.

We escaped out into the bright sunlight. Rick suggested a restaurant so we could discuss the ordeal, but I declined, having eaten more than my fill of cake. If he was hungry he should have had the sense to eat something while still there; it was too nice and unexpected a day to waste any more time inside. Still, being a good person, I offered a compromise.

"Can we pick up something at a convenience store and go sit in the park to eat? It's so beautiful out."

"Good idea," he answered, roaring down the street in excess of the speed limit, as though trying to put some distance between us and the house as fast as possible. I figured that Rick had been decidedly uncomfortable in that milieu.

"That family is crackers. So buttoned down and dysfunctional. I thought I had a disadvantaged upbringing, but at least I have some sense of reality. They give me the creeps. Are all WASPs like that?"

"No, I know some perfectly normal ones. The Whitestones are an enigma; not the family I thought they would be. Walter wasn't like them—to me, at least. However, I hold him responsible for Beth. I think she would have had a better chance at normalcy elsewhere. It's interesting; there's such an emphasis placed on doing the correct thing and no one ever considers if it's the right thing. We're branded conspicuously consumptive, yet I think we're better grounded."

"Speak for yourself."

"Why? You're not grounded?"

"Sure I am. I meant the conspicuously consumptive part."

"Yeah, right. Mr. Rolex, Lexus, Range Rover, and whatever other expensive labels you're wearing. Is that not a Gucci tie you're sporting?"

"Shut up. You win."

"I *love* winning."

We stopped at a corner bakery and Rick came out with two apple turnovers, coffee for him, and Diet Coke for me. Parking around Westmount Park was difficult, but we found a space in front of the library. I don't think anyone was inside; the lawn in front was littered with bodies, all busily reading as they lolled about—the world's first alfresco *bibliothèque*. I noticed no one else was wearing panty hose and was decidedly jealous on this hot day.

Heeding my earlier refusal to sit on the grass, Rick found us a lovely bench with the sun at our backs. I could have sat there forever. Children cavorted in the nearby playground, their nannies sitting in clusters according to nationality. Everything was calm and serene, the trees proudly displaying their newfound buds competing with those that already featured small leaves. Well-behaved dogs on leashes were leading their masters and mistresses on a bush tour, marking out the coming summer territory. The season had begun, and I pushed away the thought that the thermometer was still in danger of plummeting below the freezing point overnight. The tradition here is no planting before May 24, or the frost will kill everything. It was hard to imagine.

I gave Rick the chance to finish the first pastry but was too impatient to wait for the second.

"So what did you learn?"

Rick put the remaining turnover down on the brown bag that was serving as his napkin. He looked at it longingly, then resigned himself to the fact that I needed immediate attention and it wouldn't be worth it to make me wait. We were going to be very good friends if he continued his obedience training.

"They're a strange couple, those two. Kenneth, not Kenny or Ken, and Margaret, not Margie or Meg, have a very close relationship. They each warned me of the other's aversion to not being addressed properly. They nod and tilt their head at each other and understand the signal as paragraphs. They could probably have whole conversations without saying anything."

"But they're in separate cities, aren't they? Someone said so."

"Yes, Kenneth is a junior at Dartmouth. It suits him. And Margaret is at Vassar. Snobby kids, but obviously smart."

Rick sounded a little resentful at their opportunities, but my new self kept her mouth shut.

"Margaret is very much in school, although her parents don't know it. She's managed to land a scholarship for her senior year, based on her excellent grades, so the tuition is no problem, and works as a waitress for the rest of her upkeep. It's a heavy load, and as far as I can see she's just scraping by and not very happy about it. She's used to a grander lifestyle."

"So why would she keep it a secret from her family?"

"She said, and I quote, 'I like to get up Mother's nose. It's so improper for me to be a dropout.' Also, that getup you saw her arriving in? All costume. She has a special set of clothes designed to upset her parents. She's basically a conformist who won't give her parents the satisfaction of knowing they brought her up well. I don't understand it at all."

He looked genuinely puzzled as he took a bite of the turnover.

"I think I do," I said, giving him the chance to eat. I told him of Beth's imperious kitchen routine. "I would think that if I had the choice of impassivity or anger I might opt for the second. I don't know how Walter behaved with them, but I do know he was home very little. Beth's ire would indicate to Margaret that Beth cared. It's the only emotion she seems to show. A lot better than being ignored. What about the mysterious moocher boyfriend?"

"Long gone, but as with the rest of her pseudo-life, a fabrication perpetuated for her parents. Kenneth, on the other hand, has done all the right things. Crew, debating club, top grades, and the reputation of a big man on campus. The perfect young scion. She told me that proudly."

"How come they talked to you at all? She told me I was nobody." Until I mentioned it I hadn't realized how offensive her offhand comment had been. For a mannered family they sure could insult well. Form over content.

"I don't think they're aware of how old I am. In that room of grown-ups they looked on me as a peer."

One for Babyface.

"They were both away on Monday night in their respective cities. Or so they say, but I tend to believe them since they both told me exactly what they had been doing when Beverly called them with the news. That wasn't a good idea, by the way, especially for Margaret. She's more resentful of her mother than ever, feels she couldn't be bothered to call her personally, letting her aunt break the news."

"She's probably right. I would have reacted the same way."

"But there's something fishy about them. Or maybe it's just that I never met kids who seemingly care so little about their parents. In my neighborhood, those of us who had parents loved them or at least respected them, often through repeated beatings. It's only in later years that they come to understand the abuse and start resenting. These two have so much to be grateful for, so many opportunities at their feet—just their name will open countless doors—and all they can do is denigrate the system that created them and in which they will soon become active members, to trash their families. It's sinful." Rick looked completely outraged. It would take him a few more forays through the class system to realize it was not at all unusual.

"Aside from wasted opportunity and being spoiled, what's so suspicious about them?"

"Both asked me if I knew how long it took to get the will read and the assets distributed. They asked about double-indemnity clauses in insurance and the validity of a will if one of the legatees is indicted of the crime."

"Before I comment, why would they ask you?"

"I sort of told them I was a lawyer, a criminal lawyer."

"Why?"

"Don't know. Commodities broker sounded unclean in that house. Too close to the money. I added the criminal part as soon as I'd spoken and instantly became ashamed of myself for allowing them to get to me. Figured it was a nasty thing to be, although these days lawyer is bad enough."

So Rick hadn't settled all his demons yet. And was a sensitive person. I really liked him.

"Whatever the reason, it was probably a smart thing to do. It got you some information."

"In retrospect, I was the one supplying information."

"No, you just think you were. Beth knows what's in the will but obviously hasn't seen fit to discuss it with her children. They don't know there's no more money, and the fact that they asked you and not their uncle Winston about insurance indicates they don't want him to know they're the least bit interested. Either more of the charade or something more sinister. By the way, what's the answer to the last question?"

"As to the will, that's easy. The purported murderer ceases to exist, to all intents and purposes. His or her share reverts to the estate. It can tie things up for years. As to the insurance, that's a little trickier. The company has to pay. It has no right to be judge and jury and decide who did it. Even if the person is indicted, he hasn't been convicted and the insurance company has to pay off. A famous instance would be the Menendez brothers."

"They came to my mind also. Even before this discussion. In any event, it's a moot point as there is no insurance."

"None? How is that possible?"

"Nope. It's been canceled. Must have pissed Winston off, since he's their broker. Did you get a chance to talk to Winston at all?"

"No, I didn't. I tried when I first got to the bar, but he looked too drunk to be coherent and then I got caught up with the Duplicitous Duo."

"I couldn't get him to say anything intelligible either. Do you think he was really drunk? Could it have been an act? It looked so staged."

"I've had a lot of experience with drunks, and that weren't no playacting, ma'am."

A red-and-blue oversized ball rolled to our feet, and Rick leaned over to retrieve it. He tossed it back to a little something, I couldn't tell if it was a boy or a girl, who waved at him and smiled. The child's suspicious nanny eyed us continually for the next five minutes.

"So what did we learn?" I asked, trying to recap.

"That Walter Whitestone was a very important person. My God, the prime minister was there. At the house."

"I see Rick Fogarty was impressed."

"Sure was. That was something. Who else do you know? You can drag me along anywhere. So far your offerings, while somewhat diverse, have not been boring. This is fun." I was glad to see that his animosity toward the privileged children had dissipated and no longer colored the entire proceedings.

"Yeah, but we have to be careful. It's really none of our business, and we could get hurt."

"Get off it. You're just as interested."

"I never want to see the barrel of a gun up close and personal again." The memory made me shiver in spite of the heat.

"Oh yeah, tell me about it. What happened?"

"Another time. Just the thought of it frightens me. I don't care how good a fighter you are, a gun is terrifying. Can we drop it? I'll tell you some other time. It's too nice out to scare myself."

"I don't understand that last sentence, but okay. Anyway, it's getting late. I have a class at five."

"In what?"

"French, but don't tell anyone. I'm not as fluent as I should be."

Rick dutifully dumped our trash into the proper receptacle. Littering is severely frowned on in Westmount. It's one of the cleanest places I've ever been to. We walked toward the car over the grass, my heels sinking in with every step, but I wasn't complaining. It seemed a pity to leave. There were at least three more hours of daylight, and who knew what it would be like tomorrow. We're all gluttons for sunny days after the winter. We don't start taking them for granted until mid-June.

I WAS PEELING off the offending panty hose when the phone rang. It took me until the third ring—generally it's one and a half—to get it, as I was all entangled in sticky hose. It was nice to feel air circulation.

Susan was on the other end. I could tell immediately, since she didn't bother to say hello, just sailed right in. It was worth it.

"I was at the Barkleys' this afternoon. They'd just returned from the funeral and were discussing it. It seems there was quite a turnout. By the way, who were you with? Heather Barkley found him very attractive if a mite young. Who is it?"

"A new friend. And he's in his late thirties, so he's age-appropriate. He does look young, though."

"It must be serious if you're trotting him out to funerals. Although you might have done it to impress him with how many important people you know. I hear the prime minister and some premieres were there."

I ignored the dig.

"Yes. And then the P.M. came back to Beth's house. Even all those snooty people were in awe."

"How could you tell?"

"The ice cubes in their glasses stopped tinkling for a few seconds."

Susan giggled. It was a nice sound. "That's not what I called for, and we'll get back to it later. What do you know about Winnings?"

"Is this a trick question? Are you trying to find out if I gamble?"

Another giggle. "I mean Winnings International Corporation."

"Never heard of 'em. Why?"

"It's a pyramid scam that got shut down last week."

"Right, I read about it in the newspaper the other day. Millions of dollars involved locally, from what I understand."

"Yes, and some of that money was your ex-boss's."

"What?" Not cured yet.

"It seems that Winston Warfield, his genius brother-in-law and financial adviser, got him to invest heavily. They were guaranteeing at least a thirty-percent return, so anyone in his right mind should suspect something fishy, but Walter's mind was obviously elsewhere. Winston was getting a big finder's fee for every sucker he could reel in. There are quite a few people who are very angry with him at the moment. It was brave of him to even show his face at the funeral. I assume he was there?"

"Yes indeed. He was pickled from the start and downing them continually. Can't blame him. It must be easier to face them all in a drunken state."

"When the whole thing collapsed or deflated or whatever the proper word is, and the lists were drawn up, Walter's name appeared beside a hefty sum. I couldn't get them to tell me how much, but it should be a matter of public record somewhere. They weren't really talking to me, more to each other with me as a very interested third party who kept quiet lest they remember I was there and shut up. Not in front of the help, you know." This time a longer giggle. She was pleased as punch with herself, as she deserved to be.

"So that's where the money went. Beth said that they'd invested unwisely. More like greedily to me. I think Walter's lifestyle was getting a tad too expensive and he went for the big kill."

"And got it."

"So why did Beth ask me if Luce had gotten all the money? Could it be possible that Walter didn't tell her he'd lost it all and she found out only posthumously?"

"Bad grammar. He died, not her. Maybe she did find out, approached him, they had a fight, and she killed him. You said her alibi was idiotic."

"Could be. I just hate to think of it. I don't know why, but I don't want it to have been her." I couldn't imagine why I was on Beth's side. Maybe it was all that cleaning she had to do.

"I'll leave it with you. I called as soon as I got in the door. Now I want to change clothes. These panty hose are stifling."

"I know what you mean. I had time to take them off, and it's a blessing. Go enjoy."

I hung up and went to change the rest of my clothes. Then I opened every window in the house, making note to ask Mme Jacqueline to clean the screens. Instead of trying to figure out who killed Walter, I gave myself the evening off. I ate, I left the dishes on the counter, I read, I watched a new episode of *Homicide*, and I went to sleep quite pleased with my day.

14

SATURDAY MORNING WAS as beautiful as the day before. The weatherman predicted incoming clouds and afternoon rain, but at eight o'clock in the morning it was gloriously sunny and almost warm. My apartment was chilly; I had neglected to shut any of the windows the night before and it had been, although not frosty, quite cold. I didn't care. The sun pouring in would warm it up soon.

I donned my walking shoes, tights, and a T-shirt, with a sweatshirt over it all, then dialed my walking buddy, waking her up in the process. After five minutes of whining I persuaded her to join me, and fifteen minutes, one Diet Coke, and one cigarette later, I headed out for the mountain across the street. My friend was already waiting for me in front of the building, still a little cantankerous from having been awakened. We crossed the street and started up, sniffing the air, which was redolent with eau de skunk. This happens often in the summer when the critters come down off the forestlike parklands and try to cross Pine Avenue in search of good garbage. About once every two weeks one of them gets creamed by passing traffic. The nocturnal little guy who stank up the beautiful morning must have been on his way home when he ate the pavement, because the stench was still quite fresh. I've never minded; it gives a country feel to urban living.

We strode along the path, navigating the twists and turns on the switchback route in the company of other walkers and joggers, all minding our own business on our journeys. At the top, after short consultation, we elected to go the literal extra mile and took the road leading to and around the massive cross that dominates the east side of the peak. The structure reinforced the reality that this is indeed a Catholic city. Jacques Cartier supposedly planted the first cross in 1535, and there's been one on the site ever since. At night it's a good landmark if I'm ever lost; just aim for the lighted cruciform and I'll find my way.

After completing the circuit I thought I deserved a break, and we went into the stone chalet near the lookout to get a Diet Coke as fortification for the descent. Even though I had brought along a cigarette in case, I eschewed the pleasure. It seem too much of a pollutant in the fresh air, which was doing my lungs no end of good. Also my friend doesn't smoke, which I at first thought explained why I was more out of breath than she, until she admitted she'd been walking for the past month in an effort to lose some weight in time for her niece's wedding. She'd bought a new dress that was a bit too tight and was desperately trying to beat the clock. Looking her over carefully, I ventured that she had a good shot at it. It made her very happy.

We rested on the cement steps of the chalet for a while, and looked out over the southern part of the city. I could see the St. Lawrence River and two bridges strung across it, connecting the island to the rest of the world. In the distance, the Green Mountains of Vermont lived up to their name, and if

I'd gone to the edge, I could have seen the Adirondacks in New York. The sun was all over me, warming and delighting. Life was truly good.

Once home, I plunked myself into the wing chair by the window, breathing too rapidly for my liking. I'd thought I was in better shape. My legs felt like Jell-O and my strength was sapped. The answer was that I smoke too much, and once again, I resolved again to cut down. Not quit, but smoke less. So I lit a cigarette as I formulated a plan on how to achieve this end.

Following a long shower, which restored feeling to my lower limbs and refreshed me, I settled down to peruse the financial information Marvin Seedman had sent. No mention of any Winnings Corp.–like enterprise. Just reasonably conservative strategic planning with respectable returns. For the hundredth time I tried to figure out if I ever had to go back to work full-time, as this bout of liberty was indeed seductive, and again couldn't come up with the answer, the stock market not being predictable. After scanning a pound of documentation I decided I was in good hands and put it away to get some lunch. Walking had made me very hungry, and I hadn't had a cigarette in what felt like days but was in reality only two hours. It was already noon and I'd only had two so far today, so I was proud of myself and went to the kitchen to find something to celebrate with.

The options were indeed few, but I managed to pull something edible together. I decided that the afternoon's project would be a visit to Costco, where I could spend a pile of money for a ton of stuff I didn't need, all in the name of saving money. I love it there, especially the food samples, and often walk out poorer but not needing to eat again until the next day.

As I was about to leave, the doorbell rang. It's connected to my phone and I was on the line, trying unsuccessfully to cajole Susan into going with me, hoping she'd keep me from buying more toilet paper. I switched over and buzzed the caller in without asking who it was. Being a polite person who uses salutations and closings, I returned immediately to Susan, gracefully accepted her refusal, said good-bye, hung up, and went to the door to see who was there. Maybe someone had sent me flowers. I always hope for that, but it never happens.

Didn't get any that afternoon, either. I went to the door and waited. As soon as I heard the elevator door open I knew who it was. Joanne was giving a command performance today.

". . . the three of us. The bed really wasn't big enough since Hans and Dorf have such enormous pecs. And other parts. You wouldn't believe the permutations and combinations. And then Dorf's wife came home and we all had a big fight, throwing bowls of chocolate pudding at each other, until she decided to join us. I don't like her very much, but she tasted like a chocolate-covered cherry Popsicle and . . ."

By this time I'd dragged her inside and slammed the door behind us, effectively shutting her up. She lowered the decibel level and said, "Well, that should keep her glued to the door for a while. And should be worthy of another long letter of complaint. I didn't remember her until I got into the elevator, so it was the best I could come up with on short notice. I'll try to do better next time."

"You did fine, thank you very much. You really are going to get me thrown out." I tried to sound stern, but it's hard when you're laughing.

"So what? There are better buildings in town."

Joanne looked lovely, casually dressed in skintight jeans and a jeans shirt. She sported matching denim eyewear and a denim barrette at the side of her head, holding the honey-colored hair off her forehead. Very monochromatic and very springy.

"Hi. It's wonderful to see you. How come you're here? Wanna go to Costco with me?"

"I can't afford it. I've never been able to figure out how I can drop so much money for so much crap I don't have space for. I think I have enough toilet paper and paper towels to last until the millennium." A woman after my own heart. "In any case, I don't have much time and I have a problem and need to talk to my sensible friend."

"We may be in big trouble here."

"Seriously, I value your opinion. I think you have the ability to see things from all sides, and I'm too involved and confused to think clearly. And no, it's not sexual."

Joanne's peccadilloes have always been a great source of entertainment to me. I never judge and listen attentively, savoring every salacious detail.

She plunked her purse down on the hall table, taking the time to retrieve two chocolate bars from inside. Joanne knows that if you want anything good to eat in my house, you'd better bring it along. I took mine with no second thought. After all, I'd walked four miles this morning and I was entitled to a reward. Joanne went into the kitchen and sat down at the table.

"This place is a mess," she said, looking around in disdain.

"I was just about to clean it up," I lied. But I proceeded to do it. I turned on the tap to soak all the dirty glasses that littered the counters, searching under the sink for some washing-up liquid.

"Your dishwasher broken?"

"I forgot."

"You know, if I told people this they wouldn't believe me. You forgot you have a dishwasher? You should get down on your hands and knees and say a prayer for the continued good health of Mme Jacqueline. I think you'd disappear in your own squalor if it weren't for her."

"Don't be mean. Nobody invited you, and you have to

admit, whenever you are invited the place is spotless," I said, loading the dishwasher. It was amazing how easy it was and how much cleaner the kitchen instantly looked.

"Okay, you're right."

"You must have something very serious weighing on your mind for you to give in that easily. That and the fact that you haven't devoured your candy."

In dealing with Joanne, if there is food on the premises, it is generally understood that nothing of importance will be discussed until said food has disappeared.

She stared listlessly at the almost entire chocolate bar that sat before her, seemingly indifferent to its presence. I began to worry.

"Yes, I do," she said, shifting her gaze to her fingernails. "I simply don't know what I want."

I stopped polishing the counter, even though I was rather enjoying it. The cleanser smelled great and it was fun wiping away the cola rings. I could get into this in a big way. I put down the sponge and went to the table to sit opposite her. This did indeed sound serious.

"So what's the matter? Jacques okay?"

Jacques is Joanne's surgeon husband. Her third husband, but I think this one will be a keeper.

"Jacques is fine. Overworked, but fine."

"So what is it? Enough of this drama. Tell me."

She took a deep breath and started. "I had an offer. That's why I wasn't at the funeral yesterday. You know I would have been there otherwise."

"You missed a good one. An offer of what?"

"A job offer. Anchor for the eleven o'clock national news."

"Joanne, that's fabulous."

"Yes it is, isn't it." She sighed deeply, looking forlorn.

"So what's the problem? You've been angling for this forever. Even back in school, when you weren't going to win the Pulitzer Prize during your brilliant career at the *New York Times*, you wanted this gig. I don't understand."

"It means moving to Toronto."

"Oh, no. Of course. What are you going to do?"

"You're supposed to tell me that." She peeled some paper from her chocolate bar and bit off a small piece, not chewing but letting the confection melt in her mouth. Mine was long gone. I wanted to ask her if she had another one stashed in her bag, but it was off-topic and this was a crisis.

"I can't tell you what to do. I know if you go, I'll miss you desperately. You've been part of my life forever. But I can manage, if that's what you truly want. What does Jacques say about this?"

"I haven't told him. I need time to think about what I want before I even mention it. The thing is, he couldn't come. He's devoted to his job, and though he could probably get a good posting with more money there, he loves the hospital he's at, and I couldn't ask him to give up his life's work for me. In the scheme of things, what he does is so much more important than what I do. Mine is driven by ego, his by caring and devotion. And I really love him, Barbara. I don't want to leave him behind. On the other hand, it's such a terrific offer; all the perks I ever dreamed of and a pile of money. National recognition of my work. It's a job you keep forever and leave only if one of the U.S. networks offers you the equivalent. Look at Peter Jennings. It's really tempting."

She took another delicate bite of chocolate and sat staring out the window, lost. My heart went out to her, overtaking my selfish desire for her to stay. It was a fabulous opportunity.

"I can't tell you what to do. All I can say is that Jacques is your husband and you have to talk to him about it. It's an issue between the two of you."

"And you, too. You're my best friend, and I'll never find someone to replace you."

She actually brought tears to my eyes with that last comment. Sometimes I'm such a sap. One little compliment and I'm off. "I don't want you to go but will understand if you do." "You're right." Another heaving sigh. "I'll talk to Jacques tonight. Cook him a gourmet dinner at home with candles and soft music."

"Don't go overboard. He'll think you're dying."

Joanne smiled for the first time and proceeded to demolish the rest of the bar. Having a plan of sorts cheered her, and she returned to her normal breezy fashion.

"Okay, that's over. Now tell me all about what happened yesterday. And who were you with? And what's your version of the Harry-Harry episode?"

"You already heard about that? Less than twenty-four hours. Not bad."

I told her of the events, focusing on the Harry-Harry imbroglio, omitting Rick, and embellishing for effect when appropriate. We do this to each other, our long relationship allowing us to sort fact from fiction in a story, but enjoying the rich details.

"Do you think anyone believed you?"

"What does your source say?" In keeping with the tenor of Joanne's job, we'd long ago agreed to share any and all gossip, with the caveat of never mentioning the source. Even if it was trivial, we'd so fallen into the habit that I didn't think to ask who had told her. I was still marveling at the speed with which the information had come back to me.

"She knows better, but she did say some people looked like they wanted to believe it. He's not a very popular guy, that Harry-Harry."

"I'm glad. I can't stand him, and it makes me feel better and less vindictive to have my opinion seconded. He's awful. Any word on if he'll get Walter's position? I know he desperately wants it, and I'd hate to see him succeed. There were some people from Memphis at the funeral. They weren't at Beth's afterward, but I wonder if they heard the story. Hope so. The entire performance was unseemly, and true or not, it can't reflect well on him."

"Or you either."

"Aahh, but the difference is, I don't care," I said.

Joanne didn't forget my question, and I'd successfully avoided the subject of Rick. "No word on Walter's position yet. The airline formally announced that they would appoint his successor within the month, and I haven't heard any rumors."

"I can ask around and let you know if I come up with anything. Check with some secretaries."

"Thanks, a scoop couldn't hurt my position. If I decide to stay here, I'm going to demand a raise."

"You deserve some consolation, and money never hurts."

We chatted some more about everyone we knew, carefully avoiding the prospect of her departure to Toronto. Tomorrow she'd tell me how it went with Jacques and we could evaluate the situation further. Now that there was no need for rapt attention, I returned to the task of cleaning up the kitchen as we talked, and was actually sweeping the floor when there was a knock at the door. Not the doorbell but a knock, here in my supposedly inviolable building. I figured it had to be Susan, who'd changed her mind and had come to collect me, since she takes great pride in sneaking by the doorman or through the garage to confront me in embarrassing attire or situations. This time I was at least fully clothed in jeans and a white turtleneck, topped with a peach blazer, still in celebration of spring. It set off my hair color and perpetuated the glow of good health I had earned on my hike, which more than adequately compensated for the exorbitant price I had paid for it. Cashmere, too.

A chance to get them both. I looked over at Joanne, and

in a spate of mischief, knowing the competition for my attention that existed between these two, I said, "Can you get that, please? I want to sweep this pile into the dustpan. I'll be there in a sec."

The front door is right outside my kitchen, off the spacious foyer that also opens into the living room and a hall that leads to the rest of the apartment, so I could easily keep an ear tuned to the exchange. I swept and grinned in anticipation.

As I was dumping the dust, I heard, "Well, lookee, lookee. Look who's here." Not a suitable greeting for Susan. "Come in, gentlemen. I'm sure Barbara will be delighted to see you." It was said at high volume, obviously for the benefit of Mrs. Brooks across the hall, and I scanned the kitchen for a place to hide. Whoever it was, this couldn't be good. Joanne was enjoying it too much.

There is no hiding place in an apartment kitchen. Something else to look for at my next residence after I got thrown out of here.

In the foyer stood an abashed Detective-Sergeant Gregory Allard and a truculent Detective-Sergeant Fernand Boucherville. With a delighted Joanne in the middle.

I wasn't quite as thrilled.

"Haven't you heard of doorbells?" My mood instantly matched Boucherville's face.

"I'm sorry," Greg said. "He insisted." At the time, I didn't know he was as big a liar as I.

Boucherville didn't notice the ascribed rudeness. He was too busy trying to stare Joanne down.

"What's *she* doing here?"

"*She* was invited. This is my house and I can entertain whomever I choose. It's none of your business. What do you want?"

This was not starting well.

Joanne, on the other hand, was now in a grand old mood. Much cheerier than on her arrival. She nodded at me in thanks for the entertainment, and knowing her place, said, "Well, I'll just run along now. Leave you alone to rubber-hose her. Remember, no permanent marks. Bye-bye, Barbara. I'll speak to you in the morning. If they give you any trouble, dial nine-one-one."

"Could you please leave quietly? Please, no performance art. I'm in enough trouble for one day. Please." A lot of "pleases," in an effort to impress the point.

"Yes, ma'am." She kissed me affectionately on both cheeks, making actual contact, and left silently. I was proud of her; it must have been difficult.

I turned my attention back to the two cops, still standing uncomfortably. Boucherville was wearing his dirty trench coat, and I didn't want it on my sofa, so I asked him politely for it and hung it in the closet. He looked surprised at my manners. Or possibly that I was behaving in a civil fashion. Like Harrison-Harrison, he gets my dander up, but unlike the other it's not outright loathing on my part, just an opening adversarial stance. He gets so red so quickly that it's almost fun. In the police station or someone else's house, that is. This was my home, and I wanted to get this over with as fast as possible and get them out of there. On some level, for no good reason, because as far as I could see Boucherville was more mouth than action, he scared me. Too much of a loose cannon.

Thanks to Joanne, at least my kitchen, open to public view from the hall, was spotless.

Greg handed me the clean raincoat he carried draped over one arm. As I hung it up I looked through the kitchen and out the window and saw that it was cloudy, almost threatening. The sunny morning had faded into a gloomy afternoon, the rain imminent. Greg looked quite natty in a pale yellow shirt under a navy hand-tailored suit. A splashy tie and the expected dirty Reeboks completed the look. That suit had to have cost a fortune, and I wondered how he could possibly dress so well on his salary. I know detectives make a decent living, but he sure liked expensive clothes.

Boucherville, on the other hand, dressed like a man paying hefty alimony. A brown suit, frayed-at-the-cuffs white shirt, and a needed-to-be-cleaned solid beige tie. If he elected to spatter his food he should at least choose patterned neckwear. His feet looked better than Greg's, though. He was shod in acceptable, highly polished brown loafers. A lot of attention had gone into that footwear, and I decided it was the only area in which he felt he could outshine Greg and took advantage of it. I wondered if Greg had foot problems.

After ascertaining that neither of them wanted anything to drink, which pleased me since playing waitress for Boucherville was not a task I relished, I formally escorted them into the living room, ever the gracious chatelaine. I offered only because good manners had overridden my instincts. All that hanging around with Beth.

Boucherville scanned the room with great interest, his attention focusing on the glass door breakfront, seeming to take inventory of the contents. Did we share a passion for Waterford crystal? Maybe that, and not alimony, accounted for his sartorial distress. In the meantime, Greg picked the wing chair and then Boucherville selected the love seat, in effect forcing me to the center couch in the U-shaped configuration, ensuring that I focus on them separately. A clever ploy. It annoyed me that I'd been gotten so easily, so in retaliation I excused myself and went to the kitchen to retrieve my cigarettes. Last I knew of it Greg had quit smoking, but that was three months ago and he might have reverted. Being only the third one of the day, I had no qualms about lighting up. I had been so distracted and involved with Joanne, I'd forgotten to smoke during her entire visit. My morning's resolution to cut down might yet bear fruit.

Blowing the smoke in Greg's direction, despite the fact that I still found him attractive, I decided I'd had enough of good manners and returned to my original theme. "What do you want? Why are you here? I thought I'd gone over everything at the police station."

"We don't mean to intrude, Ms. Simons. We need to ask you a few questions and thought you'd be more comfortable answering in your own home." Greg had reverted to very formal behavior, addressing me as Ms., being disgustingly solicitous. I wasn't charmed.

"So ask away." I again blew smoke at him, and this time he winced, which pleased me no end. There was something to be said for being childish.

Boucherville cut in, causing Greg to snap his mouth shut, and so I never got to hear his response.

"What were you doing at the scene of the crime?" Boucherville asked, and not nicely either. He likes me less than I like him, which I don't understand at all. I'm not the obnoxious one. And he asked in French, probably trying to elicit an inflamed response that would lead me to tell him some important detail that I'd been holding back so he could drag me off to the clink and lock me up forever. My mind doesn't operate that well in his presence; my reactions to him are visceral. However, he hadn't been party to my recent forays to the land of good form, and my tutelage proved successful.

I responded in perfect French, which surprised him. I don't know why. Our original interrogation had been conducted in that language, so he obviously knew I was fluent and at ease with it. When I switched my glance to the other side of the coffee table I saw that Greg was equally stunned. What did they expect? I had been in public relations most of my life and knew how to play to an audience when I wanted something. This time I was seeking information but wouldn't ask directly, as I knew what the response to that would be; I hoped to get it indirectly, and being nice was my opening ploy.

With great patience, I said, "We've been over this a hundred times at the police station. My answer hasn't changed. It was an accident, a coincidence."

"It wasn't an accident, it was murder, and I don't believe in coincidences."

"I'm sorry. It's the best I can offer."

"Fernand," Greg said, "we checked it out."

"Thank you for believing me," I said. That sounds more polite than it was. I'd said it in English with heavy emphasis and in a sarcastic tone. Greg smiled and Boucherville nodded. He didn't get it.

"Were you the deceased's mistress too?" Boucherville asked. I briefly considered slapping him.

"I find that a highly insulting remark. No, I was the deceased's employee. And not while he was being made deceased."

Between my television appearance, the Harry-Harry episode, and the certainty of everyone around that I was sleeping with Walter, my image had taken a big beating in three short days.

"Can you prove that?"

What a stupid question. "Of course I can't prove it. How can anyone prove they didn't have an affair? And from what I understand, Mr. Whitestone was busy elsewhere." I made sure to use the full appellation, lest my informality be misinterpreted. Subtlety was obviously not one of Boucherville's fortes.

Greg interrupted again. "Please don't take offense. None was meant." He seemed to spend a lot of time covering his partner's faux pas. Or maybe it was the good cop/bad cop routine. Whatever it was, it didn't help. I can fight my own battles.

"A lot was taken," I muttered. Now might be the chance to get in a question. "Have you spoken to Addison Adams yet? The accountant?"

The answer was supplied by Greg, to the obvious consternation of Boucherville, who reddened to a satisfying degree. "Yes, we have. It seems the Whitestones are short of cash. Bad investments."

"Did he tell you it was in Winnings?"

"It took some leaning, but in the end he did. Client confidentiality often disappears under the threat of subpoena, where we might find additional incriminating information. After Fernand mentioned this to him, he volunteered the information that the Whitestones and the Warfields had taken a beating. Fernand can be persuasive."

"I'll bet." The idea of Boucherville confronting the tight-assed Adams amused me. I'd have to call his secretary and try to cajole all the details out of her. Joanne would love it.

"Another question," I said. I was actually getting answers and may as well try to cram as much as possible in before Boucherville stopped me, something I was sure was inevitable. "What about prints? You must have dusted the place?"

Greg smiled indulgently. It seemed to me a patronizing gesture, but it was information I was after and no time to get huffy.

"There were none on the knife itself. It had been wiped enough to smudge any identifying prints. The room gave us hundreds of prints, all over everything, many different sets, meaningless. We have no idea how long they've been there. For a bedroom, there was a lot of traffic."

"I think I can explain that. Beth has no help, she does all her own cleaning, and that's a big house. She probably only surface-dusts and tidies up the obvious mess most of the time. Anyone who's been in that room for the past year or so would probably have left some trace. Be thankful it wasn't the living room. The Whitestones did a lot of entertaining; it goes with the job. And Beth said Walter was fond of that knife, so he probably showed it off."

"That helps explain it. We're trying to match all the prints we can, but I don't think most of the people who left them, innocent or otherwise, would have them on file. I don't think we'll yield anything important."

Boucherville was not happy that Greg had said so much. He puffed himself up, obviously about to launch into another offensive question, when his pocket beeped. He took the pager out, looked at the number, and scanned the room for a phone. As he was about to reach for the one that sat on the end table right beside him, Greg said, "Fernand, I think there's another phone in the kitchen and you may prefer the privacy."

"*Bonne idée.*" He looked at me in a manner suggesting that I might be rude enough to eavesdrop and overhear something important. I'd been displaying mostly proper form so far, so although true, it was uncalled for.

As soon as he left, Greg leaned over and began speaking softly, conspiratorially. He looked adorable, blue eyes staring deeply into mine. I almost didn't hear what he said.

"I arranged for that call to Fernand. He should be gone for a few minutes. I wanted to get him out of the room so I could speak to you privately."

"You could have phoned or come yourself."

"I wanted to speak to you in person, and no, if he found out I'd been here, he would have been more suspicious of you."

"Why? What have I ever done to him?"

"He still has some unanswered questions about our last encounter. He feels there were some missing details."

"Oh" was all I said. Boucherville may be obnoxious, but he was obviously not stupid. I'd have to remember that. It was so easy to regard him as a buffoon, and that could get me into trouble.

I changed the disturbing subject and asked, "What do you want to say to me?"

"I need your help."

"The police department is seeking assistance from me?" It was incredible. He would have to do better if he thought this would put him back in my good graces. There had to be more to this. "To do what?"

"Barbara," he said. I nearly didn't bother to listen to the rest, so happy was I that he'd reverted to a first-name basis. What was wrong with me? Strange men, and he *was* strange in foppish dress and demeanor, don't usually have that effect on me. I was a middle-aged woman, and I was nearly drooling. Time to get a grip. I banished all those thoughts and forced myself to concentrate.

"This case should have been simple. An obvious act of passion. But we're having difficulty with our inquiries. Fernand's approach, while not subtle, often has good results. However, in this instance we're dealing with the most remarkably controlled people I have ever met."

"They are that," I interjected. The notion of Fernand versus that crowd made me smile. "What do you want me to do?"

"Through happenstance, you're involved. Serendipity caused it, but nevertheless you're an integral part of the investigation."

He sure spoke good English for a cop.

"Can you keep an ear to the ground for information? Can you supply me with some gossip about them? The validity of the alibis? None of the persons involved has a good one, so I'd like to hear what the speculation among their peers is. I know you're privy to more casual information than we are.

They can smell a police officer a block away, and no one will do anything but respond officially to our questions. It's a high-profile case, and we need to close it quickly. There's pressure."

"You care about gossip?"

"Yes, there's often a kernel of truth." Which again made me fret about my performance at Beth's.

Greg was obviously finished. He leaned back and eyed my cigarette package longingly.

"Still not smoking?"

"Not yet."

"Good boy. Keep it up." And I did not light up another one.

After careful consideration of his request, I took a moment to formulate my answer. In a way, he was right. I knew all the suspects, if not intimately, at least well enough to talk to them. Which I had been doing nonstop for the past few days, but that was none of his business. I'd need more time to collate the accrued information before I speculated.

"Have you looked into Cassandre Cartier? I assume you know about her."

"Yes, we've spoken to her."

"Where was she? While Mr. Whitestone was getting killed?" That didn't sound like a properly constructed phrase to me, but he didn't seem to have noticed.

"Getting her hair braided. She claims it takes twenty-four hours."

"I can believe that. It's a beautiful job. If that's indeed what she was doing. What about her boyfriend?"

"Boyfriend?"

I knew something he didn't. I liked that. "Well, maybe not boyfriend, but they looked quite chummy to me. I was not introduced, but he's a big black guy, looks like a linebacker. He was at the club when I was there." I omitted Rick from this speech, so although he didn't know it yet, he owed me one.

"You spoke to her? Barbara, listen, this isn't a game. You could get hurt. The passionate nature of this crime suggests that someone isn't as controlled as they would lead us to believe. If you get too close, you might get someone's back up and you could be next. Keep your meetings public and watch your back. You know, I didn't think this out. I was being selfish. Now that I think about it, I have no right putting you in possible jeopardy. You were lucky last time, and I wouldn't want to repeat the occurrence. Ignore what I said."

He looked so deliciously contrite that I had to come to his assistance. On the other hand, if this was his way of getting me to agree, it was very effective.

"No, I *will* be careful. And I'm sure I can get some information." I already had a lot but couldn't put it together yet. I needed more time before I shot my mouth off.

"And please stay away from Harrison Harrison."

"What? You heard about that, too?"

"I understand it was the highlight of the afternoon."

"Oh, shit." Not a mannerly word, but the first one that came to mind. I'd overdone it in my effort to be cute. Oh well, it was only Harry-Harry, and in the grand scheme of things, it didn't really matter. But it gave me the opportunity to further rattle Harry-Harry.

"I guess I should tell you," I said. "I have it on very good authority that Harrison Harrison visited Mr. Whitestone sometime on Monday night. Before Beth came home and found the body. It would be interesting to know why he went there and what transpired. If you've read the papers lately, you must be aware that they weren't on the best of terms."

"How do you know this?" Greg asked, alarmed.

"It's not important. Just believe me that it's true."

It pleased me to implicate Harry-Harry. Although I didn't

believe that he had murdered Walter, I was delighted at the prospect of his being interrogated by Boucherville. They were similar in temperament, and I could hope for a long and difficult session culminating in one or the other suffering a major coronary. Either one was acceptable.

Greg didn't want to leave it at that, and I could tell he was about to ask me something or warn me off some more, but he didn't get the chance, as Boucherville reentered at that moment. I'd been so engrossed in our conversation that I'd forgotten to keep one ear open for possibly interesting information. In any event, Greg had said he'd organized the call so it couldn't have been that important. Boucherville sat back down—I had been hoping they'd leave immediately on some kind of fabricated or actual emergency—and resumed questioning me. He asked again why I had purchased the Ride-Along and why I had chosen that night for it and a whole bunch of other repetitive questions. I answered amiably, going over everything in exquisite detail with no sign of irritation. I think it pissed him off.

Finally, after an eternity, he stood, signaling the end of my torture. I saw them both to the door, gingerly handing Boucherville his coat, not quite sure I wanted to touch it. Boucherville nodded to me and strode off down the hall. Greg held back a few seconds and said in parting, "Please be careful with your questions. Here's my card again. Call me anytime; my home number is on the back."

He shoved the card into my hand and followed his partner to the elevator as the door across the hall opened and Mrs. Brooks came out with her inevitable world's smallest trash bag.

"Lots of visitors today, I see. You're a popular girl."

Greg looked back over his shoulder to watch the interchange, but I waited until he rounded the corner and heard the elevator door close behind them before answering. A response was expected, and she wouldn't go about her business until she got it. I think she expected an explanation or an apology. Not from me, and not in a million years. Unfortunately, I couldn't think of anything clever to say, so I answered pleasantly, "Yes. I'm very lucky to have so many good friends." I think I surprised her by being so polite. And disappointed her, too.

"We don't like the police here," she said, trying to goad me so she could have something else to complain about.

"You're right. Neither do I." I went back inside and closed the door behind me, leaving her to the chore of trash disposal. I found her more enervating than the Boucherville-Allard combo. She's insidious.

In my den, I was about to slide Greg's card into my cleverly disguised-as-a-piece-of-furniture file cabinet when I thought better of it. I inspected it carefully. A duplicate of the one he'd previously given me, except that on the back, in precise lettering, he'd written his home number and pager number. I noted that the sevens were crossed in the European fashion. What did that mean? Not being able to resolve the conundrum of Greg, I slipped it into my purse. His dire warnings had spooked me. I didn't think I was in any danger since there wasn't a homicidal maniac at work here, but it wouldn't hurt to carry the card with me. In the olden days, when I was younger and more immature, I might have been tempted to call him at all hours to see if he was home, hanging up if he answered. Now, in my maturity, and with the advent of caller ID, this was no longer feasible.

Most of the day was gone. The rains had returned in a steady drizzle, darkening the apartment much too early. It was too late for Costco, so I decided that a little pampering would be in order. I switched on some lights and took a long, hot bath, not thinking about anything. Then I got ready for my date. Yes, a real live date with a man I had met during my last freelance stint. In my post-Sam mode, I had decided that it was time for me to get out more and made a conscious effort to be personable to any semiattractive or, better, available man. This guy was a labor lawyer, not bad looking, and reasonably intelligent. I wondered why I wasn't looking forward to it more.

15

I HAD A nice time on my date. He was a nice man who brought me nice flowers, then we went to a nice restaurant where the food was nice, and had nice conversation. By the time I got home I was numb from all the niceness. The thought of a weekend with Sam was seductive, and I nearly phoned him to arrange it. However, I didn't think he'd appreciate a call at one o'clock in the morning, which actually made it more tempting, but good reason made me postpone the possible pleasure until the morning when my normal equilibrium would be restored. I feared I might be too nice on the phone.

I was right. In the morning, it didn't seem such a good idea. I was slowly weaning myself from him and doing a good job of it. I lectured myself, stressing that it was a matter of exposure; if I went out with more nice men I might learn to like them. I wondered if Greg was nice.

The kitchen being clean, I tackled the bedroom. I had obviously known beforehand that I wouldn't be bringing my date home, since I hadn't bothered to tidy up for him. Now, in a misplaced fit of energy, I set about hanging up all the clothes strewn over the back of the chair and, yes, on the floor. Sexual energy totally wasted on the handling of color-coded plastic hangers. Mme Jacqueline might faint from the shock when she arrived tomorrow. Then I sorted through the closet and came up with a pile of clothes I'd never wear again and shoved them into a garbage bag to deliver to some charity. I felt very pious.

Finally, I took a shower, got dressed, and was at the kitchen table doing the *New York Times* Sunday crossword puzzle. In pen. I put it down and stared out the window for a while, checking for new spring floral arrivals. It was too high up to see if the lilies of the valley that grow like the weeds they are, were coming up beside the mansion next door. They're my official harbinger of the season, my signal that summer is on the way. I could see the St. Lawrence River sparkling in the distance, a wide band of bright blue in the sunlight. I have a spectacular view and would hate to relinquish it. I'd have to warn Joanne to curb her words in the hall; as if it would do any good. If she moved to Toronto the problem would be moot, but it wasn't a fair exchange. Golden opportunity or not, I didn't want her to go. I'd miss her too much. A lifetime of friendship made her closer than family.

Which reminded me I hadn't seen my parents all week. I called, and as expected my mother was on the other end. I don't think my father has ever answered a phone since they got married. Once, while he was on a short stay in the hospital for an appendectomy, I arrived to find him in a posh room of the Ross Pavilion of the Royal Victoria Hospital. This mausoleum-like building had originally been erected for the high muck-a-mucks of the city so they wouldn't have to mix with the rest of the patients, lest the sight of the misfortunate poor sick impede recovery, but now dedicated to anyone who has enough extra private insurance to pay for it. My mother was sitting in a comfy Naugahyde lounge chair across the spacious room, a good fifteen feet from the bed, both of them reading magazines, when the phone rang. My father, one foot away from the instrument, said, "Sally, would you get that." She got up, walked across the room, reaching for it on the third ring. She picked it up, said hello, and after listening for a second, handed him the receiver and said, "It's for you." I was astounded at the farcical scene, but both of them thought it quite normal. If I didn't call him at his office I'd never get to speak to him.

My mother, as always, was delighted to hear from me. I speak to her almost daily, yet she responds to my calls as an unexpected treat. It makes me feel good. We agreed that I should come for supper, a dubious prospect. My mother is one of the worst cooks on the face of the earth, her repertoire limited to overbroiled steak or, worse, overboiled chicken, served with a baked potato. A salad consists of a quarter slab of iceberg lettuce with a slice of tomato on the side and a bottle of Kraft Italian dressing. Both she and my father love this. In retaliation, my sister has become a gourmet cook, having done a stint at Cordon Bleu in Paris, and her husband, all 250 pounds of him, is corpulent proof of her excellence. My brother knows the phone number of every place in the city that delivers, by heart.

My offer of a treat at a good restaurant was declined. Sometimes it works. I hung up and returned my attention to the puzzle.

When the phone rang I was sure it was Joanne, calling with her decision. I was tempted to not answer, thus procrastinating unwanted results, but being me I couldn't let the machine answer.

It wasn't Joanne, it was a breathless Rick.

"They're absconding. On the move."

"What're you talking about? Where are you?"

"I'm on my car phone. Heading for the Decarie Expressway. I decided to do a little nosing around, so this morning, at seven o'clock, I parked in front of Cassie's to see what would happen. I wanted to see if the guy lived there."

"You parked your car, either the Lexus or the Range Rover, in that neighborhood and thought you'd be unobtrusive? Are you nuts?"

"I didn't think of that until I got here. I did get a lot of strange looks and people peering out of windows. On the other hand, I think I might have spooked them. Forced them to show their hand." He was breathless, talking in code, a product of too many television cop shows. I recognize the similarly afflicted.

"What happened?"

"They took off. Came flying out of the house into a taxi. Suitcases in hand. I think they're heading for the airport. I'm in close pursuit."

"Don't be too close. Keep your distance. They probably know you're there, and it could get hairy. Stay back and keep following. I'll see what I can do at this end. Which airport?"

"Dorval, I think."

"Give me your number. I'll call you back. I might be able to stall them."

"How?"

"Never mind how. We're in a hurry here. Hang up."

He did. Didn't even say good-bye, just followed orders. This relationship was going along great, if he weren't such an idiot. It was a stupid stunt. He'd obviously been caught up in the mystery and adventure of the thing and thought he'd behave like his favorite fictional detective. We'd have a long talk about responsible behavior when this was over wherein I would impress upon him the difference between reality and make-believe. The former sometimes being dangerous.

First thought was to call Pietr Korlinski, the security chief at PanCanada, but I remembered he'd said he'd be out of town, and if he was back I'd be in for a long lecture about my safety. Even though I was sitting in my own kitchen. No time for that now. I had a thought, and rushed to the den to pull out the file with all the names and phone numbers that my secretary used to dial for me. If this plan didn't work I could fall back on Pietr, phone him at home where call forwarding would find him wherever he was. Pietr does not like to be out of touch and could be a poster boy for the extensive services offered by the phone company.

It being Sunday morning, I didn't know if my quarry was working today. I hoped so. I was in luck; the phone was answered on half a ring. Over the background noise I heard, "Jeremiah Cormian. Speak."

As head of operations for the airport, Jeremiah Cormian was a man of few words and not much more patience. I'd known him for years and we'd always gotten on well. Now that I was no longer a professional acquaintance I wondered if he'd even remember me. I hoped so, since I needed his help. He's a formidable man, living and breathing airports, and can rattle off statistical information like a computer. When his wife left him last year he threw himself completely into his work, patrolling his domain seven days a week. Since it worked to my benefit, I was glad he was still exhibiting this unhealthy behavior.

"Jerry, it's Barbara Simons, from PanCanada?" It came out like a question. I'd have to be more authoritative if I wanted results.

"Formerly. What can I do for you?"

"I need your help. I have a possible situation on my hands. Two suspects might be trying to flee the country. Can you tell me if they're booked out and to where? One is called Ethel Burnsides, or she may be using her alias, Cassandre Cartier. The accompanying male's name is unknown. They're on their way to the airport now."

As previously mentioned, I'm a devout student of cop shows. I'd been firm, and my voice had stressed the urgency. As a private citizen there was no logical reason for me to demand or even get access to the requested information. If he thought about it, he'd start asking questions, and I had no time for that. My only hope was that he'd get caught up in the drama of the moment.

"Right-o. I'm heading back to the office now to access my computer. I'm almost there. Stay on the line."

That was an excellent idea, because if I hung up it would give him the chance to think about what he was doing. While not illegal, it wasn't quite right.

I waited silently while he walked. Then the background noise cut out and he returned to me.

"I'm here. Let me punch it in. What were those names again?"

I repeated them, asking him to try Burnsides first. If she was leaving the country she'd need a passport, and it would be in her rightful name. I surmised that the change had been too recent for a legal alteration. I was right.

"Got her. Can't tell about him, though. It's a list of names."

"Where's she going?"

"Booked on PanCanada 137 to Chicago. No ongoing connection, but from there you can get anywhere. Leaving at three-oh-five. It's early to be checking in. Plenty of time to catch a prior flight."

"Let's hope she's too stupid to think of it."

"Business class, I see. Tell you what, when she checks in we'll escort her to the lounge. That should keep her from changing her reservation. Folks like that."

Cassandre would love it. Make her feel important and like a big star. Also, she'd figure Rick wouldn't find her there. After all, if he was following her he'd have to park his car. They were in a taxi and could off-load at the door, while Rick couldn't abandon his vehicle on the ramp for more than three minutes without it being towed. And somehow, I thought Rick was very attached to his machinery. I was trying my best to think like everyone involved, guess at their next moves. I prayed I was right.

"Thanks, Jerry. I owe you big."

"Which you'll never be able to repay, since you're no longer at PanCanada and have very little to trade." Oh, he'd caught that. "You're an okay person, always been fair and respectful to those around, so I'm happy to help this time. Can I expect the police? Shall I alert security?"

"Just keep an eye on her. If she doesn't fall for the lounge ploy and changes to an earlier flight, see if you can have immigration stall her to give us more time. And yes, I think the police will come, but I'm not sure. Let her go if they don't show up. Then I'll apologize to you."

"None needed. How about you and me having a drink sometime, exchange war stories?"

"Sounds good to me. I have to call the police now. I'll speak to you later. Thanks a lot."

"You're welcome. But not anytime."

Another date. War stories, my foot. Did trading my personal company for services render me a fallen woman? Didn't think so. And maybe it would be fun. At least Jerry wasn't "nice." Nor was I vain enough to consider a drink with me adequate payment for the favor rendered. Stopping someone at immigration takes a lot of clout and is a mean thing to do. People get terrified. When Sam had planned to come to Montreal and invade my space to break up with me—at least that's what I thought his intentions were—I'd nearly used my connections to get him stopped at the border and sent back. I'd gone so far as to check who was on duty that day to see if there was someone sympathetic, and was on the verge of activating my nefarious plan when Sam called and canceled. I was mad enough at the letdown to consider an anonymous phone call to the DEA to have his house searched just to shake him up, but wisely thought better of it. It's true that power corrupts; just knowing I could do it was almost satisfying. Even three months later, the incident still made me angry and strengthened my resolve to sever ties.

I called Greg at home first, in hopes of avoiding police station phone-relay systems, and I got him, much to my surprise. I told him about Cassandre's planned trip and what I had arranged. He started to warn me again, then gave it up when he realized I wouldn't listen. He thanked me and rang off, not saying he'd call back later to tell me what happened. He wasn't "nice" either.

I reached Rick in his car. He was disconsolate. "I lost them. They got out in front of the PanCanada door, and I was about to follow them inside when a security officer made me move along. They don't let you park there. Now I'm in the lot, about to pull into a space, and then I'll go search for them."

I told him what I'd accomplished and then asked him to hang around and watch the festivities. The good news was that he had a pass to the lounge. Those things cost a lot of money; Rick was good to himself. I warned him not to go in until the police arrived, as Cassandre and company might recognize him and take off. He promised to obey. If Greg wouldn't tell me what was going on I wanted someone there to report every last detail; there wasn't enough time for me to get there and see for myself. Anyway, Rick had started this, so he was the one who'd have to skulk around the busy airport for a while.

"Barbara, this is the most fun I've had in a long time. Speak to you later."

If I'd felt a little guilty about appointing him sentry, I didn't anymore. The man was having a wonderful time.

"Call me as soon as they leave, alone or with the cops. And I repeat, be careful."

I sounded like Pietr.

There was another good deed I could perform. I called Joanne. She was obviously in the middle of a discussion with Jacques, her tone distant. No, she had nothing to report as yet and would get back to me later. I would have to learn patience. Not rising to the criticism, I stressed that I had not called to pry, I had a possible breaking story. That shut her up, and she started peppering me with questions. I told her my version of the story, that I had found out Cassandre and her mystery man were leaving, had set up immigration as a safety net, and had alerted the police.

"I don't have time to get a crew," she wailed.

"Call and arrange for it and get your ass out there as fast as possible. You live closer than I do. You can make it, and if they don't arrive for the big confrontation your crew should still be there in time to watch Cassandre get hauled away."

"You're right. Thanks a million. Gotta go. Bye."

I had visions of Joanne making a mad dash for the airport, stopping only at her pantry to load her purse with bribing food. Hungry airport personnel would be easy prey. I'd done good deeds on all kinds of fronts, and the day was only half gone.

I spent the next hour pacing. The kitchen was clean, my bedroom neat and tidy, so there was no housework to immerse myself in. I will not stoop to washing floors and cleaning toilets, so I paced, feeling a passing kinship for expectant fathers. The whole thing felt out of kilter. I had set into motion a chain of events, and here I was, safely at home, not able to witness the scene that I had created. It wasn't fair. I was reduced to whining when finally the phone rang.

"You really missed something." Yeah, tell me about it.

"What happened, Rick? Where are you now?"

"I just drove out of the parking lot. I'm on my way over with all the details. Should be there in about fifteen minutes. Put the coffee on."

Although he was denying me the instant gratification that I so crave, he would be here in person, so I could ask the million questions that were already forming in my mind. Not a bad resolution. But there was that problem of coffee. I hate it, hate anything remotely coffee flavored, and pay no attention to all its currently popular variations and intricacies. Mme Jacqueline drinks potfuls along with the Windex I suspect she secretly imbibes as a chaser, so I do stock it and there should be some in the freezer. I found it, and even discovered where she keeps the filters, then set about boiling water. I wanted to have the coffee ready and waiting for him when he arrived, not willing to exhibit my clumsiness with the simple project. I settled on form over content and took out the china coffeepot, with matching sugar bowl, creamer, and cup. Even added a linen luncheon-sized napkin. In front of my seat I placed the obligatory Diet Coke, albeit in a crystal goblet. In an effort not to go overboard, I eschewed the linen tablecloth but did add the silver flatware. If it tasted awful, it sure did look good.

All of this activity took about three and a half minutes, and I had resumed my pacing when the phone rang again. Joanne.

"Can't talk. Just wanted to thank you. Where'd you find that cute guy? I'll call you later."

So Joanne and Rick had finally crossed paths. It was inevitable.

And then the phone rang again. I sure was popular. I wondered if so many people generally called while I was out and didn't leave messages.

"I've got a great one for you." It was obviously Susan.

"What?" I asked, not paying much attention, as I was raptly measuring tablespoons of coffee into the filter now that the water had boiled.

"Dear sweet Beth, the bereaved herself, the paragon of all that is proper, is having an affair."

"What!" I turned my full attention to the phone, but being as dexterous as I am, was able to pour boiling water through the filter at the same time.

"Yessiree, she is."

"How do you know? Who told you?"

"Who else? Heather Barkley."

"How does she know?"

"She says she has it on very good authority, which means she wouldn't tell me or heard it third- or fourth-hand and doesn't know the source. Doesn't matter."

"Why did she?"

"What?"

"Why did she tell you? And what were you doing with her? You're not friends."

"Oh yes we are. We're coconspirators. Seems she wants her husband to sell me the Matisse and he wants to hang on to it. We had a little ladies' lunch, just the two of us, to try to figure out how to convince him to sell it. She wants to buy a condo in Palm Beach. I came up with a great plan and think I might succeed. Nice commission in the offing."

"I don't have time to ask you about that now, although I want to hear all about it. Get back to Beth."

"While Heather and I were being palsy-walsy, the conversation drifted to the Whitestones and your Harry-Harry incident. Then, with a little prompting, we slid into family gossip. I don't think these people do much of that, and it was like unleashing the floodgates. She'd had this secret inside of her and couldn't wait to blurt it out. Besides, I am no longer considered to be of the serving class, having graduated to lunch with the mistress of the house, and we don't move in the same circles, so she figured I'd be the perfect target. I sat through the rest of the meal dumbfounded, trying to keep up my end of the conversation. Couldn't get out of there fast enough to call you."

"Tell me about it."

"It's better than you think. Beth has been keeping secret company with a gentleman from Jamaica."

"A black guy?" I interrupted, thinking suspiciously of Cassandre's boyfriend and the symmetry of the thing.

"No, white. He supposedly owns a large chunk of the island. He's originally Canadian, but spends most of his time down there. This has been going on for a couple of years, yet the clincher came only last week."

She stopped speaking. This was going to be good, and it was my duty to uphold my end with the right prompts. I set the coffeepot on the stove to keep warm and prayed the doorbell wouldn't ring, that Rick had obeyed the posted speed limits or had been nailed for a ticket if he hadn't. I needed the time.

"And the clincher was . . . ?"

"Supposedly—remember this is all hearsay—last Friday, a few nights before his murder, Beth asked Walter for a divorce. She said she'd had enough of his philandering and wanted him out of her life. Now that the kids were grown up it was *her* time. Liberation at last. They were supposed to see a lawyer to discuss the settlement this week."

"There would have been no settlement. There was no money. Which would have pissed dear, sweet Beth off no end. Very interesting."

At that moment the doorbell rang. I switched over and buzzed what I assumed to be Rick in, and went back to Susan. "Sorry I can't stay on. Someone's at the door. Thanks a million for the information. The circle of suspects' motives widens daily. I'll call you later. Big kisses to Robert."

I went to the door pondering the information but didn't have time to give it much analysis, as Rick was already there. I looked behind him, and sure enough Mrs. Brooks's peephole was dark.

"Get in here," I said, snatching him inside. No patience for her now.

"Nice welcome," he said, closing the door behind him.

"It's too complicated to get into. What happened?"

"I think I ordered coffee?"

Why is it that all my friends have the same traits, the main one being to thwart me? Osmosis? After all, he'd come into contact with Joanne, so some of her genes could have leaked onto him.

"Come into the kitchen. It's on the table."

"With the good china, I see. I must be important."

Caught. "No, you're not, your information is."

Rick sat comfortably at the table and began preparing the coffee to his liking. I hoped I wouldn't get reprimanded for having half-and-half in the creamer, but it's what Mme Jacqueline favors, and *she's* important.

"No cookies?" I scanned my kitchen in panic. There were never any cookies in here. I didn't know what to do. I had the notion that if I didn't come up with the required cookies he'd take his information elsewhere. Then I regained some control over myself.

"No cookies. They're fattening, and I wasn't expecting guests. You'll have to make do. Now, please, tell me what happened."

"It started simply and quietly. I found them in the lounge where you said they'd be. They were in the large nonsmoking room, so I felt safe to sit in the smoking section. I was out of their sight, and it was more comfortable than loitering suspiciously around outside. They each had a glass of cognac in front of them, his loaded with ice. My seat offered a good view of the front door, so I could keep watch while I had a cup of coffee. They serve cookies."

I said nothing.

"Not too long later, enough for them each to get a refill,

two plainclothes detectives, accompanied by two uniformed cops and two airport security people and a man who seemed to be in charge of the place, came in. The detectives went inside while the rest waited by the front desk, the guy in charge trying to calm the apoplectic receptionist down. Then I moved to get a better view, not really caring if they saw me anymore. They couldn't run.

"The detectives approached them, and Cassandre looked furious; her boyfriend, on the other hand, looked scared. The detectives asked him who he was, but I couldn't hear the answer. I didn't want to get close enough to distract the proceedings if they recognized me. A detective took out a cell phone and called the information in to somewhere, and they sat down together to have a leisurely drink. It was all so civilized. I noticed the cops ordered coffee.

"Then came the sound of a scuffle near the entrance, but I couldn't see what was going on from my new vantage point. The boyfriend perked up, looked toward the door, and spotted me. He nudged Cassie, and she turned to stare. With an accusatory finger she pointed me out to the police. A short talk into a walkie-talkie netted me a uniformed constable as companion and a lot of stares from the rest of the innocent passengers. He must have been told only to watch me, since he didn't ask anything, just sat with me, all our eyes focused on the foursome three tables away who were chatting away like long-lost friends. At least Cassie was chatting animatedly, her braids flying around; the boyfriend, reverting to sullen, still looked scared to me and kept eyeing the room as if in search of another exit.

"The noise from the lobby suddenly got louder, a strident female voice rising above the rest. Then a woman strode in and walked to the table, addressing the more presentable of the two detectives. He said something to her and she turned around and walked back out, no longer as purposeful. On the way, she caught sight of me and my cop and detoured toward us. Then I recognized her. Joanne Cowan from the news. Isn't she your friend? My cop told her that I had nothing to say, for which I was thankful since I didn't know how much to tell her and didn't want to get distracted. Although Cassie was animated she was talking softly, and both my escort and I were straining vainly to hear. Joanne Cowan nodded, flashed a wicked smile, and went back to her post by the door. I figured she'd be back.

"We all regain our positions. So far so good. Not much is happening, but it's quite entertaining."

Rick stopped the monologue to take a sip of coffee. I felt he deserved a reward, so I went to the freezer and took out a Sara Lee banana cake that I keep in a brown paper bag so that Mme Jacqueline will not devour it. I sliced some pieces, put them on a plate with a doily, and set it in front of Rick. I knew from experience that it would thaw within five minutes.

"I knew you had to be holding back. The use of the good china indicates a woman prepared for all exigencies."

I blushed and again said nothing. Too many thoughts were whirling around in my head, and I felt if I asked questions it would distract from the narrative and he might omit something. I'd ask when he was finished.

"The cell phone rang and the rumpled detective answered. Then he stood up, and in a loud voice formally placed the boyfriend under arrest. One constable—not mine—and an airport security guard led him away. In handcuffs. Everyone in the place was excited, although no one made a sound. Too scared of being ejected and missing the show, I guess. They certainly got their money's worth for their first-class fare today."

"What about Cassandre?" I asked. I'd been silent for a very long time, and Rick had been eyeing the cake longingly. I remembered he'd said he'd taken up his original post at seven o'clock and, being a novice, surely hadn't thought to pack a lunch. All he'd probably had all day were PanCanada cookies, and I know from experience they're not great. "Take your time. Have some cake; you earned it."

He beamed, looking thirteen years old this time. One day I'd have to check his passport to see if he really was thirty-six. It didn't seem possible.

After devouring two pieces, he daintily dabbed his mouth with the napkin and proceeded.

"That was surprising. They carted the boyfriend off, but not Cassie. I guess she decided to abort her voyage, since she stood up and in a loud voice announced if they needed her further they would find her at home. And that her name was Cassandre, not Ethel, and she expected to be addressed as such. With braids flouncing, she made a dramatic, solo exit. I'm sure she never gave second thought to her luggage, which is probably on its way to Chicago as we speak."

Rick reached for another piece of cake, very pleased with himself.

"That's all?"

"No, that is not all. I need more sustenance before I continue, because you figure in the next part and you might take the food back after you hear me out."

He ate the final two slices of cake while I sat trying to divine how I'd gotten implicated. The fact that the whole encounter occurred because of my meddling hardly crossed my mind.

"After the departure of the two suspects there was only one suspicious person left. Me. All eyes were on me as the better-dressed detective came to join our table. The other one had left, presumably to get the suspect's baggage. At least that's where he said he was going. Detective-Sergeant Allard introduced himself and we had a little chat. Your name came up. By the way, I think he likes you."

I wasn't falling for that one. Anyway, I wanted to know what they had discussed and not segue into a discussion of crushes with a teenaged-looking boy.

"After checking out who I was, carefully verifying my driver's license, he of course asked me what I was doing there. Seeing no reason to lie, I told most of the truth. He was surprised to find out that I had accompanied you to the club where we first met Cassie. He said you never mentioned me in your description of the occasion. He also didn't believe that I had decided to take up surveillance on my own and not on your prompting. I should be insulted that he doesn't think me capable of independent thought. He said to thank you for your assistance and to tell you that all was under control and your assistance no longer needed. He was very formal."

Then Rick abruptly changed track and asked, "Do you think the boyfriend really did it?"

Time for me to talk. "No, I don't think so. If he had, they would have hauled Cassie away too, as an accessory. Something else was going on there. Cassie's dramatic departure doesn't sound like the act of a guilty woman who has just been confronted by the police. Lots of police, from the sound of it. She would be more unnerved. It would be a good way to go, but I don't think she has it in her. As to Detective-Sergeant Allard, he owes me for this one, whatever it is, and has no business issuing orders through you."

"I think you like him, too."

"Stop saying that idiotic thing. It's a professional relationship."

"And your profession is . . . ?"

I burst out laughing. "Let's just say our paths have crossed before. You did a good job, Rick. You shouldn't have started it in the first place, but it was great. Thanks."

I don't know why I was thanking him. He hadn't done anything for me, just gone out to satisfy his own curiosity. But he looked so sweet and happy with himself, I wanted to encourage him.

"I'm not finished."

"There's more?"

"Oh, yes indeed there is. When all the cops had left, I finished my coffee in peace, waiting for them all to get out of the airport. I didn't want to see the boyfriend being transported. The idea of jail disturbs me, and I didn't want to face the responsibility of having sent a man there."

Sensitivity or experience? There were depths yet to plumb in this friendship.

"When I thought enough time had elapsed, I left. No sooner had I walked out of the door than I was attacked."

"Joanne?"

"Yes, waiting for me politely, allowing me to finish my refreshments before being set upon. That woman can ask more questions in three seconds than I thought possible. And it wasn't about the stage show that I had just witnessed. There was nothing that I could add that she already didn't know. She was alone, the crew having probably followed the suspect to the awaiting car and then rushed off to have their film developed. She wanted to know all about us. What our relationship is, how long it's been going on, et cetera. I told her to ask you. I don't think she liked that, since she warned me, and I quote, 'Don't mess with her or I'll come after you.' Are you that fragile?"

I laughed again. Rick loved telling me this, and he smiled along. "Joanne and I are protective of each other. I think she was angry that I'd been holding back, and since I'd given her this tip she didn't feel she could yell at me for the oversight. However, she'll bide her time and then the reprimand will come. I don't mind." I chuckled some more at the notion of a thwarted Joanne.

"I have too much energy pent up," I said, suddenly standing up. "I need to get rid of it. I'm going to the gym to take it out on the machines. Coming?"

"No, thanks. I think I'll go home and take a nap. I'm exhausted."

"All that adrenaline you used up."

"Probably. Anyway, thanks for a terrific adventure and let me know if I can do anything else. I think I like this job."

"It isn't a job, it's meddling." It's amazing how I can take the other side when someone sounds like me.

"Yes, ma'am."

I saw Rick out and went to change. I brought along casual clothes since I was going to my parents' afterward, and headed for the garage. As I left I heard the snick of Mrs. Brooks's lock, but I was wearing my sneakers, so I tore down the hall and rounded the corner before she could get to me. In the distance, I heard "Barbara? I'd like to speak with you." Fat chance and never again if I can possibly help it, I thought, as the elevator door closed behind me.

The gym was uneventful, full of people I don't regularly see, most of them in their twenties, it being a Sunday afternoon and a very social time. A few others looked like they were taking it as seriously as I, but most seemed to be hanging around eyeing each other. I blocked out my surroundings, tackled the torture, and completed my routine with satisfaction.

I arrived at my parents', all showered and freshly coiffed, promptly at five-thirty. Dinner was served daily at six, never a variation. For a half hour I sat in the den with my father, discussing the vagaries of the business world. My father is a women's sportswear manufacturer, and it's probably from him that I got my love of clothes and fashion. From the time I was a little girl, he would take me to fashion shows and carefully explain what was good and what was tacky. I loved all the fancy clothes and dramatic hair and makeup and learned to be selective about my attire at much too young an age.

He complained about the latest round of bankruptcies, bemoaning that if it weren't for his export business, he'd sink. It was a lot of whining about nothing, as I carefully read his financial statements every month and know the company is in no danger of collapse. In the meantime, my mother was in the kitchen, adulterating what should have been good food.

16

W E S A T D O W N to dinner promptly at six. Tonight was an unexpected variation on a theme, overbroiled lamb chops with the regular side dishes. Canned cling peaches for dessert. My father maintains that he enjoys my mother's food and I can't figure out if he's just being polite. After all, he travels extensively, taking in the Paris collections and the Milan shows twice yearly, in search of new and wonderful designs that he can alter to suit North American tastes and sizes and then export to the United States. Thus he's had exposure to excellent cuisine, and I don't understand it. On the other hand, my parents have always stressed good manners, so that could be it. I learned long ago not to complain about the repertoire or even suggest an easy recipe. It only gets me a "Barbara, don't tell your mother what to do" or "Don't talk to your mother like that." He's fiercely protective of her, and I think they're still in love. Wonderful role models. Why I never followed their example and got married is a mystery to me. I'd spent years trying to prove I don't know what, and all it had gotten me was fired.

Conversation ceased as we tuned in to the television news, on the lookout for Joanne. My mother feels very close to her and wouldn't miss a broadcast. She's inordinately proud of Joanne, boasting of her accomplishments to all her friends. Since Joanne's parents passed away some years ago, the feeling has intensified, sometimes to the point of making her own three children a little jealous. I know it annoys my sister, their biweekly phone calls consisting mostly of my mother crowing about Joanne's latest achievements. I was no longer doing anything to brag about and my brother worked in the family business, actually running the place, but to her mind occupying a sinecure, as no one would ever be able to replace my father. In her eyes, my father was a genius. Surprisingly, it doesn't bother my brother.

Barring cataclysmic natural disaster, Sunday is a slow news day. Not much happens in the world, with even non-Christian countries taking a break. And so Joanne's piece was the lead of the day. It opened with a stand-up of Joanne outside the airport. Behind her I could see the news van that had transported her crew. Nobody had told it to move along; it must be nice to exert that kind of power. On closer inspection, I could also see Joanne's unmarked car. Now, how had she managed that? Further confirmation that Joanne was born with the parking gods devoutly on her side, a convenient space always miraculously appearing wherever she was. Now, that made me jealous.

I was so involved with the car situation that I almost forgot to listen. I refocused my attention on her, as she told us that an arrest had been made at the airport today in response to an anonymous tip. I beamed; that was me. They had netted a big one, a man on the FBI's Ten Most Wanted list. One Faustus Jones was apprehended while trying to cross the border back into the United States whence he had escaped. He was wanted for armed bank robbery resulting in homicide in

Rhode Island and Massachusetts, which meant he had killed at least two people. He had been residing in Montreal for the past six months, making a living as an itinerant jazz musician.

The scene switched to a shot of him being led into a U.S. immigration car as Joanne continued with a voice-over. So the cops had passed this one on to the Americans, letting them get credit for the arrest. Most likely, it was done to avoid costly extradition procedures, and some avaricious lawyer out there should be very unhappy with this shortcut. There was no mention or view of either Allard or Boucherville. I wondered how they felt about handing over their man to the Americans. Would they get credit for it? In this society, credit is almost as good as money.

My mother reveled in Joanne's performance, saying what a clever girl she was to have been there. I said nothing, even though the cleverness was mine. It would only have sounded like sour grapes, and the less my mother knew about my clandestine adventures the less I would get lectured. This was the woman who chided me for not dressing warmly enough. What would she say if she knew of my present participation? When I didn't remark on the event, my father looked at me suspiciously.

The television was zapped off right after Joanne's report, the rest of the world events no longer of any interest. The nights she's not on they're forced to watch the whole broadcast in anticipation. My mother asks me if she's going to be appearing that day, but I always say I don't know, and as a result, they're pretty well informed about current affairs.

The conversation turned to the funeral, and I told them about all the bigwigs in attendance. They were suitably impressed by the prime minister's having gone back to Beth's. As I never mentioned it, I don't think they knew I'd been there. Likely they thought I'd heard about the gathering from Joanne, who hadn't, and fortunately no word was mentioned of Harry-Harry.

Dinner over, it was time for *60 Minutes*. Before I settled down in the den to watch with them, I called home to check my messages. I like spending time with my parents. Aside from the terrible meals, they're good company and there's a calm feeling of serenity that pervades their apartment. The frantic pace of the outside world intrudes only through the medium of television. I always leave relaxed and happy.

There was a message from Joanne saying she and Jacques would be going out for dinner, naming the restaurant and inviting me to join them. I didn't think so; didn't want to hear any bad news.

A message from Beverly Warfield asking me to have lunch. Why? What other dirty laundry could these people possibly have? The thought passed through my mind that this adventure was seriously cutting into my gym time, and if I continued meeting people for meals I'd weigh two hundred pounds before it was over. I decided I'd wait until morning to answer that one.

Rick called to reiterate what a great day he'd had.

My walking partner called with a weather forecast, insisting that tomorrow morning would be perfect for a stroll.

Two other friends called just to say hello.

I think I got more calls that Sunday than any other day in my life, barring the occasion of my television appearance.

And lastly, Gregory Allard called, saying he could be reached at home.

That one wasn't waiting until morning, and I went to get my purse to find the card he had left me. As I dialed, I told myself I was an idiot; he simply phoned to tell me what had transpired, not to ask me out.

Sometimes miracle do happen. He answered on the first ring and sounded pleased to hear from me.

"Did you see your friend Joanne Cowan on the news?"

"I did. But I didn't see you. What happened? How come you gave him to immigration? And he had a passport?"

Greg cut me off. He chuckled and said, "I knew you'd have a million questions. How about I come over and explain everything?"

Wow! "I'm not at home now, but I can meet you somewhere for coffee."

He named a place I knew and I said I'd be there in half an hour. It would only take fifteen minutes to get there, but repairs were in order. Since I had only been coming to my parents' and they know what I look like, I hadn't put on any makeup. I rushed to the bathroom with my handbag and came out looking much better. Even an hour and twenty minutes at the gym can't give you the healthy, alert glow of artfully applied makeup. The trick is to look like you aren't wearing any, something that's hard to pull off in my mother's bathroom because of the atrocious fluorescent lighting, so I hoped I'd done it right and didn't resemble a clown. I don't know how they live with it; it casts a green tinge over everything.

I went to say good-bye to them and told them I was going home. I learned long ago never to discuss my personal life and dating habits with either of them. It saves tedious hours of discussion and advice about people who eventually disappear. I believe one's personal life should remain personal. Except Joanne's, of course, and I never told them about that. My mother would be horrified.

In the car, I fretted about the forthcoming encounter. Was this a date? I figured I'd treat it as a meeting, along the lines of the one I had with Luce Richer. I hoped I wouldn't have to face a wall. The television report was perplexing, and I had lots of questions.

Second Cup on Greene Avenue, back in familiar West-mount, has a wood fire burning all through winter. It adds atmosphere to the comfortable café and helps mask the smell of coffee. As soon as I came in the door I realized this may have been a mistake. I nearly gagged. I looked around and found Greg already seated in an easy chair at the back, in front of the spotless fireplace. No woodsy aroma tonight.

Ever the gentleman, he stood politely on my arrival and asked me what kind of coffee I would like. It's a good thing I don't drink the stuff, as there are too many choices with weird names. It's a new game of one-upmanship in the palate that has been running rampant these days and one of the few in which I don't participate. I asked for plain old boring tea, no tisanes, no infusions, no tea equivalent to the coffee madness. He looked surprised, and I realized that this reverse snobbery might put me one up after all.

As he went to the counter to get it, I checked him out. For once the ever-present Reeboks matched the rest of him. He looked positively gorgeous, dressed in faded jeans, a black turtleneck, and a black jacket that looked suspiciously like cashmere. The eyes were tricky, today they matched the faded denim perfectly, but I could have sworn they were darker last encounter. I suspected tinted contact lenses and was cheered. He might possibly be vainer than I. His expensive haberdashery relieved any qualms I had about letting him pay for me; if he could afford those clothes he could certainly spring for an extra dollar twenty-five.

Back with my tea, he regained his chair while I sat on the couch to his right. He swept the French newspaper that he had been reading off the low table in front of us, setting out the teacup, teapot, sugar bowl, and milk container with the precision of a waiter hoping for a large tip. I had neglected to tell him that I like my tea plain and didn't need all the extra stuff, so he'd brought it all. He even unfolded a paper napkin and handed it to me. Best of all, he'd brought a plate of shortbread cookies. Dinner at my parents' hadn't been all that satisfying, and the sweets looked delicious. There were six of them, and I was disappointed when I realized I was expected to share. It was fun to watch him fuss, and for some perverse reason I sent him back for an extra pot of hot water, as I like my tea weak. He went meekly, chagrined at not having thought of it. Maybe he *was* nice, which would be a shame.

Finally, we were ready to sip and chat. We started with small talk, speaking stiffly about the weather and other ridiculous topics over which we had no control. When I couldn't stand all this niceness anymore I abruptly changed the subject.

"What happened at the airport today?"

"First I want to thank you for the tip. The Americans were surprised to find him here. The last unconfirmed sighting they had was in Florida."

"It wasn't my intention, but you're welcome."

"I know. You thought you'd solved the murder, and the lovely Cassandre was skipping town to avoid arrest."

"She is lovely," I said.

"That she is. Though we let her go, I probably could have arrested her for possession of a deadly weapon, still can if you want me to. I think those nails would qualify."

I laughed. Now that we were back speaking about something real, he resumed the cute status that had been waning throughout our nice opening conversation.

"Okay, start from the beginning. What was he doing here? A passport? You gave him to immigration? How did Boucherville take that? Does he like me any better?"

"Whoa, drink your tea, eat a biscuit, and I'll tell you a story."

Sounded like a good idea to me. I relaxed and sat back in the comfortable couch, the teacup perched daintily in my hands, which left none for cookie ingestion, but a story was worth the delaying of culinary pleasure.

"I'll start with the artiste, Miss Ethel Burnsides, who gets very annoyed if you call her that. Is she a good singer?"

"Dreadful, but a magician on the fiddle."

"Even with those nails?"

"Yep. I never considered that before, but I guess she's even more talented than I first thought. It must be hard. Go on."

"Cassandre had nothing to do with the death of Whitestone. Unless she contracted it out, and I doubt if she has the money and it doesn't figure to be a professional job. She was having her hair braided, 'gettin' stentions' as she said, which I later understood to mean extensions. That southern belle accent slips in and out. There were four witnesses to this event, and in the end we had to rule her out."

"So why did you respond to my warning?" I interrupted, putting my cup down and reaching for a cookie. Cling peaches don't cut it, and I was hungry.

"For him, not her. After your first mention, we checked up on him and could find nothing on a David Green, the name he assumed here; no social insurance number, no driver's license, nothing. No records are kept at the border, so if he entered with David Green papers there would be no reason to be suspicious, nor would we have any record of it. When Boucherville and I went to interview Cassandre for a second time—we watched the house and waited until he was there— he seemed a truculent character, suspicious and argumentative, as though he'd had experience with the police. Boucherville got his prints on a glass—Cassandre is going to be angry when she finds it missing—and we ran them. When you called we hadn't heard back yet, the results were due any minute, and since you had graciously arranged to stall them, we raced out there, in case. We still had no answer when we arrived, so we joined them for drinks and chat. Ethel talked a blue streak about nothing while he glowered at us, sweating. At last we got the phone call, which identified him as Faustus Jones, and wanted."

"How could his parents do that to him? The name, I mean. He was doomed from birth. I feel sorry for him."

"Don't. He's a stone killer." Greg's voice hardened at that comment and his blue eyes flashed, showing some passion for the first time. I liked it.

"He was in possession of a fake passport under his alias, to answer your question. The plan was to fly to Chicago then catch an onward flight to Barbados. He had convinced Ethel that she would be arrested for the murder of Walter Whitestone because she was a torch singer, scum in the eyes of the rich people involved. She'd take the fall for some Westmount biggie. I presume he harped on the fact that because she was black, the police would be convinced she'd done it. She didn't say anything to that effect, I don't think it's an issue with her, but he called me 'whitey' often enough to show where his antipathies lay. Anyway, she panicked and went along with him; after all, she could become a big star in Barbados, there are so many tourists to entertain and the weather is better. Basically, I think she was scared of him and did pretty much whatever he wanted, since she no longer had Mr. Whitestone as a protector. Right now, she's plenty mad at the interruption of her big career move. She called the station and insisted that I get her luggage back; it was my fault she'd forgotten to retrieve it. I'd already made the arrangements and her suitcase should be delivered to her door in the morning. In a way, I feel bad for her. She claims, and both Boucherville and I believe her, that she had no idea that her Davy was really Faustus."

"Don't feel too sorry for her. Seems to me she's a girl who always lands on her feet." That came out sounding a little more vindictive than I had planned. "She's very beautiful and she'll find someone else soon." That sounded worse. These idiocies that I was uttering were entirely Greg's fault, his lanky body and riveting eyes putting me off-kilter. I needed to regroup, ask an intelligent question.

"How come you handed him over to immigration? To save extradition proceedings?"

"Smart lady," he said, making me inordinately happy. "Once we'd apprehended him, we consulted with Ottawa and the U.S. State Department. The FBI interceded, wanted to come up and get him, he was theirs, but even on a Sunday, or maybe because it *was* Sunday and the top brass wasn't there, so the decision making was in the hands of the second tier, who didn't have as many political points to make. It was agreed by all parties, except the FBI, who was overruled, that this would be the most efficient way of handling things. He was taken to another building for some preliminary paperwork and by now should be safely back in Boston, with immigration as the heroes."

"Do you get any credit? After all, you caught him."

"No, *you* inadvertently caught him. We won't receive any public recognition, but our personal files will note it. It'll reflect well in the upcoming performance review."

"Well, that should change Boucherville's mind about me."

Greg sat back and smiled, flashing his orthodontically perfect white teeth. They might even have been bleached. Why was I doing this? Looking for faults, belittling him in my mind, dismissing his good features. I think I was mightily attracted and trying to talk myself out of it. A cop and an amateur sleuth, which was how I'd taken to thinking about myself. How clichéd. All the books I read had them, but it was a stupid notion here in real life. But he was really attractive and real amateur sleuths didn't exist, so maybe . . .

The smile turned into a wide grin, and he said, "Nope. Now he wants to know how you got onto Faustus Jones. He's sure you know all about him, possibly may even have harbored him for a while."

"He's insane. I didn't," I sputtered. This was worse than

ever. I'd done a very good deed and could now look forward to Boucherville breathing down my neck some more. "What's he going to do about it?"

"Investigate you thoroughly. Speak to your neighbors, antagonize everyone you know." Greg was enjoying this.

Oh, no. I could just imagine the interchange with him and Mrs. Brooks. It would last hours. In my head, I again started to list the buildings I might move to.

"Don't worry. I may have exaggerated a little, but you aren't very high on his hit parade. He's sure you're holding back information. Are you?"

"No, I am not." I was indignant even if it was true.

At this moment, a server appeared and asked us if we wanted anything else. Now, Second Cup is a self-service restaurant, and we'd obviously been sitting there involved in conversation with no intention of moving toward the counter for more. If they wanted extra business they'd have to hustle for it, and Joe College had promoted himself to the position of waiter. Management should have been proud of this star employee who, if he continued his career path with such entrepreneurial enthusiasm, would soon have a franchise of his own. Greg ordered up refills and another plate of cookies since I had managed to devour five of them, leaving him the last one, which he snatched up before I could get to it. The nonwaiter reappeared almost instantly with our order—it was a slow night, with only one other couple on the premises. They were engrossed in each other, all lovey-dovey, ignoring the huge vats of café au something that sat cooling before them. This brought me back to the conjecture of the possibility of Greg and me ever becoming a couple.

I was about to be fair and offer to pay for this second round, when Greg beat me to it and pulled out his wallet. Crocodile. And brand new. I wondered who had bought it for him; it looked like something a woman would give a man for a special occasion. I'd never dared ask him if he had a girl-friend, although I'd previously ascertained that he wasn't presently married. When the coffee had been brought, the tea had been poured, and some cookies had been munched, the conversation resumed.

Greg opened with, "How did Joanne come to be conveniently there?" He knew the answer but wanted to hear me admit it.

"Come on," I chided. "You know Joanne. Do you think I could get away with not telling her? My best friend? Sorry, pal, I value my life too much."

Greg laughed again. I liked the sound and was delighted to be entertaining him. I was becoming a very good sycophant, trying a little too hard to please. "I guess you're right," he said. "She's difficult to say no to. The look on Boucherville's face when he saw her was worth the interference."

"Joanne doesn't interfere," I said defensively. "She tries to stay out of the way and do her job. She's very professional."

"Relax. It was a bad choice of words, not a reflection on her character."

"Okay." I was somewhat mollified.

I'm allowed to say anything I want to about Joanne because she's my friend, but no one else is permitted to say anything derogatory. That's a fixed rule. I decided it was time to change the subject and lighten the mood, which had suddenly become tension filled.

"Where do you live?" I asked, it being one of my favorite questions of late. Last night's date lived in a nice middle-class suburb in a nice split-level bungalow that he had retained after his not so nice divorce.

"Downtown. On de Maisonneuve. Near Atwater."

That wasn't much help, and from the lazy smile on his face he knew it. We had resumed friendly jousting. There were all sorts of buildings on that street, from modern high-rises to quaint old well-maintained buildings to some almost outright slums. I wasn't going to give him the satisfaction of asking him for more details, so I decided to go for the jugular.

"Why didn't you ever call me?"

Perfect reaction. He was so stunned that he spewed a mouthful of coffee through his nose. Just like a high school kid who drinks too much cola too fast. He grabbed a napkin, wiped his face and fortunately black sweater, not bothering to apologize for the social gaffe, faced me, and tried to look innocent as he said, "What do you mean?"

Really feeble answer.

"I mean that I haven't heard from you in three months. Except for your ordering me down to the police station that night."

"I did not order you."

I decided to lighten up and let him save some face.

"You're right, you didn't, you asked politely. Everyone involved in this thing is so polite it's driving me crazy. But back to the question. Look, I understand that you may have had some difficulty with our relationship. You put yourself out for me, straddled if not put yourself over the line to help me. I appreciate that and would have liked to have the opportunity to thank you. But in deference to the delicate nature of the situation, I waited for you to call me. You never did."

"I guess it's a fair question, one that deserves a thoughtful explanation. The truth is, I was afraid. Not afraid of you, but afraid of the fact that it had been so easy to do that for you. And while probably not legally indictable, it was wrong. Calling you would make me have to face up to it, and I wanted to put it as far behind me as fast as possible."

"I'm sorry."

"No, I'm sorry. It was childish, and I've since rethought the whole situation and come to the conclusion that I don't feel any guilt over it. But by then too much time had passed and I felt awkward about phoning. I was actually glad to see you at that grisly murder scene."

"Me, too. Even before you arrived, I hoped they'd send you."

Timing means a lot in life, and it seemed to me this was the perfect juncture from which to signal my departure. We'd both admitted enough for one night. I said it was getting late and he agreed with alacrity. I didn't offer him a lift and didn't even walk out to my car with him, deciding to make my escape after we'd said our good-byes and he headed off to the bathroom. I could have waited for him but thought it better to leave. He did say he'd call me soon. I didn't know whether I believed him.

To further confuse matters, there was a message from Sam awaiting me when I got home. He missed me, wanted to see me soon, and how did I feel about New York next week?

The big question was how *did* I feel about it?

17

ANOTHER NICE DAY; it was almost too much to ask for and very suspicious. We were going to pay for all this early good weather.

I literally tripped out of bed, falling over the shoes I had left too close to the edge. After a series of maneuvers that comprised my bouncing off the dresser and into the wall I remained upright, with another bruise to add to my collection. I am often a very colorful person as a result of my slothful habits, which I choose to interpret as congenital clumsiness.

Instead of taking a shower I donned walking clothes and called my partner, ready to submit myself to the climb and its attendant pain. It always surprises me that I continue to abuse my body in this fashion, being by nature lazy and sedentary. And I hate pain, rushing for the extra-strength Tylenol at the first sign of a headache. One of the advantages to living in Canada is that Tylenol #1 (that's the good stuff with codeine added) is sold over the counter, no prescription needed.

I got canceled. She said she didn't feel well and wouldn't be joining me today. I didn't believe that "not feeling well" part for a second. I suspected an overnight visit from her ex-husband, the man she publicly detests and runs down. The same man that we all know she clandestinely sleeps with on a regular basis. I let it pass; we're all entitled to our secrets, and this one hurt no one except possibly herself. We'd delve further into the subject on future walks, as summer and the walks warmed our seasonal friendship.

It was the perfect excuse not to go, but I was already dressed and it was beautiful, so I got out of the house before I could change my mind.

On the way up I concentrated on walking, but on the way down I thought about the events of the previous week, realizing that it had been a week ago today I had come upon the hapless Walter. The memory of the sight still made me shudder. I tried to organize all the unrelated bits of information I had gathered from diverse sources. Now that my favorite suspect Cassandre had been eliminated, and I couldn't convince myself that Harry-Harry had done it, it was time to take inventory. One by one I went through the characters involved, sorting out what I had learned from and about each, assigning motives, testing theories. It must have been the clean air and all the oxygen that filtered into my brain, because by the time I got back to the front door I thought I had figured out who the culprit was.

Now the trick was to prove my theory without getting myself killed in the process. I like my life, exercise and all, and had no desire to jeopardize it. There was no point in going to Greg with my suspicion, because it was just that. Unproven, and from his vantage point probably unprovable. He'd yell at me and tell me to butt out, which I should, but couldn't. I'd been dragged into this mess and I wanted to clean it up. And then Greg would really think I was wonderful.

The cleaning analogy should have alerted me to the fact that Mme Jacqueline would be lurking, but for some reason

I'd forgotten about her. She's such a regular part of my life that I never think about her comings and goings. Not at all interested in bikers or nuns or pyromaniacs at the moment, I headed straight for the shower, where I do my second-best thinking. By the time my hair was blown dry, my makeup applied, and I was attired in an embarrassing duster—I didn't know exactly where I was going yet—I had a semi-plan formulated. I was inordinately proud of myself as I went over all the details in my head, looking for possible slipups. I was the best detective on the planet.

As I went into the kitchen to get another Diet Coke to celebrate my intelligence, the phone rang. I was sure it was Joanne, and I was debating whether I should include her in my plot when a familiar voice said, "Good morning, Barbara. You neglected to call me back."

I hate people who open with accusations. "Who is this?" I demanded, though I was pretty sure who it was. I could match rudenesses.

"Beverly Warfield. I left a message last night."

"Oh, Beverly, hi. Yes, I got it. I came home too late to call you back. I was just about to."

"Well, can you make it?" A woman with a definite agenda. It made me curious, yet fitted perfectly with my plan.

"Sure. When and where?"

"I thought perhaps the Redpath Club. At noon. You have been there before, haven't you?"

A not so subtle put-down. It's an old established club, catering mostly to the city's upper crust. Of late it's become more open, whether out of a sense of democracy or a need for an infusion of capital I don't know, but it now boasts some ethnic names among its membership. Which is to say they finally let the Jews in, along with a smattering of French-Canadians. As sophisticated as I think I am, it intimidates me, always making me feel like an interloper. I wondered if

Bev suspected that, and had selected it for precisely that reason. It would certainly give her the upper hand, but it was her lunch invitation, so I went along. Also, I knew I wouldn't have to pay since everything was signed for by the member, and planned to order something expensive in retaliation.

"Yes, I've been there. Twelve o'clock, then. I'll meet you there." I did not offer to pick her up. Nor did I particularly like her at the moment.

As I hung up the phone rang again. This time it was Joanne.

"I just had a conversation with Beverly Warfield. Is she a snob or simply rude?" I asked.

"I never thought of her as either. I think she's smarter than her dithery appearance and quite calculated in her speech."

"Then she *did* mean to insult me. The bitch."

"What did she say?" Joanne laughed.

I told Joanne the whole conversation verbatim. It had been recent and short, so I could remember it all.

"Am I taking offense where none was meant?"

"Nope," Joanne answered. "Sounds to me like a lot was meant. I think she thought she was being subtle."

"Like a falling piano."

"Agreed. The question is why? She asks you to lunch, insults you in the process, invites you to a place that she thinks might put you ill at ease. Interesting."

"I'll find out when I get there. What about you?"

"I can't come. I have a story to edit."

"I didn't invite you. I mean what about Toronto?"

"I had a wonderful weekend with Jacques. I really love that man. You should remind me of that more often. He says if I want it I should go. He can't leave, but he doesn't want to stop me. I could come home weekends. Then he spent the rest of the time being super nice and attentive. I'm still torn, but leaning toward staying. I thought it through, weighed all possibilities, and came to the conclusion that although divinely attractive I'm no young bimbo and the odds that the U.S. networks are going to come calling at this age are slim. Once I came to that realization it colored things. Do I want to spend the rest of my days commuting to and from Toronto? I think not. Don't tell Jacques—he's being so considerate that I think I'm going to stretch it out for a few more days, but I doubt if I'll take it. I have until tomorrow to tell them, but my mind is pretty well made up. And I couldn't leave you, either."

"Oh, Joanne, I'm so glad. The thought of your leaving makes my heart hurt. I need you."

"Me, too. But I'll get you for turning me into this sentimental old fool. I feel the need for a tissue. Gotta go," she said and rang off.

It was time to get dressed. Nothing flashy would do, not that I have all that many flashy clothes, and I selected what I considered almost downright dowdy. I used to wear this outfit when labor negotiations included a visit to court. I called it my judge's togs. A mid-gray, midcalf, really boring suit. Bad length on anyone, but I had noticed most of the female lawyers wore this length under their robes. I'll bet they were thankful for those disguising gowns. The jacket wasn't much more attractive: notched collar, three plastic gray buttons. I thought of Susan saying that Beverly paid a lot for her frumpy clothes and silently agreed; this horrible thing had cost way too much money. Underneath I put on a prim white blouse with a Peter Pan collar. I was going the whole route. Gray suede pumps were the only thing on me closely resembling chic. For maximum effect I should have tied my hair back into a French knot, but I couldn't do it. So I looked like me on top and bottom and looked like a private-school mistress in the middle. Although it was warm, I took a bright blue coat out of the closet to cover the thing. I would be seen at the Redpath Club dressed like this, but nowhere else.

After I'd circled the block twice, annoyed because Joanne and her gods weren't with me, I finally found a spot just two spaces away from the door. Calculating the time, I fed three dollar coins into the meter, ensuring two hours of worry-free parking. That was as long as I would be able to endure Beverly anyway. Her implied insult still rankled.

I entered the somber lobby to find Beverly primly seated on one of the brass-studded leather chairs that dominated the space. Polished brass was the prevailing motif, with brass-topped tables that looked like expensive hubcaps, brass ashtrays with built-in matchbox holders, brass railings on the winding staircase that led to the floors above. The concierge behind the brass fronted desk wore a brown jacket with brass buttons. Everything gleamed; they were doing their bit for unemployment, as it surely took a lot of personnel to keep all that stuff polished. It smelled of cleaning fluid.

Beverly matched me, dressed in an almost identical gray suit, the same color as her hair, which made her nearly invisible. We both looked awful but totally suited to the surroundings. She stood and air-kissed me on both cheeks, not wanting to smudge her pale pink lipstick, the only sign of color on her, and you had to look hard to find it.

"You wore a coat? On such a warm day?"

I didn't want to tell her it was a disguise, so I lied. "The weatherman said it might rain." She didn't ask me which station or channel had furnished that erroneous information and I got away with it.

"We can leave it in the women's cloakroom. It's recently been remodeled," she said proudly.

I followed her into the modernized sanctum, a large room with chintz chairs and matching drapes, brass countertop in front of the brass-framed mirrors, and a large brass spittoon converted into an umbrella stand. One of the founders had to have owned shares in a brass mining venture to account for the overabundance. I hung up my coat on the inevitable brass hanger, added more lipstick to defy my increasingly gray pallor, and we headed up to the dining room.

"We can take the stairs," she said, now beaming. "We're allowed."

On my last visit I had been forced into a small, creaky, antiquated elevator that shuddered at each floor. Women were not permitted to use the staircase; maybe the flash of a well-turned ankle would be deemed incendiary, causing the men to burst aflame with passion. Along with the opening up of the membership, they had become more liberal and we were now allowed to leave our fingerprints on the brass railing. However, as we ascended I noted that they hadn't changed all the rules. On the second floor is a nice bar with a gas fire that burns all year round. A few steps off it is a casual dining room—no starched linen and no brass—serving lighter fare, which means roast beef and other red meat sandwiches. The ladies are not allowed to eat here, because important things beyond their understanding are discussed. I was getting crankier with each level.

She ushered me into the main dining room on the third floor, where we were greeted with understated dignity by the maître d' and shown to a table near a beautiful stained-glass window that splashed multicolored terrazzo patterns across the white tablecloth. The flowers matched the spray of color and it was lovely, almost making up for the second-floor insult. To Beverly's horror, my first act of bad behavior, identifying me as an outsider, was to peek under the cloth. I was relieved to see the table was wood, not brass.

We were handed leather-bound menus, and I was thwarted in my desire to order something expensive, as there were no prices beside the offerings. We could only choose from full-course meals, so I knew it had to be costly and felt better. We both selected a salad to start, mine followed by sole amandine and hers by Swiss steak, which was as close as this place came to a hamburger. A double scotch was placed before her, though I can't remember her ordering it. I thought it might have been the standard appetizer, but I didn't get one.

Beverly took a sip from her drink, then stared at the amber liquid for what seemed like ages. I stayed silent; this was her game and I was going to let her play it out. Finally, she took another sip, more like a swig this time, put the glass regretfully back down, and faced me.

"I invited you to lunch because there's something I think you should know."

"What?" An answer was called for and it was the shortest one I could think of.

She looked around the room, nodding at some people who were seated across the way. I noticed that none of the tables near us were occupied and wondered if this had been prearranged. We both spoke softly, the ambience not lending itself to strident voices. The perfect setting for a confession.

"It's about Beth. My sister-in-law has been having an affair."

Not a confession, an accusation. Still, it called for a response.

"That's old news. Why are you telling me this now?"

She looked surprised. I guess she felt that family secrets were just that. "How did you know?"

"Never mind. It doesn't matter who told me."

"Was Walter aware of this?"

"I have no idea. We never discussed his personal life."

A waiter, the same kid who worked at Second Cup, brought our salads. Two jobs and probably school, too. I had been right in my assessment of him as a comer. He recognized me and said hello, which again surprised Beverly. I wasn't meant to be on familiar terms with anyone in this place, and my knowing the waiter might brand me as a regular. I liked her discomfiture.

We picked at the green lettuce swimming in oil that lay before us. I was afraid to taste it, sure that some of the dressing would drip onto my suit or blouse and it wouldn't do to put one's napkin around one's neck here. I should have ordered the lobster so they would have given me a bib.

"Beverly, why are we having this lunch?"

"I thought I was clear. I wanted to tell you about Beth."

"Again, why?"

"I thought you should know. I'm aware of the fact that you're sticking your nose into our family business and decided I would help you. If you know about Beth's affair, then surely you must know that I disapproved. Walter was my brother and I couldn't abide her treating him so shabbily."

"He had two mistresses that I know about. *That* you approved of?"

"Oh, Barbara, he's a man. A businessman. It's to be expected."

Maybe in her circle. Definitely not in mine. This intrigued me.

"So you think it's okay for him to be unfaithful but not her?"

"Yes I do." Her tone conveyed outrage that I could think otherwise. "Men have needs." Which might explain why her husband Winston drank so much. He sure wasn't gettin' any at home. I had to control myself or I'd burst into laughter. I couldn't believe people still thought like this; Queen Victoria would adore this woman.

Beverly was now on the defensive. "Well, did you know that she had asked Walter for a divorce? More like demanded one. Walter was shocked and refused. She told me that just two days before the killing." She leaned back and gave me a vicious smile. This was her trump card, the thing that would convince me that Beth had murdered Walter.

Of course Walter didn't want a divorce. His financial disarray would then become evident to anyone, up for public scrutiny. He had to protect his image even if he equally wanted his freedom. And he would lose his free slave, which even he would realize was not replaceable. I couldn't imagine Cassandre pushing a vacuum cleaner.

"Yes, I knew that, too. I can't believe it took her so long." That was it. The fact that I already knew this deflated her. She expelled a big whoosh and grabbed for her glass, downing the rest of the scotch in two big gulps. As soon as she put the empty glass back on the table, it was whisked away and replaced by another full one. It had been done so quickly that if you blinked, you could miss it. I had the idea that Winston wasn't the only drunk in the family; she just hid her addiction better.

I got bored with the charade and decided to go for it. As I was about to speak, our salads were taken away and replaced by main courses. Beverly attacked her steak, cutting the whole thing into tiny pieces, thus giving her something to look at besides me.

"Beverly, how is Mrs. Whitestone?"

"Beth? She's fine. What do you expect?"

"Not Beth, Mrs. Whitestone senior. Your mother."

"Oh, as well as can be expected. She doesn't recognize me, although I visit her almost every day. I bring her things; she likes colorful magazines, likes to look at the pictures."

"Walter wasn't as attentive as you are, was he?"

Beverly sighed. She put her knife and fork down and looked back at me. If her food tasted like it looked, I couldn't blame her. It matched her gray suit perfectly, and I don't think that's the color meat should be. On the other hand, my sole was delicious, broiled to flakiness, in a light lemon sauce, topped with toasted almonds. The hands that had prepared this couldn't have been responsible for that awful salad.

"Walter always promised he would visit more often. She recognized us up to a month ago and was always asking for him. He was her only son."

"But you're her only daughter," I said. I know my mother feels differently about her son than her daughters, but not in a way that puts one above the other. She needs us all, and her love isn't exclusionary. I didn't understand this.

"A son is more important. He's the representative. It's a daughter's duty to care for her parents, her obligation no matter how badly they treated her. I was ignored by both my parents for most of my life. My father died fairly young, and for the last twenty years I have been devoted to my mother. She's been rather demanding, and my husband and I have had a few arguments over the fact that I spend so much time with her. She treated me like the maids she no longer had, and it made Winston furious. But what could I do, she's my mother."

A lot of hostility going on there. A lot of resentment toward her Golden Boy brother while she remained the drudge. You'd think she'd have some sympathy for Beth, who had to live with the product of that upraising. It's amazing how different people can be when it comes to separating their business lives from their home lives. This wasn't my Walter at all.

I was beginning to feel sorry for her, which wasn't a good idea. Time for the attack.

"In Mrs. Whitestone's will, the disposition of the assets is inequitable, isn't it? Considering how much time and energy you've invested?"

"How do you know that? It's none of your business."

She'd picked a good place for lunch. If we had been anywhere else that would have come out as a shriek, but in deference to her surroundings she'd kept her voice low.

"As I understand it, the bulk of her estate would go to Walter, with some smaller amount being settled on you. It is assumed that you have a husband to provide for you and it keeps the capital and investments from being diluted."

"Who told you that?" Her conversation was getting repetitive, and I guessed she deserved an answer.

"Beth did. Although I don't think she'll remember. She was talking about Walter's will, and I assume the provisions would be the same for preceding generations."

"She had no business saying anything." Beverly was upset at the display of bad form.

By now my fish was gone and Beverly's food stood before her, fifty or so small pieces of horrible-looking beef, virtually untouched. Her face was ashen, and she knocked back the second double scotch. My friendly waiter arrived to clear our plates away, offering dessert menus, which Beverly waved away. I was mad; I wanted some. The dear boy returned in seconds, placing another drink in front of Beverly and a pot of tea with attendant accoutrements in front of me. He remembered my tastes. Also, he brought a plate of delicious-looking mini fruit tarts. I wished I could tip him, but it didn't seem possible. I'd go back to find him at his other job and overtip there.

Beverly took sustenance from her third double scotch. She looked me straight in the eye and said, "I do not see how this is any of your affair. You're a meddler who should learn to mind her manners."

I ignored the reprimand, pleased I'd gotten a rise out of her.

"I think the following. I can't prove any of it at the moment, but let me tell you about it anyway. I think you invited me here to tell me about Beth's affair to allay suspicion. To point the finger at her, so to speak; make her out to be the murderer. I think you knew where Beth was that night and went over there to have it out with Walter. I know you've all taken a financial beating lately at your husband's instigation. Perhaps you went to beg for some money so Winston could pay his obligations and you could continue to hold your position in society. You may not have been aware that Walter had lost everything also. You watched the house, waited for Harrison Harrison to leave and went to talk to Walter. I don't know how you ended up in the bedroom; you might have followed him in there after he dismissed you. You got into a heated argument that got out of hand and you stabbed him. I don't think you planned to do it, I think the confrontation just escalated. Later, when you arrived at the murder scene, you said you'd gotten Beth's message. Your hair was wet and I think you'd just stepped out of the shower, possibly to wash off any blood that might have spattered onto you. How'm I doing?"

"You can't possibly believe that!" She was incredulous. "The part about the money is true, and I did go see Walter that night and we did have an argument, but when I left he was still alive. I was in the shower, trying to wash away the sordidness of our conversation, when Beth called. It had been rather ugly, a lot things that should have been left unsaid. Walter wouldn't lend me any money—I didn't know he'd been involved in Winnings Corp. also. I couldn't believe Winston had done that to him. Still, I look after Mother and I felt I deserved his protection."

"If I were you I'd stick to that story. Right to the end, which will probably be before a Superior Court judge. See if the jury buys it. See if you can add to it, though; it's too bare bones at the moment."

Beverly was frantic. "This is not something to joke about. You have to believe me. It's the truth. When I left, Walter was downstairs in the den working at his computer."

"Think about what I said, Beverly. It's only logical that

it had to be you. If you got rid of Walter the money from your mother would all go to you, therefore eliminating the probability of Beth having killed him for the legacy. With him gone, she gets nothing from the estate. We all know she didn't need his permission to get a divorce if she really wanted one. Your inviting me to lunch to implicate her indicates malice aforethought to me." Fancy words in keeping with the setting.

She stared at me, her face flat and hateful. And then something crossed it that I couldn't read: a memory, a thought, animating it for an instant.

"I did not do such a horrible thing. I wouldn't. And if you pass this supposition around I will sue you for slander. I know some powerful lawyers, and I assure you I can make it stick. I will take you for every penny you have. Do I make myself clear?"

"Yes, ma'am. Until I can prove it, I'll mention it only to the police. You'd better prepare yourself for a visit forthwith." I was starting to talk like her.

I had to get out of there. There was nothing I could do about my suspicions from here, and I couldn't bear being in her company for one more second. I was convinced I was right and wanted to talk to Greg about it, see if there was anything I'd missed that could definitely tie her to the body.

"I'm leaving," I said as I pushed my chair away from the table, taking a tart along with me for the descent. "Thank you for a not so delightful lunch."

She still had to sign off on the bill, and I wanted to get downstairs to retrieve my coat before she left. My plan was to lurk near the door and follow her, see what she was up to. She could have used the phone in the dining room to make some arrangements, but I was betting that my pastry theft would embarrass her enough to cause her to want out of there. Also, my inflammatory accusation would hang around the table like a noose. Since I did concede that the act had been unpre-

meditated and she wasn't a cold-blooded murderer who plot-
ted her every move, I was counting on her being frantic
enough to do something stupid.

She did get in the parting shot.

"Barbara, put that tart away. There is no eating on the
stairs."

I had to give her points.

18

BY THE TIME I got to the ground floor the tart had disappeared. Nobody hunted me down to tell me that I couldn't chew and walk at the same time. Much to the disgust of two women who spotted me as they were about to ascend, I licked my fingers as I reached the bottom. I hoped it would get back to Beverly.

Safely returned to flat ground, I picked up speed and tore across the lobby in search of my coat. More bad behavior. One doesn't run in such a dignified place. I was trying to tally up how many social conventions I had broken as I plowed into the cloakroom.

Right into Winston Warfield, wielding a double-barreled shotgun no less, pointed at the middle of my chest. For some reason I wasn't scared, the bulky weapon less terrifying than a pistol would have been.

"What are you doing here? This is the women's cloak-room."

It was a stupid, irrelevant thing to say. It was obvious what he was doing, but it was the only thing I could think of.

The jerk answered me. "I knew you were having lunch with Beverly. I thought she suspected me and was going to tell you about it. Ask your advice."

It surprised me how little he knew his wife. She would never, ever tell me, an outsider, that she suspected her husband. Her sister-in-law was fair game, not being the one responsible for Beverly's continued financial support or her social position.

"I hung around the lobby reading a newspaper until I heard you thundering down the stairs."

"I do not thunder," I interrupted.

"Whatever," he said, put off by the fact that I wasn't terrified. "I saw you rounding the corner at the top and slipped in here, the concierge being conveniently away from his desk. I had originally planned to follow you, but this was a better opportunity."

"You hung around the lobby with a shotgun in your hands?" I was incredulous. It's bad form to eat on the stairs or run in the lobby, but not to brandish a shotgun? What kind of crazy values did these people have?

"Don't be silly. I had it wrapped in a duffel bag."

At least the whole world hadn't gone mad. Sure enough, there was a drab khaki duffel bag on the floor by his feet.

"And what are you planning to do? Shoot me here?"

"I would suggest you stop making inane conversation. We will now proceed to my car, where we'll go for a little drive."

"Winston, this is stupid. You've been watching too much television. Real people don't go for drives with men who point shotguns. How're you going to keep me covered and drive at the same time?"

I felt my only hope was to keep him talking as long as possible. Maybe even talk him out of it.

"Do not make me out to be a cretin. You'll drive, I'll aim." He chuckled at his little joke.

"Are you drunk?" I asked, hoping he'd topple over if he was.

"I am stone cold sober," he answered primly. I'd offended him.

This was the second time I'd faced a man with a gun, and I was getting fed up with it. Where were the women bad guys? I was almost disappointed it was not Beverly, whom I had erroneously accused, taking aim at me. In any event, this was getting tiresome. For some reason I couldn't take it seriously, which I guess is not very clever. Winston was desperate and had nothing to lose—he'd lost all his money, embezzled most of his friends' money, would lose his social position in the weeks to come as the scandal unfurled, and as a capper, had murdered his brother-in-law. He was a dejected man, and I would be wise to reconsider my flip attitude and try to figure out how to get out of this.

At that moment, a woman came out of the bathroom that was en suite, through the door right beside Winston. At first her face didn't register her predicament, but as the situation dawned, panic overcame her and she began to tremble. She must watch television, too, because she didn't scream, which might have resulted in her being blasted. I'm sure she'll never go into a public toilet again.

"Get over there and stand beside Barbara," Winston said, as he prodded her in my direction with the barrel of the gun.

"Come here," I said calmly. She needed reassurance. "Stand beside me and don't say anything. We'll be okay."

"Miss Bigshot. Thinks she can talk her way out of anything. Both of you, move around this way."

What ensued was all of us creeping slowly around in a circle, ending in a reversal of positions, the frightened woman and I by the bathroom door. Winston didn't know if anyone else was in there, hadn't had the brains to watch the door while he was waiting for me to see if anyone went in. Maybe he wasn't as sober as he said he was. But he was smart enough to position us so that if there were anyone else in there, he'd be facing them as they exited. I don't know why he didn't ask the woman who'd just come out if there was someone else still there; she was so frightened I didn't think she'd have the courage to lie to him.

Talking was keeping us in here and alive, which was the best alternative.

"Winston, I know you didn't mean to kill Walter. It was an act of passion, a momentary madness. I'm sure the courts will take that into consideration." I wouldn't bet on it. Particularly after this latest escapade, even if we survived it. But I needed him to admit to it in front of this unknown woman, who was staring at me as a savior. Otherwise it would only be my speculative word against his, and as Beverly was his loyal wife, even if she was aware of the situation, I could guess what her position might be.

Winston seemed unsure as to how to proceed. It made him loquacious, the words pouring out while his mind scrambled to find a resolution to his present predicament. He now had two hostages to dispose of, one of which I didn't know if he even knew.

"Wally wouldn't loan me the money to cover everything. I told him I'd pay him back, but he wouldn't listen. I know he was busted, too, but Old Lady Whitestone won't last much longer and he could have borrowed against the inheritance to help me out," he whined, making him sound like the wimp he was.

Not good enough. I needed more.

"So you decided to kill him. That would get Beverly the money that you could then use."

"You're right. But I only thought of that afterward. At the time, all I knew was he wouldn't help me. I grabbed the knife to threaten him. I'll admit I'd had a few and wasn't thinking clearly, and he laughed at me, told me to get out of there and never come back or he'd tell Beverly how I tried to extort him. I couldn't help it. He turned his back on me to dismiss me, and I lunged. He went right down."

As the woman beside me took in the implication of his words, she looked as if she was going to faint. She grabbed my arm to hold herself up, but I shrugged it off. I needed all my limbs available in case I got an opening.

"Hang in there," I said to her. "Take a deep breath."

She breathed in and out audibly a few times and the color returned to her face. Finally, she got mad.

"Winston Warfield, you are a disgraceful man."

She would have said more, but he cut her off. "Shut up, Emily. One loudmouthed broad is enough."

That was me. Even though I'd kept the volume low. She snapped her mouth shut at the reproach and went back to trembling. I couldn't tell if it was indignation or fear.

"How're you going to get us out of here?" I asked. "We can't very well march through the lobby."

"Look behind you."

I did. There was a fire exit leading directly to the outside. I hadn't noticed it before. It had an alarm attached, along with the warning that it would sound when the door was opened. I didn't think the concierge would react to the racket quickly; we would be long gone before he even got in here. Winston's plan was beginning to make sense, and I was starting to get scared.

"Winston, we can't parade through the streets with an exposed weapon," I said.

"My car's parked right outside that door. It leads to the back of the building, to the parking lot."

I didn't know there was a lot. I could have saved the money I'd put in the meter and the price of the ticket I would get if I didn't get out of here soon. I had to stay focused.

The door behind Winston opened, and Beverly was suddenly at his side. She took in the situation calmly, realization causing a slow smile to grace her face. She didn't even glance at Winston, just looked straight at me and said, "She was right."

"Who was right?" Winston asked, worried that someone else knew about it. There were now too many people involved in what should have been a simple operation, and he was beginning to get confused. Which could work to my advantage.

"Barbara was right," she said in a flat voice. She stayed by his side, making no move to cross to the other team, whether out of loyalty or fear I wasn't sure.

"Well, almost right," I said. "The motive was correct, but the protagonist was wrong. I apologize for the inference and accusation."

"It's all right. Don't worry about it."

It was a very civilized exchange, Beverly forgiving me for my thoughtless transgressions. All in the ladies' cloakroom of the venerable Redpath Club with a shotgun center stage. It was starting to get very otherworldly, causing my head to spin.

"Beverly, get over there with them."

"Winston, you can't mean that!"

"Move."

Beverly came over to our side and we three shooting ducks stood all in a row. Beverly was furious. This was the ultimate breach of trust, and really bad manners to boot.

"Beverly," I said. "Don't worry. He won't shoot you. If you die he won't get the money he needs; it'll all go to Kenneth, Walter's son. He'll get rid of us and then you two can go back to your cozy lives." That was a guess on my part, but a logical assumption.

"Of course I wouldn't hurt you, darling," he said. "You're my wife."

"This is the first time you've called me darling in years; you've gone mad. When Barbara explained her theory I knew it had to be you. It brought to mind the bloody handkerchief I found in your pocket. I assume you used it to wipe your prints off the knife and bloodied it in the process." Her voice was forceful but devoid of censure. She looked at him with pity, the weak husband who'd finally stepped over the line and would need to be reprimanded at a later date, in private.

Winston was looking a little unsure. "I told you I had a nosebleed. It's the truth."

"You had no such thing. Unless you fell over in a drunken stupor, and I notice you've been drinking less this past week. I thought you were trying to economize, but I now see you were trying to stay sober long enough to figure out how to get out of this situation you created. You were the one who kept trying to implicate Beth, discussing the situation with me and subtly pointing in her direction, trying to assign guilt. Barbara, I'm sorry I dragged you into this. Now I feel weak in the knees and am going to sit down. Shoot me if you want to. I don't care."

We all took courage from her speech, the woman beside me pulling herself up to her five-foot-two-inch maximum, her face now defiant.

Winston was confused. He couldn't shoot his wife for a plenitude of reasons, one of them being this was not the proper place for such an act. A now dejected Beverly, true to her words, crossed the room and plunked herself down in a chintz chair. Winston's eyes followed her.

I figured this was my chance. The air was full of confusion; no one could remember the parts they were supposed to play. Winston's script had gone massively awry. Even though he'd been sober at its inception, he wasn't computing well. There were too many variables for his generally pickled brain to assimilate.

While his eyes were on Beverly, his face pleading, I took

two steps forward and knocked the barrel of the shotgun aside with my right arm. He didn't let go, but at least it wasn't pointed at me anymore. Before he could do anything, my right foot shot out, sideways, just as Rick had taught me, and I got him full in the solar plexus with all my weight behind it. The high-heeled pump was an added bonus, as it punctured his skin and blood spurted. He looked down at his bleeding middle in shock as he slowly sunk to the ground. I wasn't finished. I was mad and I was showing off my new skills, so I leaned over and chopped him in the neck with the side of my right hand. I don't know what I connected with and it hurt like hell, but Winston's lights went out. As an added bonus, he bumped his head on the corner of the brass counter during his descent. More blood.

Quickly I picked up the gun, aiming it in the general direction of Beverly, who sat numbly, staring at the proceedings with the disdainful look that I had become familiar with, making no effort to help her husband. Still, I didn't fully trust her.

I turned to the other woman and said, "Emily, I'm Barbara, and I'm sorry you had to be subjected to this. Now I need a favor. Winston is going to come to at any second, and he's going to be mightily pissed."

She giggled, and I knew I had her.

"What I need for you to do is sit on him. Unfortunately you may get some blood on you, but I'll pay for the dry cleaning."

"Hang the blood and the cleaning. It will be my pleasure. By the way, nice to meet you." She bopped across the room and plunked herself, all two hundred pounds of herself, onto Winston, effectively pinning him. All his air went out in a whoosh.

"Shut up," Emily said to the inert Winston. "That's a disgusting sound." And she giggled again. "Barbara, in return for the use of my ample girth I have one favor to ask."

"Shoot."

"No, don't shoot," she said, this time accompanied by full-bodied chuckles. This was the adventure of her lifetime, and she was going to savor every last detail. "Will you come to dinner at my house next week? Nobody's going to believe this, and I need a corroborating witness. Particularly the part where I sit on him."

"Absolutely. I like your style," I answered.

Beverly now looked torn, considering whether she should come to the aid of her inert husband, despising him at the same time. After all, he had murdered her brother.

I trained the gun on her and said, "Beverly, I don't know how to shoot this thing. I don't know how long it's been in disuse and what the consequences of firing it are. I could miss you, the recoil could send me flying, the bullet could ricochet and knock off nice Emily here. I don't want to do it, but you must know by now that I am tenacious, and if I perceive you as a threat, I will. I'm now going to use the phone and expect you to remain seated there like a good girl. I don't feel like sitting on you."

"Why not? It's fun," Emily piped up from her position. I liked this woman.

I went to the phone, the gun aimed in the general vicinity of Beverly, and dialed 911. I really hoped she wouldn't do anything stupid and force me to discharge the thing. We could all get killed. However, probably taking her cue from Beth's previous example, she sank into catatonic staring, eyes focused on the chintz cabbage roses.

I explained the situation to the answering operator, and suggested she ask the arriving cops to show some discretion as they pounded into the Redpath Club. This was a place of quiet dignity. She was probably used to crackpots calling, as she didn't laugh in my ear, just calmly reassured me that the police would be there soon. I'm sure she thought I was nuts, but Emily laughed some more, which made me happy. I'd inadvertently put her through a lot and owed her for sitting on Winston.

It was difficult maneuvering everything, because I had the phone jammed in my neck. With one hand I tried to keep the gun steady and pointed at Winston, while I searched my purse with the other. After severing the connection with 911, I found what I wanted and consulted it with a quick glance. One eye still on Winston, I dialed. After a series of intermediaries, Detective-Sergeant Gregory Allard came on the line.

"Greg, get over here. Have I got a present for you!"